## PRAISE FOR SPUR AWARD-WINNING AUTHOR MATT BRAUN



**"Matt Braun is one of the best!"**
**—Don Coldsmith, author of the Spanish Bit series**

**"Braun tackles the big men, the complex personalities of those brave few who were pivotal figures in the settling of an untamed frontier."**
**—Jory Sherman, author of *Grass Kingdom***

## ACTING THE PART . . .

Lillian finally joined the fight. After a struggle to cock both hammers on the shotgun, she found it required all her strength to raise the heavy weapon. She brought it to shoulder level, trying to steady the long barrels, and accidentally tripped both triggers. The shotgun boomed, the double hammers dropping almost simultaneously, and a hail of buckshot sizzled into the charging Indians. The brutal kick of the recoil knocked Lillian off her feet.

A warrior flung out his arms and toppled dead from his pony. The others swerved aside as buckshot simmered through their ranks like angry hornets. Their charge was broken not ten feet from the overhang, and Fontaine and Chester continued to blast away with their Henry repeaters . . .

## St. Martin's Paperbacks Titles by Matt Braun

Wyatt Earp
Black Fox
Outlaw Kingdom
Lords of the Land
Cimarron Jordan
Bloody Hand
Noble Outlaw
Texas Empire
The Savage Land
Rio Hondo
The Gamblers
Doc Holliday
You Know My Name
The Brannocks
The Last Stand
Rio Grande
Gentleman Rogue
The Kincaids
El Paso
Indian Territory
Shadow Killers
Buck Colter
Kinch Riley
Deathwalk
Hickok & Cody

# THE WILD ONES

## MATT BRAUN

St. Martin's Paperbacks

THE WILD ONES



ISBN: 0-312-98133-3

Printed in the United States of America

St. Martin's Paperbacks edition / January 2002

St. Martin's Paperbacks are published by St. Martin's Press, 175 Fifth Avenue, New York, NY 10010.

10 9 8 7 6 5 4 3 2 1

IN MEMORY OF ALL THOSE LOST AT
THE WORLD TRADE CENTER
AND THE PENTAGON
SEPTEMBER 11, 2001

# THE WILD ONES

# Chapter 1

THE TRAIN was some miles west of Boonville. Lillian sat by the window, staring out at the verdant countryside. She thought Missouri looked little different from Indiana or Ohio, though perhaps not so flat. Her expression was pensive.

September lay across the land. Fields tall with corn, bordered by stands of trees, fleeted past the coach window under a waning sun. There was a monotonous sameness to the landscape, and the clickety-clack of steel wheels on rails made it all but hypnotic. She wondered if she would ever again see New York.

Chester, her brother, was seated beside her. Three years older, recently turned twenty-two, he was a solid six-footer, with chiseled features and a shock of wavy dark hair. His head bobbed to the sway of the coach and his eyes were closed in a light slumber. He seemed intent on sleeping his way through Missouri.

Alistair Fontaine, their father, was seated across from them. A slender man, his angular features and leonine head of gray hair gave him a distinguished appearance. He was forty-four, an impeccable dresser, his customary attire a three-piece suit with a gold watch chain draped over the expanse of his vest. He looked at Lillian.

"A penny for your thoughts, my dear." Lillian loved the sound of her father's voice. Even as a young child, she had been entranced by his sonorous baritone, cultured and uniquely rich in timbre. She smiled at him.

"Oh, just daydreaming, Papa," she said with a small shrug. "I miss New York so much. Don't you?"

"Never look back," Fontaine said cheerfully. "Westward the sun and westward our fortune. Our brightest days are yet ahead."

"Do you really think so?"

"Why, child, I have no doubt of it whatever. We are but stars following our destiny."

She sensed the lie beneath his words. He always put the best face on things, no matter how dismal. His wonderfully aristocratic bearing gave his pronouncements the ring of an oracle. But then, she reminded herself, he was an actor. He made reality of illusion.

"Yes, of course, you're right," she said. "Abilene just seems like the end of the earth. I feel as though we've been . . . banished."

"Nonsense," Fontaine gently admonished her. "We will take Abilene by storm, and our notices will have New York clamoring for our return. You mark my words!"

Chester was roused by his father's voice. He yawned, rubbing sleep from his eyes. "What's that about New York?"

"I was telling Lillian," Fontaine informed him. "Our trip West is but a way station on the road of life. We've not seen the last of Broadway."

"Dad, I hope to God you're right."

"Never doubt it for a moment, my boy. I have utter faith."

Lillian wasn't so sure. On the variety circuit, *The Fontaines*, as they were billed, was a headline act. Her earliest memories were of traveling the circuit of variety theaters throughout the Northeast and the Eastern Seaboard. Originated in England and imported across the Atlantic, variety theaters were the most popular form of entertainment in America.

A child of the theater, Lillian had been raised among performers. Her playmates were the offspring of chorus girls, song-and-dance men, comics, contortionists, and acrobats. At an early age, she and Chester became a part of the family troupe, acting in melodramas with their parents and sometimes accompanying their mother in song. The family ensemble presented entertainment for the masses, something for everyone.

Alistair Fontaine played to popular tastes by appearing in the sometimes-histrionic melodramas. At heart, he considered himself a tragedian, and his greatest joy was in emoting Shakespearean soliloquies in full costume. Yet it was his wife, Estell Fontaine, who was the true star of the show. Her extraordinary voice rendered audiences spellbound, and she might have had a career in opera. She chose instead her family. And the variety stage.

The magnitude of her stardom became apparent just three months ago, in the early summer of 1871. A bout of influenza quickly turned to pneumonia, and two days later she died in a New York hospital. Her loss devastated Alistair, who stayed drunk for a week, and left Lillian and Chester undone by grief. Estell was the bulwark of the family, wife, mother, and matriarch. They were lost without her, emotionally adrift. Yet, strangely, made somehow closer by her death.

Their personal tragedy was compounded in their professional lives. With Estell gone, the Fontaines soon discovered they were no longer a headline act. Her voice was the stardust of the show, and without her, they were suddenly unemployable anywhere on the variety circuit. Theater owners were sympathetic, but in the months following Estell's death there were no offers for an engagement, even on the undercard. Their booking agent suggested they try the budding variety circuit in the West.

Alistair Fontaine was at first opposed and not a little offended. But then, after three months without work and facing poverty, he reluctantly agreed. Their agent finally obtained a booking in Abilene, Kansas, the major railhead for shipping Texas cattle. Whatever was to be learned of their destination was to be found in the pages of the *Police Gazette*. Abilene was reported to be the wildest town in the Wild West.

Today, watching her father, Lillian wasn't at all convinced that he had reconciled himself with their situation. In off moments, she caught him staring dully into space and sensed his uncertainty about their trip West. Even more, she knew his posturing and his confident manner were meant to reassure herself and Chester. His oft-repeated assertion that they would return to New York and Broadway was fanciful, a dream at best.

She longed for the counsel of her mother.

"When's our next stop?" Chester abruptly asked. "I wouldn't mind a hot meal for a change."

There was no dining car on the train. A vendor periodically prowled the aisles, selling stale sandwiches and assorted sundries. Their last decent meal had been in St. Louis.

Fontaine chuckled amiably. "I fear you'll have a wait, my boy. We're scheduled to arrive in Kansas City about midnight."

"Wish it was New York instead."

"Be of stout heart, Chet. Think of us as thespians off on a grand adventure."

Lillian turned her gaze out the window. Abilene, for all her father's cheery bluster, hardly seemed to her a grand adventure. The middle of nowhere sounded a bit more like it.

She, too, wished for New York.

The train hurtled through the hamlet of Sweet Springs. Coupled to the rear of the engine and the tender were an express car and five passenger coaches. As the locomotive sped past the small depot, the engineer tooted his whistle. On the horizon, the sun dropped toward the rim of the earth.

A mile west of town, a tree had been felled across the tracks on the approach to a bridge. The engineer set the brakes, wheels grinding on the rails, and the train jarred to a screeching halt. The sudden jolt caught the passengers unawares, and there was a moment of pandemonium in the coaches. Luggage went flying from the overhead racks as women screamed and men cursed.

Then, suddenly, a collective hush fell over the coaches. From under the bridge where trees bordered a swift stream, a gang of riders burst out of the woods. Five men rode directly to the express car, pouring a volley of shots through the door. Another man, pistol drawn, jumped from his horse to the steps of the locomotive. The engineer and the fireman dutifully raised their hands.

Four remaining gang members, spurring their horses hard, charged up and down the track bed. Their pistols were cocked and pointed at the passengers, who stared openmouthed through the coach windows. No shots were fired, but the men's menacing attitude and tough appearance made the message all too clear. Anyone who resisted or attempted to flee the train would be killed.

"My God!" Alistair Fontaine said in an awed tone. "The train is being robbed."

Lillian shrank back into her seat. Her eyes were fastened on the riders waving their pistols. "Are we in danger, Papa?"

"Stay calm, my dear," Fontaine cautioned. "I daresay the rascals are more interested in the express car."

The threat posed by the armed horsemen made eminent good sense to the passengers. Like most railroads, the Kansas Pacific was not revered by the public. For years, eastern robber barons had plundered the West on land grants and freight rates. A holdup, according to common wisdom, was a matter between the railroad and the bandits. Only a fool would risk his life to thwart a robbery. There were no fools aboard today.

From the coaches, the passengers had a ringside seat. They watched as the five men outside the express car demonstrated a no-nonsense approach to train robbery. One of the riders produced a stick of dynamite and held the fuse only inches away from the tip of a lighted cigar. Another rider, whose commanding presence pegged him as the gang leader, gigged his horse onto the roadbed. His voice raised in a shout, he informed the express guards that their options were limited.

"Open the door or get blown to hell!"

The guards, much like the passengers, were unwilling to die for the Kansas Pacific. The door quickly slid open and they tossed their pistols onto the ground. Three of the robbers dismounted and scrambled inside the express car. The leader, positioned outside the car, directed the operation from aboard his horse. His tone had the ring of authority, brusque and demanding. His attitude was that of a man accustomed to being obeyed.

"Holy Hannah!" one of the passengers exclaimed. "That there's the James boys. There's Jesse himself!"

Jesse and Frank James were the most famous outlaws in America. Their legend began in 1866, when they rode into Liberty, Missouri, and robbed the Clay County Savings Association of $70,000. It was the first daylight bank robbery in American history and created a furor in the nation's press. It also served as a template by which the gang would operate over the years ahead, robbing trains and looting banks. Their raids were conducted with military precision.

A master of propaganda, Jesse James frequently wrote articulate letters to editors of influential midwestern newspapers. The letters were duly reprinted and accounted, in large measure, for the myth that "he robbed from the rich and gave to the poor." Comparisons were drawn between Jesse and Robin Hood, the legendary outlaw of Sherwood Forest. Not entirely in jest, newspaper editorials made reference to "Jesse and his merry band of robbers."

Tales were widely circulated with regard to Jesse's charitable nature toward the poor. The loot taken in the robberies, so he contended in his letters, was simply liberated from the coffers of greedy bankers and corrupt railroads. In time, with such tales multiplying, Jesse became known as a champion of the oppressed and the downtrodden. To backwoods Missourians and gullible Easterners alike he came to represent a larger-than-life figure. A Robin Hood reborn—who wore a six-gun and puckishly thumbed his nose at the law.

The holdup took less than five minutes. The robbers inside the express car emerged with a mail sack that appeared painfully empty of cash. There was a hurried conference with their leader, and his harsh curses indicated his displeasure. He dismounted, ordering one man to guard the train crew, and waved the others toward the passenger coaches. They split into pairs, two men to a coach, and clambered up the steps at the end of each car. The leader and another man burst through the door of the lead coach.

A murmur swept through the passengers. The two men were instantly recognizable, their faces plastered on wanted dodgers from Iowa to Texas. Jesse and Frank James stood at the front of the car, brandishing cocked pistols.

"Sorry to trouble you folks," Jesse said with cold levity. "That express safe was mighty poor pickin's. We'll have to ask you for a donation."

Frank lifted a derby off the head of a notions drummer. He started down the aisle, the upturned hat in one hand and a pistol in the other. His mouth creased in a sanguine smile as passengers obediently filled the hat with cash and gold coins. He paused where the Fontaines were seated.

Lillian blushed under his appreciative inspection. She was rather tall, with enormous china blue eyes and exquisite features. Vibrant even in the face of a robber, she wore her tawny hair upswept, with fluffs of curls spilling over her forehead. Her demure dimity cotton dress did nothing to hide her tiny waist and sumptuous figure. She quickly averted her eyes.

"Beauty's ensign"—Frank James nodded, still staring at her—"is crimson in thy lips and in thy cheeks."

Alistair Fontaine was an avid reader of periodicals. He recalled a curious item from the *Police Gazette*, noting the anomaly that robber and mankiller Frank James was a student of Shakespeare. He rose as though taking center stage.

"M'lord," he said in a mellifluous voice. "You see me here before you a poor man, as full of grief as age, wretched in both."

"King Lear," Frank said, grinning. "I take it you fancy the Bard."

"A mere actor," Fontaine replied modestly. "Known to some as a Shakespearean."

"Well, friend, never let it be said I'd rob a man that carries the word. Keep your money."

"Frank!" Jesse snapped. "Quite jawin' and tend to business. We ain't got all night."

Frank winked slyly at Fontaine. He went down the aisle and returned with the derby stuffed to overflowing. Jesse covered his retreat through the door and followed him out. Some moments later the gang mounted their horses and rode north from the railroad tracks. A smothered sun cloaked them in silty twilight.

The passengers watched them in stunned silence. Then, as though a floodgate was released, they began babbling to one another about being robbed by the James Boys. Chester shook his head in mild wonder.

"Some introduction to the Wild West," he muttered. "I hope Abilene's nothing like that."

Lillian turned to her father. "Oh, Papa, you were wonderful!"

"Yes," Fontaine agreed. "I surprised myself."

Twilight slowly faded to dusk. Fontaine stared off at the shelterbelt of woods where the riders had disappeared. Abruptly, his legs gone shaky with a delayed reaction, he sank down into his seat. Yet he thought he would remember Frank James with fondness.

It had been the finest performance of his life.

# Chapter 2

Abilene was situated along a dogleg of the Smoky Hill River. The town was a crude collection of buildings, surrounded by milling herds of longhorn cattle. The Kansas plains, flat as a billiard table, stretched endlessly to the points of the compass.

The Fontaines stepped off the train early the next afternoon. They stood for a moment on the depot platform, staring aghast at the squalid, ramshackle structures. Eastern newspapers, overly charitable in their accounts, labeled Abilene as the first of its kind. One of a kind. A cowtown.

"Good heavens," Fontaine said in a bemused tone. "I confess I expected something more . . . civilized."

Lillian wrinkled her nose. "What a horrid smell."

There was an enervating odor of cow dung in the air. The prairie encircling Abilene was a vast bawling sea of longhorns awaiting shipment to eastern slaughterhouses, and a barnyard scent assailed their nostrils. The pungency of it hung like a fetid mist over the town.

"Perhaps there's more than meets the eye," Fontaine said, ever the optimist. "Let's not jump to hasty conclusions."

Chester grunted. "I can't wait to see the theater."

A porter claimed their steamer trunks from the baggage car. He muscled the trunks onto a handcart and led the way around the depot. The Kansas Pacific railroad tracks bisected the town east to west, cleaving it in half. Texas Street, the main thoroughfare, ran north to south.

Lillian was appalled. Her first impression was that every storefront in Abilene was dedicated to separating the Texan cattlemen from their money. With the exception of two hotels, three mercantile emporiums, and one bank, the entire business community was devoted to either avarice or lust. The street was lined with saloons, gambling dives, and dancehalls.

The boardwalks were jammed with throngs of cowhands. Every saloon and dancehall shook with the strident chords of brass bands and rinky-dink pianos. Smiling brightly, hard-eyed girls in gaudy dresses enticed the trailhands through the doors, where a quarter bought a slug of whiskey or a trip around the dance floor. The music blared amidst a swirl of jangling spurs and painted women.

"Regular circus, ain't it?" the porter said, leading them past hitch racks lined with horses. "You folks from back East, are you?"

"New York," Fontaine advised him. "We have reservations at the Drover's Cottage."

"Well, you won't go wrong there. Best digs this side of Kansas City."

"Are the streets always so crowded?"

"Night or day, don't make no nevermind. There's mebbe a thousand Texans in town most of the trailin' season."

The porter went on to enlighten them about Abilene. Joseph McCoy, a land speculator and promoter, was the founder of America's first cowtown. Texans were beef-rich and money-poor, and he proposed to exchange Northern currency for longhorn cows. The fact that a railhead didn't exist deterred him not in the least. He proceeded with an enterprise that would alter the character of the West.

McCoy found his spot along the Smoky Hill River. There was water, and a boundless stretch of grassland, all situated near the Chisholm Trail. After a whirlwind courtship of the Kansas Pacific, he convinced the railroad to lay track across the western plains. In 1867, he bought 250 acres on the river, built a town and stockyards, and lured the Texas cattlemen north. Four years later, upward of 100,000 cows would be shipped from Abilene in a single season.

"Don't that beat all!" the porter concluded. "Dangblasted pot o'gold, that's what it is."

"Yes indeed," Fontaine said dryly. "A veritable metropolis."

The Drover's Cottage was a two-story structure hammered together with ripsawed lumber. A favorite of Texas cowmen, the exterior was whitewashed and the interior was sparsely decorated. The Fontaines were shown to their rooms, and the porter lugged their steamer trunks to the second floor. They agreed to meet in the lobby in an hour.

Lillian closed the door with a sigh. Her room was appointed with a single bed, a washstand and a rickety dresser, and one straight-backed chair. There were wall pegs for hanging clothes and a grimy window with tattered curtains that overlooked Texas Street. The mirror over the washbasin was cracked, and there was a sense of a monk's cell about the whole affair. She thought she'd never seen anything so dreary.

After undressing, she poured water from a pitcher into the basin and took a birdbath. The water was tepid and thick with silt, but she felt refreshed after so many days on a train. Then, peering into the faded mirror above the washstand, she rearranged her hair, fluffing the curls over her forehead. From her trunk, she selected undergarments and a stylish muslin dress with a lace collar. She wanted to look her best when they went to the theater.

Her waist was so small that she never wore a corset. She slipped into a chemise with a fitted bodice and three petticoats that fell below the knees. Silk hose, ankle-high shoes of soft calfskin, and the muslin dress completed her outfit. On the spur of the moment, she took from the trunk her prize possession, a light paisley shawl purchased at Lord & Taylor in New York. The shawl, exorbitantly expensive, had been a present from her mother their last Christmas together. Lillian wore it only on special occasions.

Shortly after three o'clock the Fontaines entered the Comique Variety Theater. The theater was a pleasant surprise, with a small orchestra pit, a proscenium stage, and seating for 400 people. Lou Gordon, the owner, was a beefy man with a walrus mustache and the dour look of a mortician. He greeted the men with a perfunctory handshake and a curt nod. His eyes lingered on Lillian.

"High time you're here," he said brusquely. "You open tomorrow night."

Fontaine smiled. "Perfect timing, my dear chap."

"Hope for your sake your booking agent was right. His wire said you put on a good show."

"I have every confidence you will be pleased. We present a range of entertainment for everyone."

"Such as?"

"All the world's a stage." Fontaine gestured grandly. "And all the men and women merely players. They have their exits and their entrances. And one man in his time plays many parts."

Gordon frowned. "What's that?"

"Shakespeare," Fontaine said lightly. *"As You Like It."*

"Cowhands aren't much on culture. Your agent said you do first-rate melodrama."

"Why, yes, of course, that, too. We're quite versatile."

"Glad to hear it." Gordon paused, glanced at Lillian. "What's the girl do?"

"Lillian is a fine actress," Fontaine observed proudly. "And I might add, she has a very nice voice. She opens our show with a ballad."

"Cowhands like a pretty songbird. Just don't overdo the Shakespeare."

"Have no fear, old chap. We'll leave them thoroughly entertained."

"You know Eddie Foy?" Gordon asked. "Tonight's his closing night."

"We've not had the pleasure," Fontaine said. "Headliners rarely share the same bill."

"Come on by for the show. You'll get an idea what these Texans like."

"I wouldn't miss an opportunity to see Eddie Foy."

Fontaine led the way out of the theater. He set off at a brisk pace toward the hotel. "The nerve of the man!" he said indignantly. "Instructing me on Shakespeare."

Lillian hurried to stay up. "He was only telling you about the audience, Papa."

"We shall see, my dear. We shall indeed!"

* * *

The chorus line kicked and squealed. They pranced offstage, flashing their legs, to thunderous applause from the crowd. The house was packed with Texans, most of them already juiced on rotgut liquor. Their lusty shouts rose in pitch as the girls disappeared into the wings.

The orchestra segued into a sprightly tune. The horns were muted, the strings more pronounced, and the audience quieted in anticipation. Eddie Foy skipped onstage, tipping his derby to the crowd, and went into a shuffling soft-shoe routine. The sound of his light feet on the floor was like velvety sandpaper.

Foy was short and wiry, with ginger hair and an infectious smile. Halfway through the routine, he began singing a bawdy ballad that brought bursts of laughter from the trailhands. The title of the song was *Such a Delicate Duck.*

> *I took her out one night for a walk*
> *We indulged in all sports of pleasantry and talk*
> *We came to a potato patch; she wouldn't go across*
> *The potatoes had eyes and she didn't wear no drawers!*

Lillian blushed a bright crimson. She was seated between her father and brother, three rows back from the orchestra. The lyrics of the song were far more ribald than anything she'd ever heard in a variety theater. Secretly, she thought the tune was indecently amusing, and wondered if she had no shame. Her blush deepened.

Foy ended the soft-shoe number. The orchestra fell silent with a last note of the strings as he moved to center stage. Framed in the footlights, he walked back and forth with herky-jerky gestures, delivering a rapid comedic patter that was at once risque and hilarious. The Texans honked and hooted with rolling waves of laughter.

On the heels of a last riotous joke, the orchestra suddenly blared to life. Foy nimbly sprang into a high-stepping buck-and-wing dance routine that took him cavorting around the stage. His voice raised in a madcap shout, he belted out a naughty tune. The lyrics involved a girl and her one-legged lover.

Toward the end of the number, Foy's rubbery face stretched wide in a clownish grin. He whirled, clicking his heels in midair, and skipped offstage with a final tip of his derby. The audience whistled and cheered, on their feet, rocking the walls with shrill ovation. Foy, bouncing merrily onto the stage, took three curtain calls.

The crowd, still laughing, began filing out of the theater. Fontaine waited for the aisle to clear, then led Lillian and Chester backstage. They found Foy seated before a mirror in his dressing room, wiping off greasepaint. He rose, turning to greet them, as Fontaine performed the introductions. His mouth split in a broad smile.

"Welcome to Abilene," he said jauntily. "Lou Gordon told me you're opening tomorrow night."

"Indeed we are," Fontaine affirmed. "Though I have to say, you'll be a hard act to follow. You're quite the showman."

"Same goes both ways. The Fontaines have some classy reputation on the circuit back East."

"The question is, will East meet West? We certainly had an education on Texans tonight."

Foy laughed. "Hey, you'll do swell. Just remember they're a bunch of rowdies at heart."

"Not to mention uncouth," Fontaine amended. "I'm afraid we haven't your gift for humor, Eddie. Gordon warned us that culture wouldn't play well in Abilene."

"You think I'd try the material you heard tonight in New York? No sir, I wouldn't, not on your tintype! You have to tailor your material to suit your audience. Westerners just like it a little . . . raunchy."

"Perhaps it's herding all those cows. Hardly what would be termed a genteel endeavor."

"That's a good one!" Foy said with a moonlike grin. "Nothing genteel about cowboys. Nosiree."

"Well, in any event," Fontaine said, offering a warm handshake. "A distinct pleasure meeting you, Eddie. We enjoyed the show."

"All the luck in the world to you! Hope you knock'em in the aisles."

"We'll certainly do our very best."

Fontaine found the way to the stage door. They emerged into a narrow alley that opened onto Texas Street. Lillian fell in between the men and glanced furtively at her father. She could tell he was in a dark mood.

"How enlightening," he said sourly. "I hardly think we'll follow Mr. Foy's advice."

"What would it harm, Papa?" Lillian suggested. "Melodrama with a few laughs might play well."

"I will not pander to vulgarians! Let's hear no more of it."

On the street, they turned toward the hotel. A group of cowhands, ossified on whiskey, lurched into them on the boardwalk. The Texans stopped, blocking their way, and one of them pushed forward. He was a burly man, thick through the shoulders, with mean eyes. He leered drunkenly at Lillian.

"Lookee here," he said in a rough voice. "Where'd you come from, little miss puss? How about we have ourselves a drink?"

"How dare you!" Fontaine demanded. "I'll thank you to move aside."

"Old man, don't gimme none of yore sass. I'm talkin' to the little darlin' here."

Chester stepped between them "Do as you're told, and quickly. I won't ask again."

"Hear that, boys?" the cowhand said, glancing at the other Texans. "Way he talks, he's from Boston or somewheres. We done treed a gawddamn Yankee."

"Out of our way."

Chester shoved him and the cowhand launched a murderous haymaker. The blow caught Chester flush on the jaw and he dropped to his knees. The Texan cocked a fist to finish him off.

A man bulled through the knot of trailhands. He was tall, with hawklike features, a badge pinned to his coat. His pistol rose and fell, and he thunked the troublemaker over the head with the barrel. The Texan went down and out, sprawled on the boardwalk.

"You boys skedaddle," the lawman said, motioning with the pistol. "Take your friend along and sober him up."

The cowboys jumped to obey. None of them said a word, and they avoided the lawman's eyes, fear written across their faces. They grabbed the fallen Texan under the arms and dragged him off down the street. The lawman watched them a moment, then turned to the Fontaines. He knuckled the brim of his low-crowned hat.

"I'm Marshal Hickok," he said. "Them drunks won't bother you no more."

Lillian was fascinated. His auburn hair was long, spilling down over his shoulders. He wore a frock coat, with a scarlet sash around his waist, a brace of Colt pistols tucked cross-draw fashion into the sash. His sweeping mustache curled slightly at the ends.

Hickok helped Chester to his feet. Fontaine introduced himself, as well as Lillian and Chester. The marshal nodded politely.

"I reckon you're the actors," he said. "Heard you start at the Comique tomorrow."

"Yes indeed," Fontaine acknowledged. "I do hope you will attend, Marshal."

"Wouldn't miss it for all the tea in China."

"Allow me to express our most sincere thanks for your assistance tonight."

"Never yet met a Texan worth a tinker's damn. Pleasure was all mine."

Hickok again tipped his hat. He walked off upstreet, broad shoulders straining against the fabric of his coat. Fontaine chuckled softly to himself.

"Do you know who he is?"

"No," Lillian said. "Who?"

"Only the deadliest marshal in the West. I read about him in *Harper's Magazine*."

"Yes, but who is he, Papa?"

"My dear, they call him Wild Bill Hickok."

# Chapter 3

A JUGGLER dressed in tights flung three bowie knives in a blinding circle. The steel of the heavy blades glittered in the footlights as he kept them spinning in midair. His face was a study in concentration.

The Comique was sold out. Tonight was opening night for *The Fontaines*, and every seat in the house was taken. The crowd, mostly Texas cowhands, watched the juggler with rapt interest. They thought he might slip and lose a finger.

The juggler suddenly flipped all three knives high in the air. He stood perfectly still as the knives rotated once, then twice, and plummeted downward. The points of the blades struck the floor, embedded deep in the wood, quivering not an inch from his shoes. The Texans broke out in rollicking applause for his death-defying stunt.

The orchestra blared as the juggler bowed, collecting his knives, and skipped off the stage. A chorus line of eight girls exploded out of the wings, squealing and kicking as the orchestra thumped louder. The girls were scantily clad, bosoms heaving, skirts flashing to reveal their legs. They bounded exuberantly around the stage in a high-stepping dance routine.

Lillian stood in the wings at stage right. She was dressed in a gown of teal silk, with a high collar and a hemline that swept the floor. Her heart fluttered and her throat felt dry, a nervous state she invariably experienced before a performance. Her father appeared from backstage, attired in the period costume of a Danish nobleman. His hands lightly touched her shoulders.

"You look beautiful," he said softly. "Your mother would have been proud of you."

"If only I had Mama's voice. I feel so . . . inadequate."

"Simply remember what your mother taught you. You'll do fine, my dear. I know you will."

Her mother had had an operatic voice, with the range of a soprano. Lillian's voice was lower, a husky alto, and her mother had taught her how to stay within her range, lend deeper emotion to the lyrics. Yet she never failed to draw the comparison with her mother, and in her mind she fell short. On her best nights, she was merely adequate.

The chorus line came romping offstage. The curtain swished closed, and Lou Gordon stepped before the footlights, briefly introducing his new headliner act. When the curtain opened, Lillian was positioned center stage, her hands folded at her waist. By contrast with the chorus girls, she looked innocent, somehow virginal. The orchestra came up softly as she opened with *Darling Nelly Gray.*

*There's a low green valley*
*On the old Kentucky shore*
*There I've whiled happy hours away*
*Sitting and singing by the cottage door*
*Where lived my darling Nelly Gray*

Something extraordinary happened. A hushed silence fell over the audience as her clear alto, pitched low and intimate, filled the hall. She acted out the song with poignant emotion, and her sultry voice somehow gave the lyrics a haunting quality. She sensed the cowhands were captivated, and she saw Wild Bill Hickok watching intently from the back of the theater. She played it for all it was worth.

*Oh, my darling Nelly Gray*
*Up in heaven there they say*
*They'll take you from me no more*
*I'm coming as angels clear the way*
*Farewell now to the old Kentucky shore*

There was hardly a dry eye in the house. The Texans were Southerners, many having served under the Confederate flag during the late war. They were caught up in a melancholy tale that was all the more sorrowful because of Lillian's striking good looks. She held them enthralled to the last note, and then the theater vibrated to rolling applause. She took a bow and bowed a final time before disappearing into the wings. The Texans chanted their approval.

*"Lilly! Lilly! Lilly!"*

The curtain closed as the clamor died down. Gordon again appeared before the footlights, announcing that the famed thespian Alistair Fontaine would now render a soliloquy from Shakespeare's masterpiece *Hamlet*. A moment later the curtain opened with Fontaine at center stage, bathed in the cider glow of a spotlight from the rear of the theater. He struck a classic profile, arresting in the costume of a Danish prince. His voice floated over the hall in a tragic baritone.

*To be, or not to be: that is the question:*
*Whether 'tis nobler in the mind to suffer*
*The slings and arrows of outrageous fortune,*
*Or to take arms against a sea of troubles,*
*And by opposing end them? To die, to sleep . . .*

The cowhands in the audience traded puzzled glances. They knew little of Shakespeare and even less of some strangely dressed character called Hamlet. Though they tried to follow the odd cadence of his words, the meaning eluded them. Fontaine doggedly plowed on, aware that they were restive and quickly losing interest. He ended the passage with a dramatic gesture, his features grimly stark in the spotlight. The Texans gave him a smattering of polite applause.

The finale of the show was a one-act melodrama titled *A Husband's Vengeance.* Chester played the husband and Lillian, attired in a cheap print dress, the attractive wife. Fontaine, following a quick change from Danish prince to top-hatted villain, played a lecherous landlord. In Scene 1, Chester and Lillian's love-struggling-against-poverty was established for the audience. In Scene 2, with the husband off at work, the lustful landlord demanded that the wife surrender her virtue for the overdue rent or be evicted. The crowd hissed and booed the villain for the cad he was.

Scene 3 brought the denouement. Chester returned from work to discover the landlord stalking his wife around the set, with the bed the most prominent item of furniture in the shabby apartment. The husband, properly infuriated, flattened Fontaine with a mighty punch and bodily tossed him out the door. The cowhands jumped to their feet, whooping and hollering, cheering the valorous conquest of good over evil. Then, to even greater cheers, the curtain closed with Chester and Lillian clinched in a loving embrace. The crowd went wild.

The show might have ended there. But the Texans almost immediately resumed their chant. They stood, shouting and stomping, the jingle of their spurs like musical chimes. Their voices were raised in a collective roar.

*"We want Lilly! We want Lilly! We want Lilly!"*

Lou Gordon hastily improvised an encore. After a hurried backstage conference with Lillian, he ran out to distribute sheet music to the orchestra. Some minutes later the curtain opened with Lillian center stage, still costumed in the cheap print dress. A hush settled over the audience as violins' from the orchestra came up on *Take Back the Heart.* Her dulcet voice throbbed with emotion.

*Take back the heart that thou gavest*
*What is my anguish to thee?*
*Take back the freedom thou cravest*
*Leaving the fetters to me*
*Take back the vows thou hast spoken*
*Fling them aside and be free*
*Smile o'er each pitiful token*
*Leaving the sorrow for me*

The ballad went on with the story of unrequited love. By the time she finished the last stanza, hardened Texans were sniffling noisily and swiping at tears. Their thoughts were on mothers and sisters, and girlfriends left behind, and there was no shame among grown men that night. Lillian bowed off the stage to tumultuous applause.

Gordon caught her as she stepped into the wings. "Little lady, from now on you're Lilly Fontaine! You hear what I'm saying—*Lilly Fontaine!*"

Lillian was in a daze. Her father was waiting as she turned backstage. He enfolded her into his arms, holding her close. His voice was a whisper.

"Thou art thy mother's glass, and she in thee calls back the lovely April of her prime."

"Oh, Papa!" She hugged him tightly. "You know that's my favorite of all the sonnets."

Fontaine grinned. "Your mother and the Bard would be proud of you."

She desperately hoped it was true.

Hickok was waiting at the stage door. The alleyway was deep in shadow, faintly lighted by a lamppost from the street. He knuckled the brim of his hat.

"Evenin'," he said pleasantly. "You folks put on a mighty good show. Liked it a lot."

"Why, thank you, Marshal," Fontaine said. "We're delighted you enjoyed yourself."

Hickok shrugged. "Figured I'd see you back to your hotel. Things get a little testy on the streets this late at night."

"How kind of you, Marshal. As it happens, Mayor McCoy invited Chester and myself for a drink. Perhaps you wouldn't mind escorting Lillian."

Joseph McCoy, the town founder, was also Abilene's mayor. His invitation, extended backstage following the show, did not include Lillian. Women of moral character never patronized saloons.

"Be an honor, ma'am," Hickok said, nodding to Lillian. "A lawman don't often get such pleasurable duty."

Lillian batted her eyelashes. "How very gallant, Marshal."

On the street, Fontaine and Chester turned north toward the Alamo Saloon. The Alamo catered to wealthy Texas cattlemen and local citizens of means. Lillian and Hickok walked south along the boardwalk.

"Tell me, Marshal," Lillian said, making conversation. "Have you been a peace officer very long?"

"A spell," Hickok allowed. "I was sheriff over at Hays City before I came here. How about you?"

"Pardon?"

"How long you been in variety work?"

"Oh, goodness, all of my life. I was born in the theater."

Hickok looked at her. "You was *born* in a theater?"

"A figure of speech," Lillian said gaily. "I started on the stage when I was five. The theater's all I've ever known."

"Well, now, don't that beat all."

A young man stopped in front of them. He was dressed in cowboy gear, a pistol holstered at his side. His eyes were cold slate blue, and Lillian placed him at about her own age. He gave Hickok a lopsided smile.

"How's tricks, Wild Bill?"

"Tolerable, Wes," Hickok said shortly. "You stayin' out of trouble?"

"Yeah, I'm on my good behavior. Wouldn't do to get on your bad side, would it now?"

"Never figured you any other way."

"Well, I'll see you around, Marshal. Don't take any wooden nickels."

The young man stepped around them, never once looking at Lillian. As they moved on, she darted a glance at Hickok. His expression was somber.

"How strange," she said. "I really don't think he likes you."

"Miss Lillian, the feeling's mutual."

"Who is he?"

"John Wesley Hardin," Hickok said. "Got himself a reputation as a gunman down in Texas. I warned him to mind his manners here in Abilene."

"Gunman?" Lillian said, shocked. "You mean he killed someone?"

"More'n one, so folks say."

"He doesn't look old enough."

"They raise'em quick in Texas."

Hickok bid her good night in the lobby of the Drover's Cottage. From her father she knew that Hickok himself was a notorious gunman. Apparently, a raft of dime novels had been written about his exploits on the frontier, dubbing him the "Prince of Pistoleers." She wondered how many men he had killed.

Upstairs, she undressed and changed into a nightgown. She got into bed, too exhilarated for sleep, remembering the applause. In her most fanciful dreams, she would never have imagined the reception she'd received tonight. The thought of men shedding tears at the sound of her voice made her shiver. She closed her eyes and fervently prayed it would last. An image of her mother formed. . . .

A gunshot brought her out of bed. She realized she'd fallen asleep, dreaming of her mother. There was no noise from the street, and she thought it must be late.

She went to the window, still confused by the gunshot, and looked out. Three rooms down from hers, she saw a man leap from the window and land heavily on the boardwalk. He jumped to his feet.

The spill of light from a lamppost momentarily froze his features. She recognized him as the young man she'd seen earlier, John Wesley Hardin. She saw now that he appeared disheveled, shirttail flapping, boots in one hand, his pistol in the other. He searched the street in both directions, spotting no one, and then sprinted off in his stocking feet. He disappeared around the corner.

Some minutes later she heard voices in the hall. She opened the door a crack and saw her father and Chester, barefoot, their nightshirts stuffed into their trousers. Other men, similarly awakened from sleep, were gathered before a door two rooms down from hers. They all turned as Hickok pounded up the stairs into the hall, his gun drawn. He brushed past them, entering the darkened room. A moment later lamplight glowed from the doorway.

"Good Lord!" her father exclaimed. "He's been shot."

Hickok stepped out of the room. His features were grim as he looked around at the men. "Anybody see what went on here?"

There were murmurs of bewilderment, men shaking their heads. Then, stuffing his pistol back in his sash, Hickok saw Lillian peering out of her door. He walked down the hall.

"Miss Lillian," he said. "Some poor devil's been shot and killed in his own bed. You hear anything unusual?"

"I saw him," Lillian said on an indrawn breath. "The gunshot awoke me and I went to my window. It was the young Texan you and I met on the street earlier. He leapt out the window of his room."

"You talkin' about Wes Hardin?"

"Yes, the one you said was a gunman."

"Where'd he go?"

"Why, he ran away," Lillian replied. "Around the corner, by the mercantile store."

"I'm most obliged for your help."

Hickok hurried to the stairwell. Fontaine and Chester, who were listening to the conversation, entered her room. She explained how she'd met Hardin and later recognized him as he fled the hotel. Fontaine slowly wagged his head.

"I'm sorry, my dear," he said, clearly shaken. "I've brought you to a place where murderers lodge just down the hall."

"Oh, Papa," she said quickly. "You mustn't blame yourself. It might have happened anywhere."

"I am reminded of the Bard by this dreadful affair. 'As flies to wanton boys, are we to the gods; they kill us for their sport.' "

Chester snorted. "Shakespeare should have seen Abilene!"

Several days later they learned the truth. John Wesley Hardin, after a drunken night on the town, was annoyed by the rumbling snores of a hotel guest in the next room. Hardin fired through the wall and killed the man where he lay fast asleep. Then, rather than face Hickok, he fled on foot to a cowcamp outside Abilene. From there, he made good his escape to Texas. He was eighteen years old.

Lillian, thinking back on it, was struck by how very little changed with time. Shakespeare, nearly three centuries before, had penned an axiom for all time.

Wanton boys, like the gods, still killed for sport.

# Chapter 4

A BRILLIANT sun stood fixed at its zenith. The weather was moderate for late September, with cottony clouds drifting westward against an azure sky. The bawling of cows was constant from the stockyards near the railroad siding.

Hickok arrived at the hotel shortly before one o'clock. Lillian was waiting in the lobby, wearing a corded cotton dress with delicate stripes worked into the fabric. She carried a parasol and wore a chambray bonnet that accentuated her features. She gave him a fetching smile as he tipped his hat.

"I see you're punctual, as always."

"Never keep a lady waiting," Hickok said smoothly. "All ready to see the sights?"

"Oh, yes, I'm so looking forward to it."

Outside, on the boardwalk, she took his arm. They drew stares from passersby as they walked south along Texas Street. After a fortnight at the Comique, Lillian was the talk of the town. The *Abilene Courier* referred to her as a "chanteuse," and beguiled cowhands flocked to her performances. The theater was sold out every night.

The town was no less interested in her curious relationship with Hickok. He was a womanizer of some renown, having carried on liaisons with several ladies since arriving in Abilene. Even more, at thirty-four, he was fifteen years Lillian's senior, and the difference was the source of considerable gossip. Yet, for all anyone could tell, it was a benign relationship. Hickok appeared the perfect gentleman.

Lillian was attracted to him in the way a moth flirts with flame. She knew he was dangerous, having been informed by her father that he had killed at least a dozen men, not including Indians. He was a former army scout and deputy U.S. marshal and lionized by the press as the West's foremost "shootist." The term was peculiar to the frontier, reserved for those considered to be mankillers of some distinction. Other men crossed him at their own peril.

For all that, Lillian found him to be considerate and thoughtful, gentle in a roughhewn sort of way. Her father at first forbade her to see Hickok, and she deflected his protests with kittenish artifice. She was intrigued as well by Hickok's reputation as a womanizer, for she had never known a lothario, apart from Shakespeare's plays. One of the chorus girls at the Comique told her Hickok had lost his most recent lady friend to a Texas gambler named Phil Coe. Lillian thought, perhaps, the loss accounted for his courtly manner. He was, she sensed, a lonely man.

Every night, Hickok escorted her from the theater back to the Drover's Cottage. There, assured she was safe, he left her in the lobby and went about his duties as marshal. On three occasions, before the evening show at the Comique, he had invited her to dinner at the restaurant in the hotel. Today, leaving his deputy, Mike Williams, to police Abilene, he had invited her for an afternoon ride in the country. They had never been alone together or far from her father's sight, and she somehow relished the experience. She felt breathlessly close to the flame.

The owner of the livery stable was a paunchy man, bald as a bullet. He greeted Hickok with a nervous grin and led them to the rig, hired for the afternoon. Hickok assisted her into the buggy, which was drawn by a coal black mare with ginger in her step. He had a good hand with horses, lightly popping the reins, urging the mare along at a brisk clip. They drove east from town, on a wagon trace skirting the Smoky Hill and the Kansas Pacific tracks. Dappled sunlight filtered through tall cottonwoods bordering the river.

On the southeast corner of the town limits, they passed what was derisively known as the Devil's Addition. Abilene, with hordes of randy cowhands roaming the streets, attracted prostitutes in large numbers. The decent women of the community, offended by the revelry, demanded that the mayor close down the bordellos. Joseph McCoy, ever the pragmatist and fearful of inciting the Texans, banished the soiled doves instead to an isolated red-light district. The cowhands simply had to walk a little farther to slake their lust.

Lillian stared straight ahead as they drove past the brothels. She was no innocent, even though she had managed to retain her virginity despite the advances of handsome and persuasive admirers on the variety circuit. She knew men consorted with prostitutes and that the world's oldest profession could be traced to biblical times. Sometimes, wakeful in the dark of night, she tried to imagine what services the girls provided to their clientele. She often wished she could be a fly on the wall, just for a moment. She thought she might learn wicked and exotic secrets.

One secret she already knew. Her mother had taught her that the way to a man's heart was through his vanity. Men loved nothing quite so much as talking about themselves and their feats, imagined or otherwise. A woman who was a good listener and expressed interest captivated men by the sound of their own voices. Lillian had found what seemed an eternal axiom to be no less true with Wild Bill Hickok. She turned to him now.

"I've been wondering," she said with an engaging smile. "Why do people call you Wild Bill?"

"Well," Hickok said, clearly pleased by her interest. "One time durin' the war I had to fight off a passel of Rebs and swim a river to make my escape. The Federal boys watchin' from the other side was plumb amazed. They up and dubbed me Wild Bill."

"What a marvelous story!"

"Yeah, ceptin' my name's not Bill. It's James."

"James?" Lillian said, looking properly confused. "Why didn't they call you Wild *Jim?*"

"Never rightly knew," Hickok said. "The name stuck and I've been tagged with it ever since. Finally got wore out tryin' to set folks straight."

"I think James is a fine name."

"So'd my ma and pa."

Lillian urged him on. "So you were with the Union army?"

"Worked mostly as a scout behind enemy lines. The Rebs would've shot me for a spy if I'd ever got caught."

"How exciting!"

Hickok brought the buggy to a halt. They were stopped on a low bluff, overlooking the river and the prairie. The grasslands stretched endlessly in the distance, broken only by the churned earth of the Chisholm

Trail. A herd of longhorns, choused along by cowhands, plodded north toward Abilene.

"How beautiful!" she said. "I wish I were a painter."

"You're mighty pretty yourself." Hickok casually placed his arm on top of the seat behind her. "Somebody ought to paint you."

Lillian felt his fingers brush her shoulder. She thought she might allow him to kiss her, and then, just as quickly, she changed her mind. She knew he wouldn't be satisfied with a kiss.

"I'm simply fascinated by your work," she said, shifting slightly in the seat. "Do you enjoy being a peace officer?"

The question distracted Hickok. She seemed genuinely interested, and young as she was, she was probably impressionable. Talking about himself might lead to more than a kiss.

"Guess every man's got his callin'," he said with a tinge of bravado. "Turns out I'm good at enforcin' the law."

"Yes, but everyone out here carries a gun. Aren't you sometimes afraid . . . just a little?"

Hickok explained the code of the West. There were no rules that governed conduct in a shootout, except the rule of fairness: A man could not fire on an unarmed opponent or open fire without warning. Apart from that, every man looked for an edge, some slight advantage. The idea was to survive with honor intact.

"Not likely I'll ever be beat," he bragged. "Don't you see, I've already got the edge over other men. I'm Wild Bill."

Lillian at first thought he was joking. But then she realized he was serious, deadly serious. She wished her mother were there, for how they would have laughed. Wild Bill Hickok proved the point.

No man, given an attentive female, could resist tooting his own horn.

The spotlight bathed Lillian in an umber glow. She stood poised at center stage, the light caressing her features, the audience still. The house was again sold out, and every cowhand in the theater stared at her with a look of moony adoration. The orchestra glided into *The Rose of Killarney* as her voice filled the hall.

> *There's a spot in old Ireland still dear to my*
> *heart*
> *Thousands of miles 'cross the sea tho I'm*
> *forced to part*
> *I've a place now in the land of the free*
> *Tho the home there I shall never forget*
> *It brings a tear for thoughts I so regret*
> *When I bid goodbye to the rose of Killarney*

Her eyes roved over the audience. At the rear of the hall, she saw Hickok in his usual post by the door. Even in the midst of the song, she wondered if he regretted the loss of a kiss, having talked about himself all the way back to town. When she finished the last stanza, the crowd whooped and shouted, their hands pounding in applause. The spotlight followed her as she bowed her way offstage.

Fontaine came on next with a piece from *The Merchant of Venice*. The audience slumped into their seats, murmuring their displeasure, as though Shakespeare were an unwelcome guest at an otherwise festive occasion. Then, suddenly, the door at the rear of the hall burst open with a resounding whack. A cowboy, mounted on a sorrel gelding, ducked low through the door and rode down the center aisle. He caterwauled a loud, screeching Rebel yell.

Hickok was only a step behind. He levered himself over the horse's rump with one hand, grabbed a fistful of shirt with the other, and yanked the cowboy out of the saddle. The Texan hit the floor on his back, and as he scrambled to his feet, Hickok thumped him across the head with a pistol. The impact of metal on bone sounded with a mushy *splat*, and a welter of blood geysered out from the cowboy's scalp. He dropped into the arms of a man seated directly beside the aisle.

The horse reared at the railing of the orchestra pit. Terrified, the members of the orchestra dived in every direction, scattering horns and violins. By now thoroughly spooked, the gelding whirled around, wall eyed with fright, and started up the aisle. Hickok stepped aside, whacking him across the rump, and the horse bolted out of the theater. As he went through the door, the Texans in the audience erupted from their seats, angered that Hickok had spoiled the fun. All the more, they were outraged by his treatment of the cowboy.

"You sorry sonovabitch!" someone yelled. "You got yours comin' now!"

A knot of cowhands jammed into the aisle. Hickok backed to the orchestra pit, pulling his other Colt. He leveled the pistols on the crowd.

"Stop right there!" he ordered. "I'll drill the first man that comes any closer."

"You cain't get us all!" one of the cowhands in the front rank shouted. "C'mon, boys, let's rush the Yankee bastard."

A shotgun boomed from the rear of the theater. The Texans turned and saw Hickok's deputy, Mike Williams, standing in the doorway. Plaster rained down from a hole in the ceiling, and he swung the double-barrel scattergun in a wide arc, covering the crowd. Hickok rapped out a command.

"Everybody back in your seats!" he barked. "Any more nonsense and I'll march the whole bunch of you off to jail."

"Yore jail ain't that big, Hickok!"

"Who wants to try me and find out?"

No one seemed inclined to accept the offer. Order was restored within minutes, and the Texans, still muttering, slowly resumed their seats. Hickok walked up the aisle, both pistols trained on the audience, and stopped at the door. Mike Williams, who was a beefy man with a thatch of red hair, gave him a peg-toothed grin. They stood watching as the crowd settled down.

The Fontaines went directly into a melodrama titled *A Dastardly Deed.* When the play was over, Lillian came back onstage alone, for her nightly encore was by now part of the show. In an effort to further dampen the cowhands' temper, she sang their favorite song, *Dixie*. She sang it not as a stirring marching ballad but rather as a plaintive melody. Her voice was pitched low and sad, almost mournful.

*I wish I was in the land of cotton*
*Old times there are not forgotten*
*Look away! Look away! Look away, Dixieland!*

The Texans, unrepentant Confederates to a man, trooped out of the theater in weepy silence. They jammed into saloons along the street, drinking maudlin toasts to the Bonnie Blue Flag and blessing the gracious sentiment of Lilly Fontaine. Some of them, after a few snorts of popskull, wandered off to the Devil's Addition. There they found solace in the arms of whores.

Hickok escorted Lillian, as well as Fontaine and Chester, back to the hotel. He bid them a solemn good night, his features grave, and rejoined Mike Williams on the street. His manner was that of a man off to do battle, and the Fontaines fully expected to hear gunshots before the night was done. They went to their rooms wondering if the Texans would leave well enough alone.

Later, lying awake in the dark, Lillian was reminded of Abilene's former marshal. One of the chorus girls had related the gory end of Hickok's predecessor, Tom Smith. By all accounts a respected peace officer, Smith had gone to arrest a homesteader, Andrew McConnell, on a murder warrant. McConnell waylaid the marshal, grievously wounding him with a Winchester rifle. As Smith lay helpless, McConnell hefted an ax and chopped off his head. Abilene gave the slain lawman a stately funeral.

Lillian shuddered at the image. Still, the grisly death of Tom Smith helped her to better understand Hickok. Tonight's incident at the theater was part and parcel of what he'd tried to explain on their buggy ride that afternoon.

Wild Bill Hickok lived by a code ancient even in olden times: Do unto them before they do unto you.

# Chapter 5

THE EVENING of October 5 was brisk and clear. A full moon washed the town in spectral light and stars dotted the sky like diamond dust. Texas Street was all but deserted.

A last contingent of cowhands wandered from saloon to saloon. Earlier that day the final herd of longhorns had been loaded at the stockyards and shipped east by train. The trailing season was officially over, for the onset of winter was only weeks away. Two months, perhaps less, would see the plains adrift with snow.

The mood was glum at the Comique. Abilene, the first of the western cowtowns, was sounding the death knell. The railroad had laid track a hundred miles south to Wichita, a burgeoning center of commerce located on the Arkansas River. By next spring, when the herds came north on the Chisholm Trail, Wichita would be the nearest railhead. Abilene would be a ghost town.

Lou Gordon planned to move his operation to Wichita. With the coming of spring, he would reopen the Comique on the banks of the Arkansas and welcome the Texans with yet another variety show. He had offered the Fontaines headliner billing, for Lillian was now a star attraction with a loyal following. But that left the problem of where they would spend the winter and how they would subsist in the months ahead. So far, he'd uncovered only one likely alternative.

Alistair Fontaine was deeply troubled. Though he usually managed a cheery facade, he was all but despondent over their bleak turn of fortune. Upon traveling West, he had anticipated a bravura engagement in Abilene and a triumphant return to New York. Yet his booking agent, despite solid notices in the *Abilene Courier,* had been unable to secure a spot for them on the Eastern variety circuit. A hit show in Kansas kindled little enthusiasm among impresarios on Broadway.

Fontaine saw it as a descent into obscurity. To climb so high and fall so far had about it the bitter taste of ignominy. He'd begun life as John Hagerty, an Irish ragamuffin from the Hell's Kitchen district of New York. Brash and ambitious, he fled poverty by working his way up in the theater, from stagehand to actor. Almost twenty-five years ago, he had adopted the stage name Alistair Fontaine, lending himself an air of culture and refinement. Then, seemingly graced, he had married Estell.

Yet now, after thirty years in the theater, he was reduced to a vagabond. The descent began with Estell's untimely death and the realization that he was, at best, a modest Shakespearian. In Abilene came the discovery that his daughter, though a lesser talent than her mother, nonetheless brought that indefinable magic to the stage. But he hadn't foreseen the vagaries of a celebrated return to New York or the growth of the railroad and the abrupt demise of Abilene. He wasn't prepared to winter in some primitive outpost called Dodge City.

The crowd for tonight's show was sparse. There were fewer than a hundred cowhands still in Abilene and perhaps half that number in the audience. The melodrama finished only moments ago, Fontaine and Chester stood in the wings, watching Lillian perform her encore. For their last night in Abilene, she had selected as her final number a poignant ballad titled *The Wayfarer*. She thought it would appeal to the Texans on their long journey home, south along the Chisholm Trail. Her voice gave the lyrics a sorrowful quality.

*The sun is in the west,*
*The stars are on the sea,*
*Each kindly hand I've pres't,*
*And now, farewell to thee.*
*The cup of parting done,*
*'Tis the darkest I can sip.*
*I have pledg'd them ev'ry one*
*With my heart and with my lip.*
*But I came to thee the last,*
*That together we might throw*
*One look upon the past*
*In sadness ere I go*

On the final note, the cowhands gave her a rousing ovation. They rose, calling out her name, waving goodbye with their broad-brimmed hats. She smiled wistfully, waving in return as the curtain closed, throwing them a kiss at the last moment. Her eyes were misty as she moved into the wings, where Fontaine and Chester waited. She swiped at a tear.

"Oh, just look at me," she said with a catch in her throat. "Crying over a bunch of cowboys."

"Well, it's closing night," Chester consoled her. "You're entitled to a few tears."

"I feel like crying myself," Fontaine grumped. "We've certainly nothing to celebrate."

"Papa!" Lillian scolded gently. "I'm surprised at you. What's wrong?"

"We are not traveling to New York, my dear. To paraphrase Robert Burns, the best laid schemes of mice and men often go awry."

"Yes, but Lou felt almost certain he could arrange a booking in Dodge City. It's not as though we're out of work."

"Dodge City!" Fontaine scoffed. "Gordon seemed quite chary with information about the place. Other than to say it is somewhere—*somewhere*—in western Kansas."

Chester grinned. "Dad, you were talking about a grand adventure when we came out here. This way, we get to see a little more of the West."

"And it's only for the winter," Lillian added. "Lou promised an engagement in Wichita in the spring."

Fontaine considered a moment. "I've no wish to see more of the West. But your point is well taken." He paused, nodding sagely. "Any engagement is better than no engagement a'tall."

Lou Gordon appeared from backstage. Over the course of their month in Abilene, he had become a friend, particularly where Lillian was concerned. He felt she was destined for big things on the variety stage. He extended a telegram to Fontaine.

"Got a wire from Frank Murphy just before the show. He's agreed to book you for the winter."

"Has he indeed?"

Fontaine scanned the telegram. His eyes narrowed. "Two hundred dollars a month! I refuse to work for a pauper's wages."

"Lodging and meals are included," Gordon pointed out. "Besides, Alistair, it's not like you've got a better offer."

"Papa, please," Lillian interceded. "Do we really have a choice?"

"I appear to be outnumbered," Fontaine said. "Very well, Lou, we will accept Mr. Murphy's parsimonious offer. How are we to accomplish this pilgrimage?"

Gordon quickly explained that railroad tracks had not yet been laid into western Kansas. He went on to say that he'd arranged for them to accompany a caravan of freight wagons bound for Dodge City. He felt sure they could make an excellent deal for a buggy and team at the livery stable. With the loss of the cattle trade, everything in Abilene was for sale at bargain prices.

"A buggy!" Fontaine parroted. "Good Lord, I'd given it no thought until now. We'll be sleeping on the *ground*."

"Afraid so," Gordon acknowledged. "You'll be cooking your own meals, too. The hardware store can supply you with camp gear."

"Is there no end to it?" Fontaine said in a wounded voice. "We are to travel like . . . Mongols."

Chester laughed. "No adventure as grand as an expedition. Nostradamus has nothing on you, Dad."

"I hardly predicted a sojourn into the wilderness."

"How marvelous!" Lillian clapped her hands with excitement. "We'll have such fun."

Fontaine arched an eyebrow. He thought perhaps her mother had missed something in her training. There was, after all, a certain limit to hardship.

Overland travel was hardly his idea of fun.

* * *

Hickok checked his pocket watch. He rose from behind his desk in the jailhouse and went out the door. He walked toward the theater.

All evening he'd been expecting trouble. As he passed the Lone Star Saloon, he glanced through the plate glass window. Phil Coe and several cowhands were standing at the bar, swilling whiskey. He wondered if Coe would at last find courage in a bottle.

Their mutual antagonism went back over the summer. Coe was a tinhorn gambler who preyed on guileless cowhands by duping them with friendship and liquor. Hickok, sometime in early July, put out the word that Coe was a cardsharp, the worst kind of cheat. He gulled fellow Texans in crooked games.

The charge brought no immediate confrontation. Hickok heard through the grapevine that Coe had threatened his life, but he suspected the gambler had no stomach for a fight. Coe retaliated instead by charming a saloon girl widely considered to be Hickok's woman and stealing away her affections. The animosity between the men deepened even more.

Word on the street was that the last of the Texans planned to depart town tomorrow. Coe, whose home was in Austin, would likely join them on the long trek down the Chisholm Trail. Without cowhands for him to fleece, there was nothing to hold Coe in Abilene any longer. So it made sense to Hickok that trouble, if it came at all, would come tonight. Coe, to all appearances, was fueling his courage with alcohol.

Hickok turned into the alley beside the Comique. He intended to see Lillian safely back to the hotel, just as he'd done every night since she arrived in Abilene. He planned to apply for the job of marshal in Wichita, and he thought that might have some bearing on their future. Lou Gordon was opening a variety theater there, and Hickok assumed the Fontaines would tag along. He would arrange to talk with her about it in the next day or so. Tonight, given the slightest pretext, he would attend to Phil Coe.

The stage door opened as he moved into the alleyway. Lillian stepped outside, accompanied by her father and brother. He greeted Fontaine and Chester as she waited for him by the door. Her features were animated.

"Aren't you the tardy one," she said with a teasing lilt. "You missed my last performance."

"Not by choice," Hickok begged off. "Had some business that needed tendin'."

"Wait till you hear our news!"

Lillian was eager to tell him about their plans. She fantasized that he would join them on the trip, perhaps become the marshal of Dodge City. She wasn't sure she loved him, for she still had no idea of what love was supposed to feel like. But she was attracted to him, and she knew the feeling was mutual, and she thought there was a good man beneath the rough exterior. A trip west together would make it even more of an adventure.

"What news is that?" Hickok asked.

"Well, we just found out tonight we're going—"

A gunshot sounded from the street. Then, in rapid succession, two more shots bracketed through the still night. Hickok was moving even as the echoes died away.

"Stay here!" he ordered. "Don't go out on the street."

"Where are you—"

"Just stay put!"

Hickok rushed off into the darkness. He moved to the far end of the alley, turning the corner of the building across from the Comique. Headed north, he walked quickly to the rear of the third building and entered the back door of the Alamo Saloon. He hurried through the saloon, startled customers frozen in place as he drew both pistols. He stepped through the front door onto the boardwalk.

Phil Coe stood in the middle of the street. A dead dog lay on the ground at his feet, the earth puddled with blood. He had a bottle in one hand and a gun in the other, bantering in a loud voice with four Texans who were gathered around. He idly waved the bottle at the dog.

"Boys, there lies one tough scutter. Never thought it'd take me three shots to kill a dog."

"Hell, it didn't," one of the cowhands cackled. "You done missed him twice."

"What's going on here, Coe?"

The men turned at the sound of Hickok's voice. He was framed in a shaft of light from the door, the pistols held loosely at his sides. Coe separated from the Texans, a tall man with handsome features, his mouth quirked in a tight smile. He gestured with the bottle.

"No harm done, Marshal," he said. "Just shot myself a dog, that's all."

"Drop your gun," Hickok told him. "You're under arrest."

"What the hell for?"

"Discharging firearms within the town limits."

"Bullshit!" Coe flared. "You're not arresting me for shootin' a goddamn dog."

"I won't tell you again—drop it."

Coe raised his pistol and fired. The slug plucked the sleeve of Hickok's coat and thunked into the saloon door. He extended his right arm at shoulder level and the Colt spat a sheet of flame. Coe staggered backward, firing another round that shattered the Alamo's window. Hickok shot him again.

A crimson starburst spread over the breast of Coe's jacket. His legs tangled in a nerveless dance, and he slumped to the ground, eyes fixed on the starry sky. Footsteps clattered on the boardwalk as a man bulled through a crowd of onlookers, gun in hand, and hurried forward. Hickok caught movement from the corner of his eye, the glint of metal in silvery moonlight. He whirled, reflexes strung tight, and fired.

The man faltered, clutching at his chest, and tumbled off the boardwalk into the street. One of the onlookers, a railroad worker, eased from the crowd and peered down at the body. His face went taut and he turned to Hickok with an accusing stare. "It's Mike Williams!" he shouted. "You've killed your own deputy."

A look of disbelief clouded Hickok's features. He walked to the body and knelt down, pistols dangling from his hands. His hard visage seemed to crack, and he bowed his head, shoulders slumped. The onlookers stared at him in stony silence.

The Fontaines watched from the alleyway. They had witnessed the gunfight, then the senseless death of a man rushing to help his friend. Fontaine was reminded of a Greek tragedy, played out on the dusty street of a cowtown, and Chester seemed struck dumb. Lillian had a hand pressed to her mouth in horror.

Fontaine took her arm. She glanced one last time at Hickok as her father led her away. Chester followed along, still mute, and they angled across the street to the Drover's Cottage. The desk clerk was standing in the door, drawn by the gunshots, on the verge of questioning them. He moved aside as they entered the lobby, reduced to silence by the expression on their faces. They mounted the stairs to their rooms.

Some while later, changed into her nightgown, Lillian crawled in bed. She felt numb with shock, her insides gone cold, and she pulled the covers to her chin. She had never seen a man killed, much less two in a matter of seconds, and the image of it kept flashing through her mind. The spectacle of it, random violence and death, was suddenly too much to bear. She closed her eyes to the terror.

A thought came to her in a moment of revelation. She could never love a man who so readily dealt in killing. The fantasy she had concocted was born of girlish dreams, silly notions about honor and knights of the plains. She saw now that it was all foolish whimsy.

Tomorrow, she would say goodbye to Wild Bill Hickok.

# CHAPTER 6

THE CARAVAN stretched nearly a mile along the river. The broad, rushing waters of the Arkansas tumbled over a rocky streambed that curved southwestward across the plains. A fiery sun tilted lower toward the distant horizon.

Lillian was seated between her father and Chester. She wore a linsey-woolsey dress with a fitted mantle coat that fell below her knees. The men were attired in whipcord trousers, plaid mackinaws, and wide-brimmed slouch hats. They looked like reluctant city folk cast in the role of pioneers.

Their buckboard, purchased in Abilene, was a stout four-wheeled vehicle designed for overland travel. The rig was drawn by a team of horses, one sorrel and one dun, plodding along as though hitched to a plow. The storage bed behind the seat was loaded with camp gear, food crates, and their steamer trunks. The goods were lashed securely and covered with a tarpaulin.

"Ah, for the outdoor life," Fontaine said in a sardonic tone. "My backsides feel as though I have been flailed with cane rods."

Chester, who was driving the buckboard, chuckled aloud. "Dad, you have to look on the bright side. We're almost there."

"How would you know that?"

"One of the teamsters told me this morning."

"Well then, we have it from an unimpeachable source."

"Honestly!" Lillian said with a perky smile. "Why do you complain so, Papa? I've never seen anything so wonderful in my life." She suddenly stopped, pointing at the sky. "There, look!"

A hawk floated past on smothered wings. Beyond, distant on the rolling plains, a small herd of buffalo grazed placidly beneath wads of puffy clouds. The hawk caught an updraft, soaring higher into the sun. Lillian watched it fade away against a lucent sky.

"Oooo," she said softly, her eyes round with wonder. "I think it's all so . . . so magnificent."

"Do you really?" Chester said all too casually. "I'll wager you don't think so when you have to do your business. You sure look mortified, then."

"You're such a ninny, Chester. I sometimes wonder you're my brother."

Her indignation hardly covered her embarrassment. There were fifty-three wagons in the caravan and more than a hundred men, including teamsters, laborers, and scouts. The upshot, when she needed to relieve herself, was scant privacy and a desperate search for bushes along the river. She absolutely dreaded the urge to pee.

Yet, apart from the matter of privacy, she was content with their journey. Fifteen days ago, south of Abilene, they had joined the freight caravan on the Santa Fe Trail. The muleskinners were a rough lot, unaccustomed to having a woman in their company, and at first standoffish. But Josh Ingram, the wagon master, welcomed them into the caravan. He worked for a trading firm headquartered in Independence, Missouri.

The Santa Fe Trail, pioneered in 1821, was a major trading route with the far southwest. The trail began in Independence, crossing the Missouri line, and meandered a hundred-fifty miles across Kansas to the great northern bend of the Arkansas. The trail then followed the serpentine course of the river for another hundred-twenty miles to Fort Dodge and the nearby civilian outpost, Dodge City. From there, the trail wound southwest for some five hundred miles before terminating in Santa Fe, the capital of New Mexico Territory. Hundreds of wagons made the yearly trek over a vast wilderness where no railroads yet existed.

Lillian was fascinated by the grand scheme of the venture. One aspect in particular, the Conestoga wagons, attracted her immediate attention. Over the campfire their first night with the caravan, Josh Ingram explained that the wagons dated back to the early eighteenth century. Developed in the Conestoga River Valley of Pennsylvania, the wagons bore the distinctive touch of Dutch craftsmen. The design, still much the same after a hundred and fifty years, had moved westward with the expansion of the frontier.

The wagon bed, as Ingram later showed her, was almost four feet wide, bowed downward like the hull of a ship. Overall, the wagon was sixteen feet in length, with immense wheels bound by tire irons for navigating rough terrain. The wagon box was fitted with oval wooden bows covered by sturdy canvas, which resulted in the nickname prairie schooner. Drawn by a six-hitch of mules, the wagons regularly carried up to 4,000 pounds in freight. The trade goods ran the gamut from needles and thread to axes and shovels and household furniture.

Late every afternoon, on Ingram's signal, the wagons were drawn into a four-sided defensive square. So far west, there was the constant threat of Indian attack and the imperative to protect the crew as well as the livestock. There were army posts scattered about Kansas, and west of Fort Dodge, where warlike tribes roamed at will, cavalry patrols accompanied the caravan. But an experienced wagon master looked to the defense of his own outfit, and before sundown the livestock was grazed and watered. Then everyone, man and beast, settled down for the night within the improvised stockade.

The Fontaines made their own small campfire every evening. They could have eaten with the crew, for the caravan employed a full-time cook. But the food was only passable, and Lillian, anxious to experience life on the trial, had taught herself to cook over open coals. The company scouts, who killed a couple of buffalo every day to provision the men, always gave Lillian the choice cuts from the hump meat. Chester took care of the horses, and Fontaine, adverse to menial chores of any nature, humbled himself to collect firewood along the river. He then treated himself to a dram from his stock of Irish whiskey.

By sundown, Lillian had the cooking under way. She worked over a shallow pit, ringed with rocks and aglow with coals scooped from the fire. Her battery of cast-iron cookware turned out stews and steaks and sourdough biscuits and an occasional cobbler made from dried fruit. Fontaine, who had appointed himself armorer, displayed a surprising aptitude for the care and cleaning of weapons. In Abilene, the hardware store owner had convinced him that no sane man went unarmed on the plains, and he'd bought two Henry .44

lever-action repeaters. His evening ritual included wiping trail dust from the rifles.

"Fate has many twists," he said, posing with a rifle as he looked around at the camp enclosed by wagons. "I am reminded of a passage from *King Lear*."

Lillian glanced up from a skillet of sizzling steaks. She knew he was performing and she was his audience. "Which passage is that, Papa?"

" 'When we are born we cry that we are come to this great stage of fools.' "

"You believe our journey is foolhardy?"

"We shall discover that by the by," Fontaine said, playing the oracle. "Some harbinger tells me that our lives will never again be the same."

"Evenin', folks."

Josh Ingram stepped into the circle of firelight. He was a large man with weathered features and a soup-strainer mustache. He nodded soberly to Fontaine.

"Figgered I'd best let you know. Our scouts cut Injun sign just before we camped. Wouldn't hurt to be on guard tonight."

Fontaine frowned. "Are we in danger of attack?"

"Never know," Ingram said. "Cheyenne and Kiowa get pretty thick out this way. They're partial to the trade goods we haul."

"Would they attack a caravan with so many men?"

"They have before and they doubtless will again. Don't mean to alarm you overly much. Just wanted you to know."

"We very much appreciate your concern."

Ingram touched his hat, a shy smile directed at Lillian. "Ma'am."

When he walked off, Fontaine stood for a moment with the rifle cradled over his arm. At length, he turned to Lillian and Chester. "I daresay we are in for a long night."

Chester took the other Henry repeater from the buckboard. He levered a shell into the chamber and lowered the hammer. "Wish we had practiced more with these rifles. I'd hate to miss when it counts."

"As the commander at Bunker Hill told his men, wait until you see the whites of their eyes. What worked on British Red Coats applies equally well to redskins."

Lillian thought it a witty pun. She knew her father's levity was meant to allay their fears. She was suddenly quite proud of him.

Alistair Fontaine was truly a man of many parts.

A noonday sun was lodged like a brass ball in the sky. The caravan followed a rutted track almost due west along the river. Scouts rode posted to the cardinal points of the compass.

The Fontaines' buckboard was near the front of the column. Josh Ingram, mounted on a blaze-faced roan, had stopped by not quite an hour ago with a piece of welcome news. He'd told them the caravan, by his reckoning, was less than twenty miles from Fort Dodge. He expected to sight the garrison by the next afternoon.

Lillian breathed a sigh of relief. The likelihood of confronting Indians seemed remote so close to a military post. Even more, from a personal standpoint, she would no longer have to suffer the indignity of squatting behind bushes to relieve herself. Her spirits brightened as she began thinking about the civilized comforts—

A scout galloped hell for leather over a low knoll to the north. He was waving his hat in the air and his bellow carried on the wind. *"Injuns! Injuns!"*

Ingram roared a command at the lead wagon. The teamster sawed hard on the reins and swung his mules off the trail. The wagons behind followed along, the drivers popping their whips, and the column maneuvered between the river and the rutted trace. The lead wagon spliced into the rear wagon minutes later, forming a defensive ring. Chester halted the Fontaines' buckboard in the center of the encircled caravan.

A war party boiled over the knoll even as the men jumped from their wagons. The massed Indians appeared to number a hundred or more, and they charged down the slope, whipping their ponies, at a dead run. The warriors rapidly deployed into a V-shaped formation and fanned out into two wings. They thundered toward the caravan whooping shrill battle cries.

The men behind the barricaded wagons opened fire. Before them, the buckskin-clad horde swirled back and forth, the wings simultaneously moving left and right, individual horsemen passing one another in opposite directions. The warriors were armed for the most part with bows and arrows, perhaps one in five carrying an ancient musket or a modern repeater. A cloud of arrows whizzed into the embattled defenders.

Ingram rushed about the wagons shouting orders. Fontaine instructed Lillian to remain crouched on the far side of the buckboard, where she would be protected from stray arrows. He left her armed with a Colt .32 pocket pistol he'd bought in Abilene, quickly showing her how to cock the hammer. She watched as he and Chester joined the men behind the barricade, shouldering their rifles. Here and there mules fell, kicking in the traces, pincushioned with feathered shafts. The din of gunfire quickly became general.

Ten minutes into the battle the warriors suddenly retreated out of rifle range. Several teamsters lay sprawled on the ground, dead or wounded, and beyond the wagons Lillian saw the bodies of dark-skinned braves. She thought the attack was over and prayed it was so, for neither her father nor Chester had suffered any wounds. Then, with hardly a respite, the Indians tore down off the knoll, again splitting into two formations. Lillian ducked behind the buckboard, peering over the seat, racked with shame and yet mesmerized at the same time. She was struck by something splendid and noble in the savage courage of the Indians.

A man stumbled away from one of the wagons, an arrow protruding from his chest. In the next instant, a lone brave separated from the horde and galloped directly toward the wagons. He vaulted his pony over a team of mules, steel-tipped lance in hand, and landed in the encirclement. All along the line men were firing at him, and Lillian, breath-taken, thought it was the most magnificent act of daring she'd ever seen. Suddenly he spotted her, and without a moment's hesitation he charged the buckboard, lance raised overhead. She froze, ready to crawl beneath the buckboard, and then, witless with fear, cocked the hammer on the small Colt. She closed her eyes and fired as he hurled the lance.

The warrior was flung forward off the back of his pony. He crashed onto the seat of the buckboard, a feather in his hair and a hole in his forehead, staring with dead eyes at Lillian. She backed away, oddly fixated on the war paint covering his face, her hands shaking uncontrollably. She couldn't credit that she had shot him—between the eyes—actually killed a man. The lance quivered in the ground at her side, and she knew she'd been extraordinarily lucky. A mote of guilt drifted through her mind even as she lowered the pistol. Yet she had never felt so exhilarated, so giddy. She was alive.

The Indians seemed emboldened by the one warrior's suicidal charge. Their ponies edged closer to the wagons, and the sky rained wave upon wave of arrows. Here and there a brave would break ranks and charge the defenders, whooping defiance, only to be shot down. But it appeared the Indians were working themselves into a fever pitch, probing for a weak spot in the defenses. There was little doubt that they would attempt to overrun the wagons and slaughter everyone in savage struggle. Then, so abruptly that it confounded defenders and attackers alike, the din of gunfire swelled to a drumming rattle. A bugle sounded over the roar of battle.

The Indians were enveloped from the rear by massed cavalry. Fully two troops of horseback soldiers delivered a withering volley as they closed on the warriors at a gallop. The lines collided in a fearsome clash, and the screams of dying men rose eerily above the clatter of gunfire. Lillian saw a cavalry officer with long golden ringlets, attired in a buckskin jacket, wielding a saber slick with blood. The warriors were caught between the soldiers and a wall of gunfire from the wagons, and scores of red men toppled dead from their ponies. Others broke through the line of blue coats and fled across the plains in disorganized retreat. A small group, surrounded at the center of the fight, was quickly taken prisoner.

One of the captured warriors was tall and powerfully built. His features were broad and coarse, as though adzed from dark wood, and his eyes glittered with menace. Lillian watched, almost transfixed, as the cavalry officer with the golden hair reined through the milling horses and stopped near the tall warrior. He saluted with his bloody saber.

"*Hao,* Santana," he said crisply. "We have you now."

The warrior stared at him with a stoic expression. After a moment, the officer wiped the blood from his saber with a kerchief and sheathed the blade in his saddle scabbard. He spun his horse, a magnificent bay stallion, and rode toward Josh Ingram and the men at the wagons. He reined to a halt, touched the brim of his hat with a casual salute. His grin was that of Caesar triumphant.

"Gentlemen," he said smartly. "The Seventh Cavalry at your service."

"The Seventh!" someone yelled. "You're Custer!"

"I am indeed."

Ingram stepped over a dead mule. "General, I'm the wagon master, Josh Ingram. We're damned glad to see you and your boys. How'd you happen on this here fracas?"

Custer idly waved at the tall warrior. "Mr. Ingram, you are looking at Santana, chief of the Kiowa. We've been trailing him and his war party for near on a week." He paused with an indulgent smile. "You are fortunate we were not far behind. We rode to the sound of gunfire."

"Mighty glad you did, General. We might've lost our scalps."

"Yes, where Santana's concerned, you're entirely correct. He keeps his scalping knife sharply honed."

Lillian had joined her father and Chester. She listened to the conversation while studying the dashing cavalry officer. Finally, unable to contain herself, she whispered to Fontaine, "Who is he, Papa?"

"The greatest Indian fighter of them all, my dear. George Armstrong Custer."

"Thank God he came along when he did."

Fontaine smiled. "Thank God and the Seventh Cavalry."

# CHAPTER 7

THE FONTAINES were quartered in a billet normally reserved for visiting officers. There were two bedrooms and a sitting room, appointed in what Lillian assumed was military-issue furniture. She stood looking out the door at the garrison.

Fort Dodge was situated on a bluff overlooking the Arkansas. To her immediate front was the parade ground, and beyond that the post headquarters. Close by were the hospital and the quartermaster's depot and farther on the quarters for married officers. The enlisted men's barracks and the stables bordered a creek that emptied into the river. Everything looked spruce and well tended, orderly.

The caravan, accompanied by the cavalry, had arrived earlier that afternoon. The wagons were now encamped by the river, preparations under way to continue tomorrow on the Santa Fe Trail. Colonel Custer, courteous to a fault, had arranged for the Fontaines to stay the night in the officers' billet. Upon discovering they were actors, he had invited them to his quarters for dinner that evening. He seemed particularly taken with Fontaine's mastery of Shakespeare.

Fontaine, on the way to the fort, had spoken at length about the man many called the Boy General. He informed Lillian and Chester that their host was the most highly decorated soldier of the late Civil War. A graduate of West Point, his gift for tactics and warfare resulted in an extraordinary series of battlefield promotions. From 1862 to 1865, a mere three years, he leaped from first lieutenant to major general. He was twenty-five years old when the war ended.

Gen. Philip Sheridan personally posted Custer to the West following the Civil War. Though his peacetime rank was that of lieutenant colonel, he retained the brevet rank of major general. A splendid figure of a man, he was six feet tall, with a sweeping golden mustache, and wore his hair in curls that fell to his shoulders. He had participated in campaigns against the Plains Tribes throughout Kansas and Nebraska, culminating in a great victory in Indian Territory. There, on the Washita River, Custer and the Seventh Cavalry had routed the fabled Cheyenne.

Josh Ingram, listening to Fontaine's dissertation on Custer, had pointed out a parallel with Santana, the Kiowa war chief. His Indian name, *Se-Tain-te*, meant White Bear, bestowed on him after a vision quest. A blooded warrior at twenty, he began leading raids along the Santa Fe Trail and as far south as Mexico. He ranged across the frontier, burning and pillaging, leaving in his path a legion of scalped settlers and dead soldiers. What Custer was to the army Santana was to the Kiowa: a bold, fearless leader who dared anything, no matter the odds.

Lillian, reflecting on it as the sun went down over the parade ground, thought there was a stark difference. Santana, with his four followers who were captured in yesterday's battle, was in chains in the post stockade. George Armstrong Custer, victorious in every battle he'd ever fought, was yet again lauded for his courage in the field. She recalled him saying that he "rode to the sound of gunfire," and she mused that he was a man who thrived on war. She wouldn't be surprised if he one day replaced William Tecumseh Sherman as General of the Army. Custer, too, was a leader who never reckoned the odds.

Capt. Terrance Clark, Custer's adjutant, called for the Fontaines as twilight settled over the post. He was a strikingly handsome man, tall and muscular, resplendent in a tailored uniform. He shook hands with Fontaine and Chester and bowed politely to Lillian. Outside, he offered her his arm and led them across the parade ground in the quickening dusk. His manner somehow reminded her of Adonis, the young hero of Greek mythology. A warrior too handsome for words.

Custer's home was a military-style Victorian, with a pitched roof, square towers, and arched windows. The furniture in the parlor was French Victorian, with a rosewood piano against one wall flanked by a matching harp. The study was clearly a man's room, the walls decorated with mounted heads of antelope and deer and framed portraits of Custer and Gen. Philip Sheridan. The bookshelves were lined with classics, from Homer, to Shakespeare, to James Fenimore Cooper.

Elizabeth Custer was a small, attractive woman, with dark hair and delicate features. She insisted on being called Libbie and welcomed the Fontaines as though she'd never met a stranger in her life. She informed them that she was thrilled to have a troupe of professional actors in her home. Hardly catching her breath, she went on to say that she and the general were amateur thespians themselves. Lillian gathered that Libbie Custer, at least in public, referred to her husband only by rank.

"We have such fun," she rattled on. "Our last playlet was one written by the General himself. And he starred in it as well!"

"Libbie makes too much of it," Custer said with an air of modesty. "We stage amateur theatricals for the officers and their wives. Life on an army post requires that we provide our own entertainment."

"How very interesting," Fontaine observed. "And what was the subject of your production, General?"

Custer squared his shoulders. "I played the part of a Cheyenne war chief and one of the officers' wives played my . . . bride." He paused, suddenly aware of their curious stares. "We depicted a traditional Indian wedding ceremony. All quite authentic."

"I must say that sounds fascinating."

"Hardly in your league, Mr. Fontaine. Perhaps, after dinner, you would favor us with a reading from Shakespeare. We thirst for culture here on the frontier."

Fontaine preened. "I would be honored, General."

"By the by, I forgot to ask," Custer said. "Where will you be performing in Dodge City?"

"We are booked for the winter at Murphy's Exchange."

Fontaine caught the look that passed between Custer and his wife. Lillian saw it as well, and in the prolonged silence that followed she rushed to fill the void. Her expression was light and gay.

"We so wanted to see something of the frontier. And the timing is perfect, since we're between engagements until next spring. We open then at the Comique Theater in Wichita."

A manservant saved the moment. He appeared in the doorway of the dining room, dressed in a white jacket and blue uniform trousers, and announced dinner. Libbie, ever the gracious hostess, tactfully arranged the seating. Fontaine and Chester were placed on one side of the table, and Lillian was seated on the other, beside Captain Clark. Custer and Libbie occupied opposite ends of the table.

Dinner opened with terrapin soup, followed by a main course of prairie quail simmered in wine sauce. Throughout the meal, the Custers peppered their guests with questions about their life in the theater. Fontaine, though flattered, gradually steered the discussion to Custer's military campaigns against the warlike tribes. The conversation eventually touched on yesterday's engagement with the Kiowa.

"A sight to behold!" Fontaine announced, nodding to Libbie. "Your husband and the Seventh Cavalry at a full charge. I shan't soon forget the spectacle."

"*Au contraire*," Libbie said, displaying her grasp of French. "The General tells me your daughter was the heroine of the day." She cast an almost envious glance at Lillian. "Did you really shoot an Indian, my dear?"

Lillian blushed. "I'll never know how," she said with open wonder. "I closed my eyes when I fired the gun— and then . . . he practically fell in my lap."

Everyone laughed appreciatively at her candid amazement. Lillian was all too aware of Captain Clark's look of undisguised infatuation. He stared at her as if she were a ripe and creamy éclair and he wished he had a spoon. She noted as well that he wore no wedding ring.

After dinner, the men retired to the study for cigars and brandy. Lillian and Libbie conversed about New York and the latest fashions, discreetly avoiding any mention of the Fontaines' upcoming appearance at Murphy's Exchange. A short while later, the men joined them in the parlor. Captain Clark, rather too casually, took a seat beside Lillian on the sofa.

Fontaine required no great coaxing to perform. He positioned himself by the piano, his gaze fixed on infinity, and delivered a soliloquy from *King Richard II*. Custer and Libbie applauded exuberantly when he finished, congratulating him on the nuance of his interpretation. Then, with Libbie playing the piano, Lillian sang one of the day's most popular ballads. Her voice filled the parlor with *'Tis Sweet to Be Remembered*.

Terrance Clark watched her as though he'd seen a vision.

Dodge City was five miles west of Fort Dodge. A sprawling hodgepodge of buildings, it was inhabited principally by traders, teamsters, and buffalo hunters. Thousands of flint hides awaited shipment by wagon to the nearest railhead.

Late the next morning, when the Fontaines drove into town, they were dismayed by what they saw. Nothing had prepared them for a ramshackle outpost that looked as though it had been slapped together with spit and poster glue. Abilene, by comparsion, seemed like a megalopolis.

"To paraphrase the Bard," Fontaine said in a dazed voice. "I have ventured like wanton boys that swim on bladders. Far beyond my depth, my high-blown pride at length broke under me."

Chester nodded glumly. "Dad, no one could have said it better. We'll be lucky if we don't drown in this sinkhole."

The permanent population of the Dodge City looked to be something less than 500. At one end of Front Street, the main thoroughfare, were the Dodge House Hotel and Zimmerman's Hardware, flanked by a livery stable. Up the other way was a scattering of saloons, two trading companies, a mercantile store, and a whorehouse. The town's economy was fueled by buffalo hunters and troopers of the Seventh Cavalry. Whiskey and whores were a profitable enterprise on the edge of the frontier.

Fontaine directed Chester to the Dodge House. There were no porters, and they were forced to unload the buckboard themselves. Fortunately, it was a one-story building, and after registering with the desk clerk, they were able to slide their steamer trunks through the hall. Their rooms were little more than cubicles, furnished with a bed, a washstand, one chair, and a johnny pot. The clerk informed them the johnny pots would be emptied every morning.

Still shaking his head, Fontaine instructed Chester to take the buckboard to the livery stable. He expressed the view that it would not be prudent as yet to sell the horses and the buckboard. Their escape from Gomorrah, he noted dryly, might well depend on a ready source of transport. An hour or so later, after unpacking and changing from their trail clothes, they emerged from the hotel with their trepidation still intact. The men were attired in conservative three-piece suits and the Western headgear they had adopted while in Abilene. Lillian wore a demure day dress and a dark woolen shawl.

Murphy's Exchange was located across from one of the trading companies. Three buffalo hunters, lounging out front, gave them a squinted once-over as they moved through the door. The establishment was a combination saloon, dance hall, and gaming dive. Opposite a long mahogany bar were faro layouts and poker tables. A small stage at the rear overlooked a dance floor, with a piano player and a fiddler providing the music. Saloon girls in full war paint mingled with the crowd.

All conversation ceased as the soldiers and hide hunters treated Lillian to a slow inspection. She had the sinking sensation that they were undressing her with their eyes, layer by layer. Frank Murphy, the proprietor, walked forward from the end of the bar. He was a toadish man, short and stout, with jowls covered by muttonchop whiskers. His jaw cranked in a horsey smile, revealing a gold tooth, as he stopped in front of them. He regarded the finery of their clothes.

"From your duds," he said, flashing his gold tooth, "I'd say you're the Fontaines. Welcome to Dodge City."

"Thank you so much," Fontaine replied. "Our arrival was delayed by a slight skirmish with Kiowa brigands."

"Yeah, the word's all over town. Custer and his boys pulled your fat out of the fire, huh?"

"An apt if somewhat colloquial description."

"Well, you're here now and that's all that counts."

"Indeed we are."

Fontaine stared a moment at the miniature stage. His arm swept the room with a patrician gesture. "There is no sin but to be rich; there is no vice but beggary."

"Uh-huh," Murphy said, stroking his whiskers. "That wire I got about you folks, from Lou Gordon? He said you was partial to Shakespeare."

"Yes, I understand, Mr. Murphy. For the sake of your clientele, tread lightly with the verse."

"I guess it's sort of like bitin' into a green persimmon. A little bit goes a long ways."

"A green persimmon?" Fontaine said thoughtfully. "I've not heard the expression before. Is it a bitter fruit?"

"Right tasty when they're ripe," Murphy said. "A green one'll make your mouth pucker up worse'n wormwood."

"I have no doubt you dispense sound advice, Mr. Murphy. However, from the look of your customers, a dab of culture and a hot bath would do wonders. Charity demands that I acquaint them with the Bard."

"Don't say I didn't warn you."

"Consider your duty done."

Murphy turned his attention to Lillian. "You must be Lilly, the singer Gordon told me about. His wire said you're better'n good."

"How nice of him," Lillian said with a dimpled smile. "I'll certainly do my best, Mr. Murphy."

"Hope you've got some racy numbers in your songbook. The boys don't come here for church hymns."

"I sing all the popular ballads. The audiences in Abilene weren't disappointed."

"Hide hunters are a rougher lot than cowhands. Maybe just a little something off-color?"

"No, I'm afraid not."

"Too bad." Murphy examined her outfit. "Maybe you've got a dress that don't dust the floor. The boys like to see some ankle."

Lillian glanced at her father, clearly uncomfortable. Fontaine quickly intervened. "We are what we are, Mr. Murphy. Neither ribald nor risqué is included in our repertoire."

Murphy considered a moment. He thought he'd made a bad deal but saw no practical remedy. October was almost gone, and the chances of importing another act for the winter were somewhere between slim and none. He decided there was nothing for it.

"Guess we'll have to make do," he grouched. "I'm a man of my word, so I'll still pick up the tab for your lodging and your eats. Just try to gimme a good show."

"Have no fear," Fontaine said stiffly. "We never fail to entertain."

Outside, Fontaine led the way back toward the hotel. Lillian and Chester were silent, aware that his dour mood had turned even darker. He finally grunted a saturnine laugh. His expression was stolid.

"I believe our employer lacks confidence."

"Who cares?" Chester said. "We're a far cry from Broadway."

"You miss the point entirely, my boy."

"What point is that?"

"We are the Fontaines, and we thrive on challenge. Need I say more?"

Lillian thought that said it all.

# Chapter 8

Fontaine proved to a prophet. By the end of the week, Murphy's Exchange was the most popular spot in town. The other saloons were all but empty.

Every night, at show time, the house was packed. The audience, mainly buffalo hunters and soldiers, suffered through Shakespeare with only occasional jeers. The melodrama usually held their interest, though that was hardly the reason for their presence. They were there to see Lilly Fontaine.

Frank Murphy was the most amazed man in town. To his profound shock, he discovered that burly cavalrymen and rancid-smelling hide hunters all had a soft spot. A tender ballad, sung by a young innocent with the face of an angel, left them a-sea in memories of lost and long-ago yesterdays. Even the saloon girls wept.

The nature of the men made it all the more astounding. Buffalo hunters, who traveled where others feared to tread, lived from day to day. They wandered the plains, constantly under the threat of Indian attack, for they killed the beasts that were the very sustenance of nomadic tribes. The horse soldiers, even more inured to brutality, were in the business of killing Indians. Sentiment seemed lost in the scheme of things.

Yet none among them was so hardened that memory of gentler times failed. All of which made Frank Murphy the happiest saloonkeeper in Dodge City. Winters were harsh on the plains, with blizzards that sometimes left the land impassable, locked in snow and ice. The freezing cold drove men into town, often for weeks on end, seeking sanctuary from polar winds howling out of the north. The longer they stayed, the more they spent, and Murphy saw it as the winter of great fortune. He'd cornered the trade with Lilly Fontaine.

Lillian sometimes felt guilty. She was flattered by all the attention and adored the appreciative cheers of men who watched her perform. But she was saddened for her father, whose love of Shakespeare played to an unreceptive audience. He jokingly referred to them as "buffoons and jackanapes" and tried to slough off their indifference with nonchalant humor. Still, she knew he was disheartened, often embittered, while at the same time he gloried in her success. Her father's pride merely served to underscore her guilt.

On Monday morning, Fontaine's pride was put to the test. They were in his room, rehearsing the lines of a new melodrama he'd written, when someone knocked on the door. Fontaine moved across the room, opening the door, freshly inked script still in hand. A portly man in a checkered suit stood in the hallway.

"Mr. Fontaine," he said, "I'm Joe Porter. I own the Lucky Star Saloon and I'd like to talk to you."

"May I inquire the purpose of your call, Mr. Porter?"

"Let's just say it's a private matter. I'd sooner not discuss it standin' here in the hall. Could I come in a minute?"

"Of course."

Fontaine held the door. Porter entered, hat in hand, nodding mechanically to Chester. He smiled warmly at Lillian. "Miss Fontaine, a pleasure to see you."

"How may we assist you?" Fontaine asked. "I believe you said it was a private matter."

"Well, sir, just to be truthful, it's a business matter. I'd like to hire you folks over to the Lucky Star."

"As you must know, we are currently engaged."

"Yessir," Porter confirmed. "Everybody in a hundred miles knows about your daughter. And you and your boy, too, naturally."

Fontaine pursed his mouth. "I believe that rather nicely covers it, Mr. Porter."

"No, not just exactly it don't. What would you say if I was to offer you twice what Frank Murphy's payin' you?"

"I would have to say . . . no, thank you."

"Then name your price, if that ain't enough. I'd pay pretty near anything to have your girl singin' at the Lucky Star."

"Mr. Porter."

"Yeah?"

"We are not available," Fontaine said firmly. "We accepted a winter's engagement at Murphy's Exchange. We intend to honor our commitment."

"Look here," Porter insisted. "Your girl's runnin' the rest of us saloon owners out of business. We don't get no trade till your show's over every night. It just ain't fair."

"I most sincerely regret the inconvenience."

"Hell's bells, you gotta have a price! Name it!"

"Good day, Mr. Porter."

Fontaine opened the door. Porter gave him a look of bewildered disbelief, then marched out with a muttered curse. When the door closed, Fontaine turned back into the room. His gaze settled on Lillian.

"You appear to have the town bedazzled, my dear."

"I'm sorry, Papa," she said, genuinely contrite. "So very sorry."

"Never apologize for your talent. You deserve all the accolades one might imagine."

"What about the money?" Chester interjected. "Porter would have paid through the nose. We may never get another offer like that."

Fontaine smiled. "I daresay Mr. Murphy will be open to renegotiation. He most certainly will not be pleased, but then . . . business is business."

There were no secrets in a small town. Joe Porter made the mistake of grumbling about his unsatisfactory meeting with the Fontaines. The news spread on the moccasin telegraph, and Frank Murphy heard of it long before the noon hour. He took it as a personal affront.

"Tryin' to steal away my trade!" he huffed to one of the bartenders. "I always knew Joe Porter was a no-good sonovabitch."

Murphy's Exchange and the Lucky Star were located catty-corner from each other on Front Street. Porter, as was his custom, took his noon meal at the Silver Dollar Café, three doors down from his establishment. Shortly before one o'clock, he emerged from the café and turned upstreet. He had a toothpick wedged in the corner of his mouth.

Murphy stepped from the door of his saloon. He held a Colt Navy revolver at his side, and cognizant of the rules in such affairs, he prudently avoided being tagged a bushwhacker. He issued the proper warning to his opponent.

"Porter!" he shouted. *"Defend yourself!"*

Porter, taken by surprise, nonetheless reacted with dispatch. His stout legs pumping, he sprinted along the boardwalk as he drew a pistol from his waistband. Murphy fired, imploding a storefront window, and Porter winged a wild shot in return. He barreled through the door of the Lucky Star, diving for cover. Murphy wisely retreated within his own saloon.

The gunfight soon evolved into siege warfare. Murphy and Porter, after emptying their revolvers, switched to repeating rifles. They banged away at one another with more spirit than accuracy, bullets whizzing back and forth across the intersection. All along Front Street people took cover in saloons and dance halls, watching the duel as though it were some new and titillating spectator sport. By two o'clock, the windows in both Murphy's Exchange and the Lucky Star were reduced to shards of glass.

There was no law in Dodge City. The town was not incorporated and lacked either a city council or a town marshal. Law enforcement was the province of deputy U.S. marshals, who only occasionally wandered into western Kansas. An hour or so into the siege, someone decided a stray bullet would eventually claim the life of an innocent bystander. The military seemed the most likely solution, and a rider was dispatched to Fort Dodge. The onlookers settled down to await developments.

Capt. Terrance Clark, at the head of a cavalry troop, rode into town late that afternoon. He dismounted the company, stationing troopers armed with Springfield rifles around the intersection. The sight of fifty soldiers and the threat of military reprisal got the attention of Murphy and Porter. Clark arranged a cease-fire and then, ordering the saloonkeepers to lay down their arms, coaxed them into the street. There he negotiated a truce, which concluded with the two men reluctantly shaking hands. The onlookers applauded the end of what would later be called the Darlin' Lilly War.

Before departing town, Captain Clark seized the opportunity to call on Lillian at the hotel. She was already aware of the reason for the shooting and highly embarrassed rather than flattered. Yet her spirits were restored when he invited her to a military ball, two weeks hence at Fort Dodge. She was planning her wardrobe before he was out the door.

Terrance Clark, for his part, felt like clicking his heels. He'd taken the first step in his campaign to capture Lilly Fontaine.

*I have done the state some service, and they know 't;*
*No more of that. I pray you, in your letters,*
*When you shall these unlucky deeds relate,*
*Speak of me as I am; nothing extenuate,*
*Nor set down aught in malice: then, must you speak*
*Of one that lov'd not wisely but too well.*

The lines from *Othello* fell on deaf ears. Fontaine, in blackface and costumed as a Moorish nobleman, wrung agony from every word. The buffalo hunters and soldiers in the audience stared at him as if he were a field slave, strangely dressed and speaking in foreign tongues. He slogged on through the soliloquy.

There were times, alone on the stage, when Fontaine despaired that the majesty of the words had the least effect. He wondered now if the men watching him had any comprehension that he—Othello—had murdered Desdemona, a faithful wife falsely accused of betrayal. He despaired even more that he was acting out the tragedy for an audience of one. Himself.

The crude stage in Murphy's Exchange had no curtain. When he completed his oration, Fontaine paused with dramatic flair and then bowed his way offstage. The crowd, by now resigned to his nightly histrionics, gave him a smattering of applause. The fiddler and the piano player struck up a sprightly tune, allowing him time to run backstage and hurriedly scrub off the blackface. Saloon girls circulated with bee-stung smiles, pushing drinks.

The windows fronting the saloon, now empty holes, had been boarded over. The pitched battle that afternoon was all the talk, and Frank Murphy found himself something of a celebrity. He had, after all, defended what was rightfully his, and other men admired a man who would not tolerate insult. The crowd tonight was even larger than normal, standing-room-only and spilling out onto the boardwalk. Everyone wanted to see the sweet young temptress now known as Darlin' Lilly.

Lillian was repulsed by the whole affair. She thought it sordid and tawdry, and she felt soiled by the nickname bestowed on her just that afternoon. Earlier, when she performed her first number, she'd fixed her gaze on the front wall, ignoring the crowd. Where before she had given them the benefit of the doubt, she suddenly found the men brutish and coarse, rough vulgarians. She felt they stripped her naked with their loutish stares.

The melodrama that evening was titled *The Dying Kiss*. Fontaine, who recognized his limitations as a playwright, had plagiarized freely from Shakespeare's *Romeo and Juliet.* Lillian and Chester played the tragic young lovers, and Fontaine, casting himself as the villain of the piece, played the girl's father. The buffalo hunters and soldiers, caught up in what was a soppy tearjerker, roundly booed Fontaine off the stage. The final scene, when the lovers' suicide left them in eternal embrace, made tough men honk into their kerchiefs. Saloon girls wept so copiously they spoiled their war paint.

The audience gave the cast three curtain calls, albeit sans the curtain. Then, as though the brotherhood of men were of a single mind, they began chanting, *"Lilly! Lilly! Lilly!"* Lillian performed a quick change of costume, slipping into one of her two silk gowns, royal blue with white piping. The piano player and the fiddler, by now thoroughly rehearsed on her numbers, segued into Stephen Foster's immortal classic, *Beautiful Dreamer*. Her voice resonated poignantly through the saloon.

*Beautiful dreamer, wake unto me*
*Starlight and dew drops are waiting for thee*
*Sounds of the rude world heard in the day*
*Lulled by the moonlight have all passed away*

The crowd hung on her every word. The saloon was still as a church, the men and saloon girls a hushed tableau. Her face was turned as to the heavens and her eyes shone with emotion. On the last note there was an instant of impassioned silence, and then the audience erupted in raucous adulation and cheers. She bowed low, her features radiant.

A buffalo hunter lurched forward from the front of the crowd. His eyes were bloodshot with liquor and he drunkenly hoisted himself onto the stage. He spread his arms wide, reaching for her, and like a bull in rut bellowed, "Darlin' Lilly!" She backed away, unnerved and frightened, moving toward the wings. He lumbered after her.

She saw another man leap over the footlights. His features were wind-seamed, ruggedly forceful under a thatch of sandy hair and a bristling mustache. Though he wasn't a tall man, he was full-spanned through the shoulders, his wrists thick as a singletree. He grabbed the hide hunter by the collar, jerked him around, and lashed out with a splintering blow to the jaw. Clubbed off his feet, the hunter crashed to the floor.

The man stooped down, lifting the drunk by the collar and the seat of the pants. He walked to the footlights, carrying his load like a sack of potatoes, and hurled the buffalo hunter off the stage. Saloon girls squealed and men scattered as the inert form tumbled across the dance floor and skidded to a halt. The crowd roared with laughter as the man on the stage grinned and neatly dusted his hands. Their voices raised in a rowdy chant.

*"Cimarron! Cimarron! Cimarron!"*

Waving them off, the man turned and strode across the stage. Lillian noted he was dressed in the rough work clothes worn by the other buffalo hunters. But unlike them, his clothing was clean and freshly pressed and he smelled faintly of barber's lotion. His eyes crinkled with amusement as he stopped in front of her. He doffed his hat.

"Sorry for the trouble," he said, holding her gaze. "Some of these boys get liquored up and lose their heads." He paused, still grinning. "I'm Cimarron Jordan."

"How do you do," Lillian said warmly. "You saved me from a most unpleasant experience. Thank you so much."

"Why, anybody would've done the same for a pretty lady like yourself. No thanks necessary."

"Are you a buffalo hunter, Mr. Jordan?"

"That I am," Jordan said with amiable good humor. "Hope you haven't got nothin' against hunters."

"Oh, no, apart from the anarchy of Dodge City. I've never lived in a place where there isn't any law."

"Miss Lilly, you just whistle and I'll be your lawdog. Anytime a'tall."

Lillian sensed the magnetism of the man. He seemed to radiate strength and a quiet, but certain, force of character. She was amazed at herself that she found him attractive, although somewhat rough around the edges. She amazed herself even more by inviting him backstage to meet her father and brother. His unusual name intrigued her as well. Cimarron!

She thought she would ask him about that later.

# Chapter 9

"I WON'T have it! Goddammit, it's Saturday night!"

"Lower your voice," Fontaine said curtly. "I will not permit you to curse at my daughter."

Murphy glowered at him. "Why'd she wait till tonight to tell me? I'd like to hear you answer that."

"For the very reason we see exhibited in your behavior. You are an intemperate man."

"You and your highfalutin words. What's that mean?"

"Quite simply, it means you are a hothead. You lack civility."

The Friday night show had concluded only moments ago. Lillian, with her father and Chester still in their melodrama costumes, had caught Murphy backstage. She explained as politely as possible that she had been invited to a military ball tomorrow night, Saturday night, at Fort Dodge. She asked for the night off.

"Tell me this," Murphy said gruffly. "When'd you get this invitation?"

"Two weeks ago," Lillian replied. "The day Captain Clark stopped you from killing Mr. Porter. He asked me while he was in town."

"And you waited till now to tell me?"

"Father has already explained that. I knew you wouldn't be . . . pleased."

*"Pleased!"* Murphy echoed. "You know good and well, Lilly—"

Lillian interrupted him. "I've told you over and over. I will not be called Lilly."

"All right then, Lillian, you know Saturday night's the biggest night of the week. And everybody in town turns out to hear you sing."

"I still have to have the night off."

Lillian was determined. After three weeks in Dodge City, she longed for the refinement and decorum that could be found only at Fort Dodge. Terrance Clark and sometimes Cimarron Jordan occasionally took her for afternoon buggy rides in the country. But she hadn't had a free night since she'd arrived in town. She meant to stand her ground.

"Let's be reasonable," Fontaine interceded. "We have performed every night—including Sunday, I might add—for three weeks running. Lillian deserves a night to herself."

Murphy laughed derisively. "You just don't get it, do you? Lillian's pipes are what draws the crowd. No songs, no crowd, no business!"

"On the contrary," Fontaine said indignantly. "Chester and I are perfectly capable of providing the entertainment for one night. We are, after all, actors."

Chester nodded eagerly. "I can even do a soft-shoe routine. I started practicing after we saw Eddie Foy in Abilene. I'm pretty good."

Fontaine and Lillian looked at him. Neither of them was aware that he had the slightest interest in dance routines. He had never once alluded to it, and so far as they knew, he had no talent as a hoofer. They could only conclude he'd been practicing secretly in his room at the hotel.

"There you have it," Fontaine jumped in with a confident air. "Chester will perform a soft-shoe number, with accompaniment from the piano. I will present a special rendering from Shakespeare. Perhaps something from *Macbeth.*"

"You're cracked, the both of you," Murphy growled. "You think anybody's gonna stick around to watch a couple of hams trod the boards? Lillian goes on and that's that!"

"No," Lillian said adamantly. "I insist on a night off."

"Well, insist all you want, little lady, but the answer's no. That's final."

"Then I quit."

Murphy looked as though his hearing had failed him. Fontaine and Chester, equally shocked, appeared speechless. The three men stared at her in startled apprehension.

"You leave us no choice," Lillian said, her eyes on Murphy. "We are forced to give you notice as of tonight. I feel quite sure Mr. Porter will welcome us to the Lucky Star."

"You'd do that to me!" Murphy exploded. "You'd take it across the street to that four-flusher—after I made you a star?"

"You made nothing," Lillian informed him. "We were The Fontaines long before we arrived in Dodge City."

Fontaine and Chester were struck dumb. The girl they'd known all their lives seemed to have stepped over the threshold into womanhood. She sounded eerily like her mother, quiet and strong and utterly certain of herself. They knew she wasn't bluffing.

Frank Murphy knew it as well. His toadish features mottled, and for a moment it appeared he would strangle before he recovered his voice. But he finally got his wits about him and recognized who was who in the scheme of things. He offered her a lame smile.

"Don't blame me if we have a riot on our hands. Hope you enjoy yourself."

"I'm sure I shall."

The officers' mess had been cleared of furniture for the occasion. Gaudy streamers festooned the ceiling, and several coats of wax, buffed since early morning by enlisted men, had brought the floor to a mirror polish. The regimental band, attired in gold-frogged uniforms, thumped sedately under the baton of a stern-eyed master sergeant.

Terrance Clark held Lillian at arm's length. He stiffly pushed her around the dance floor, neither light on his feet nor an accomplished dancer. Although perfectly tailored, splendid in a uniform bedecked with sash and medals, he was nonetheless overshadowed by his partner. As they moved about the floor, other men kept darting hidden glances at her. The women, more direct than their husbands, stared openly.

Lillian had dressed carefully for the ball. Her hair was arranged in an *en revanche* coiffure of ribbons and silk flowers, a French style she had copied from a ladies' periodical. Her svelte figure was stunningly displayed in the better of her two gowns, the teal silk with dark lace at the throat. Draped around her neck was her most prized possession, a string of black deep-sea pearls presented to her mother by her father on their tenth wedding anniversary. Lillian thought her mother would approve.

Tonight was her first formal ball. She'd never before kept company with a man, her mother wisely shielding her from the many Don Juans who populated variety theaters. Captain Clark, an officer and a gentleman, had assured her father she would be properly chaperoned during her stay at Fort Dodge. Arrangements had been made for her to spend the night with Colonel and Mrs. Custer, and Clark would drive her back to town Sunday morning. Still, chaperone or not, she wasn't worried about Terry Clark. His intentions were perhaps too honorable.

The band segued into a waltz. Custer claimed the dance while Libbie glided away on the arms of Clark. Lillian discovered that Custer was nimble of foot, clearly a veteran of ballroom engagements. He held her lightly, his golden ringlets bobbing as they floated off in time to the music. His mustache lifted in a foxy smile.

"I trust you are enjoying yourself."

"Oh, yes, very much."

"Excellent." Custer stared directly into her eyes. "Permit me to say you look ravishing tonight."

"Why, thank you," she said with a shy smile. "You're much too kind, General."

"A beautiful woman needs to be told so on occasion. Don't you agree?"

"You flatter me."

"Hardly more than you deserve."

By now, Lillian knew from gossips in town that Custer has an eye for the ladies. There were rumors he kept an Indian mistress tucked away somewhere, though he was circumspect around Fort Dodge. She'd also heard that his great victory over the Cheyenne was actually the massacre of a harmless band led by the peace chief Black Kettle. She chose not to believe the latter, for she remembered his valor the day he had rescued her from the Kiowa war party. But she accepted the story about his roving ways with women.

Long ago, her mother had warned her about smooth-talking men who could charm the birds out of the trees. She understood, though her mother had deftly employed a metaphor, that it was girls who were too often charmed out of their drawers. The world was full of glib, sweet-talking flatterers—George Armstrong Custer not being the first one she'd met—and she had long since taken her mother's lesson to heart. She would not be charmed out of her drawers.

Yet, on a moment's reflection, she realized that Custer was simply flirting. She was in no danger tonight, for Libbie rarely let her husband out of her sight. To put a point on it, Libbie reclaimed him as soon as the waltz ended. The foursome stood talking awhile, and then Custer, with Libbie on his arm, wandered off to mingle with the other guests. Clark suggested the refreshment table.

A grizzled sergeant served them punch from a crystal bowl. Their cups in hand, Clark led her across the room, where a row of chairs lined the dance floor. He chose a section with mostly empty chairs and courteously waited for her to be seated. She knew he wanted to be alone with her and sensed he had something on his mind. But Terry, as he insisted she call him, was not one of the smooth talkers and usually took the time to organize his thoughts. He finally got his tongue untied.

"Are you happy in Dodge City?" he asked. "I mean, do you enjoy theater work?"

Clark had only attended one show, and she'd intuited that he was disturbed by her working conditions. "I enjoy singing," she replied, pausing to take a sip of her punch. "I can't say I enjoy performing in a saloon."

"Army life is a good deal different." Clark seemed unaware of his awkward non sequitur. "Probably the main reason I chose a career as a soldier."

"Oh?" She wondered where he was trying to lead the conversation. "How is the army different?"

"Well, take this ball, for example. There's never a dull moment, and always something cultural to hold your interest. Do you see what I mean?"

"Like the ball?"

"Yes, and the theatricals we put on for ourselves. Not to mention our discussion groups on classical literature. And picnics in the summer and the evenings we get together for sing-alongs. You'd really enjoy that."

"I'm sure I would."

"The army's a fine life," he said with conviction. "Wonderful people, educated and intelligent, a stimulating culture. You couldn't ask for a better life."

All in a rush, Lillian realized he was trying to sell her on the army life. Or more to the point, the joys of the life of an army *wife*. He was, she saw in sudden comprehension, working himself around to a proposal. She thought it was a marvelous compliment, unbelievably flattering. He was so earnest, so handsome—and yet . . .

"Oh!" She sprang to her feet as the band swung into a lively tune. "Don't you just love a Virginia Reel!"

Before Clark knew what hit him, she had set their punch cups on an empty chair. She laughed, taking his hands, and pulled him onto the dance floor. There seemed no alternative but that she keep him dancing all night.

She wasn't yet ready to hear his proposal.

A warm sun flooded the streets of Dodge City. The weather was nonetheless brisk, for it was the middle of November and a chilly breeze drifted across the plains. Lillian wore her linsey-woolsey dress with a heavy shawl.

Jordan called for her at one o'clock. She'd arrived at the hotel with only enough time to change clothes. The drive back from Fort Dodge had required artifice and a good deal of chatter on her part. Terrance Clark had yet to complete the thought he'd started last night.

Fontaine had gently chided her about being a social butterfly. Out with the army last night, he slyly teased, and off with the buffalo hunter today. Still, he trusted her to do what was right and offered no real objection. He was secure in the knowledge that her mother had raised her to be a lady.

Today, with a buggy rented from the livery, Jordan drove west along the Arkansas. He and his crew of skinners returned to town every ten days or so with a load of hides. Lillian had learned that his nickname—Cimarron—derived from the fact that he was the only buffalo man willing to cross the Cimarron River and hunt in Indian Territory. His given name was Samuel.

She knew as well, from talking with the saloon girls, that he was widely admired by the other buffalo hunters. His daring had made him a legend of sorts, for he had returned time and again with his scalp intact from a land jealously guarded by hostile tribes. He was no less a legend for his ferocity in saloon brawls, though the girls vowed he'd never been known to start a fight. His temper, once unleashed, quickly ended any dispute.

Lillian found him different than his reputation. With her, he was quiet and gently spoken and always a gentleman. Today was their third ride into the country, and he'd never attempted to make advances, not even a kiss. He went armed with a pistol, and he carried his Sharps buffalo rifle whenever they traveled outside Dodge City. But she had never seen his violent side, and she sometimes wished he would try to kiss her. She found him a very attractive man.

Jordan stopped the buggy on a low rise some ten miles west of town. Off in the distance, a herd of buffalo numbering in the thousands slowly grazed southward against the umber plains. He explained that the herds migrated south for the winter, taking refuge in Palo Duro Canyon or on the vast uncharted wilderness known as the Staked Plains. At length, his explanation finished, he turned to her with a quizzical smile.

"How'd you enjoy the dance last night?"

"Very much," she said, taken aback. "How did you know where I went?"

"Well, I got to town expectin' to see you in the show. I asked your dad about it, thinkin' maybe you was sick. He told me you was sweet on that soldier-boy, Clark."

"Oh, that's just like Papa! He knows very well it's not true."

"Simmer down," Jordan said with an amused chuckle. "I was only funnin' you."

Lillian looked at him. "You don't care much for the army, do you? I've noticed you never speak to the soldiers in Murphy's. Why is that?"

"The cavalry tries to stop me from crossin' into Injun country. There's some treaty or another that says nobody's supposed to hunt down there."

"But you do it anyway?"

"I reckon somebody's got to keep the soldier-boys on their toes."

"You're shameless."

Her tone was light. Still, his casual manner made her wonder again at the violence of the frontier. The army fought the Indians, and the Indians pillaged settlements, and the buffalo hunters provoked the tribes even more with the slaughter of the herds. Hardly a night went by that hide hunters and soldiers weren't evolved in a brawl, just for the sheer deviltry of it. Everyone, white and red, fought everyone else.

First in Abilene, and now in Dodge City, it seemed to her that men fought without any great rhyme or reason. There was no real effort on anyone's part to live in peace, and the hostility inevitably led to more bloodshed. Of course, she had killed a Kiowa warrior—who thought he was justified in trying to kill her—so she had no right to be critical. But it all struck her as such a waste.

"Where'd you go?" Jordan asked. "You look like you're a million miles away."

"Oh, just daydreaming," Lillian fibbed. "Nothing important really."

"Thinking about that fancy ball last night?"

"No, actually, I was thinking about you. Am I the only one who calls you Samuel?"

"Most folks don't even know my real name."

"Then I want to know even more. How did you become a buffalo hunter?"

"That's a long story."

"We have all afternoon."

Jordan, like most men, was easily prompted to talk about himself. She listened, nodding with interest, seemingly all attention. Yet her mind was a world away, another time and another place. A time of gentler memory.

She longed again for the sight of New York.

# CHAPTER 10

THE PLAINS were blanketed with snow. The air crackled with cold, and there were patches of ice along the banks of the Arkansas. Clouds the color of pewter hung low in the sky.

The Fontaines arrived shortly after eleven o'clock. They were bundled in heavy coats and lap robes, their breath like frosty puffs of smoke. An orderly rushed out to take charge of the buckboard and team as they stopped before the house. Libbie Custer met them at the door.

"Merry Christmas!" she cried gaily. "Come in out of the cold."

"Yes, Merry Christmas," Lillian replied, hugging her fondly. "Thank you so much for having us."

"Indeed," Fontaine added heartily. "You are the very spirit of the season for strangers far from home. We feel blessed by your charity."

"Don't be silly," Libbie fussed. "Now, get out of those coats and come into the parlor. Everyone's waiting."

Their coats were hung in the vestibule. Libbie led them into the parlor, where a cheery blaze snapped in the fireplace. Custer moved forward, his hand outstretched, followed by Clark. His manner was jovial.

"Here you are!" he said, shaking their hands. "To quote our friend Dickens, 'God bless us every one!' Welcome to our home."

Chester went to warm himself by the fire. Custer nodded to a manservant, who shortly returned with a tray of hot toddies in porcelain mugs. The mix of brandy, water, and sugar, heated with a red-hot poker, brought a flush to Lillian's face. Clark raised his mug in a toast.

"Merry Christmas," he said cordially. "You look lovely today."

"You're being gallant," she said with a smile. "I'm sure my nose is red as an apple. I thought I would freeze before we got here."

"I'm afraid it will be even colder when you drive back."

"Yes, but as you know, there's no rest for actors. The show must go on, even on Christmas night."

"We could change that easily enough. All you have to do is say the word."

Lillian avoided a reply. Over the past month Clark had proposed on several occasions, and each time she had gently turned him down. She was still attracted to him, just as she was to Jordan, who continued to court her whenever he was in town. But the thought of being stranded in Kansas, marriage or not, made her shudder. She looked for a way to change the subject.

"Oh, what a marvelous tree!" she said, turning to Libbie. "Why, it's absolutely gorgeous."

Libbie brightened. "I sent all the way to Chicago for some of the ornaments. I'm so happy you like it."

George Armstrong Custer was not a man to do things by half-measure. In mid-December, he'd had a fir tree imported from Missouri, freighted overland with a consignment of military stores. Libbie had decorated the tree with cranberries and popcorn strung together on thread and gaily-colored ribbon bows. Her most treasured ornaments, ordered from Chicago, were white satin angels with gossamer wings and shiny glass balls. The tree was crowned with a silver papier-mâché star.

The Custers were childless, but Christmas was nonetheless a time of celebration. Watching them, it occurred to Lillian that there was something childlike about the couple. They were forever inventing reasons for gala parties, amateur theatricals, or nature outings that often involved a dozen or more officers and their wives. Yet Christmas was clearly their favorite festivity of the year, eclipsing even the Fourth of July. The tree, imported all the way from Missouri, stood as testament to their Yuletide spirit.

The hot toddies were apparently a tradition in the Custer household. Apart from wine with dinner, women seldom drank hard liquor in the company of men. But Custer insisted, and before an hour was out Lillian felt as though her head would float away from her shoulders. Libbie coaxed her into singing a Christmas carol, and she managed to get through it without missing a note. She was giddy with delight.

Fontaine, who needed little prompting, was then asked to perform. To their surprise, he selected a poem written by Clement C. Moore, one that had gained enormous popularity in recent years. He positioned himself beside the tree and recited the poem with a Shakespearean flair for the dramatic. His silken baritone filled the parlor.

*Twas the night before Christmas, when all*
*through the house*
*Not a creature was stirring—not even a mouse;*

*The stockings were hung by the chimney with care,*
*In hopes that St. Nicholas soon would be there . . .*

"Bravo!" Custer yelled when Fontaine finished the last line. "Never have I heard it done better. Never!"

Libbie was reduced to tears. Lillian, still lightheaded from the hot toddies, was amazed. Apart from Shakespeare, she had no idea that her father had ever committed anything to memory. She glanced at Chester, who offered her an elaborate shrug. He seemed equally nonplussed.

The manservant, with impeccable timing, announced dinner. The table was decorated with greenery, bight red berries, and tall colored candles. A roasted goose, its legs tied with red and green bows, lay cooked to a crisp on a large serving platter. Custer, wielding a carving knife as though it were a cavalry saber, adeptly trimmed the bird. After loading their plates, he waited for the manservant to pour wine. He hoisted his glass.

"You honor Libbie and I with your presence on the day of Our Lord's birth. Merry Christmas!"

Everyone clinked glasses and echoed the sentiment. The serving bowls were passed and their plates were soon heaped with stuffing, winter squash, cranberry sauce, mashed potatoes, and a rich oyster gravy. Fontaine offered his compliments to the chef, though the army cook in the kitchen had never been seen on any of their visits to the house. The manservant kept their wineglasses full.

Lillian was acutely conscious of Clark seated on her right. He hadn't spoken since their earlier conversation in the parlor, when she'd blithely evaded his reference to marriage. His manner was sullen, and while the others ate with gusto, he merely picked at his food. No one else seemed to notice, but she saw Libbie glance at him several times during the meal. He drained his wineglass every time it was replenished.

Later, after dessert, the men retired to the study for cigars and brandy. Clark was bleary-eyed with wine on top of hot toddies and scarcely looked at Lillian as he walked from the room. Libbie led her into the parlor, where they seated themselves on a sofa before the fireplace. The gaiety of the party seemed diminished for Lillian, and she scolded herself for having hurt Clark with an unintentional rebuff. There was an awkward silence as she stared into the flames.

"I couldn't help but notice," Libbie finally said. "Did you and Terrance have words?"

Lillian smiled wanly. "I'm sure you knew he asked me to marry him."

"Yes, he mentioned it to the general."

"I've told him no any number of times. I think he realized today it's really final."

"What a shame," Libbie said sadly. "Terrance would make a fine husband."

"I know," Lillian said, a tear at the corner of her eye. "I just hate it, but I'm not ready for marriage. I haven't yet sorted out my own life."

"How do you mean?"

"Oh, it seems I'll never see New York again. And I so wanted a stage career."

"Aren't you scheduled to play Wichita next spring?"

"Wichita isn't New York," Lillian said fiercely. "I really loathe performing for cowboys and buffalo hunters, and drunken, brawling men. Everything in the West is so crude and . . . uncivilized."

"Yes, unfortunately, it is," Libbie agreed. "I often have those same feelings myself." She hesitated, considering. "Tell me, have you given any thought to Denver?"

"Denver?" Lillian looked at her. "Isn't that somewhere in Colorado? The mountains?"

"My dear, you have never seen anything like it. The Rockies are absolutely stunning, and Denver itself is really quite cosmopolitan. A very sophisticated city."

"Honestly?"

"Oh, goodness yes," Libbie said earnestly. "Theater, and opera, and shops with all the latest fashions. And scads of wealthy men. Just scads!"

Lillian's face lit up. "It sounds like the answer to a dream."

"Well, for someone who wants a career on the stage, it's perfect. I just know you would be a sensation there."

"Would you tell Father about it? Would you, please?"

"You mean, how grand and sophisticated it is? Perhaps a little hyperbole?"

"Yes! Yes!"

"Why, of course. What are friends for?"

The men trooped in from the study. Lillian caught Chester's eye and warned him to silence with a sharp look. Then, artful as a pickpocket, she got her father seated on the sofa. She gave the general's wife a conspiratorial wink.

Libbie Custer began her pitch on the wonders of Denver.

* * *

Murphy's Exchange was mobbed. The blizzard a few days past had driven every buffalo hunter on the plains into Dodge City. They decided to stay and celebrate Christmas.

Their idea of celebrating the Christ Child's birth was little short of heathen. The first stop was a saloon, where they got modestly tanked on rotgut whiskey. The second was a whorehouse, where the girls baptized them in ways unknown to practicing Christians. After a carnage of drinking, gambling, and whoring, they were ready at last for Christmas night. They came, en masse, to see Darlin' Lilly.

Lillian was beside herself with excitement. On the drive back from Fort Dodge, her father had spoken of little else but Denver. Libbie Custer's glowing account had left him intrigued by the thought of a cosmopolitan oasis in the heart of the mountains. The general, not to be outdone by his wife, had embellished the Mile High City with an aura of elegance second to none. His comments added authority to an already dazzling portrait.

The marvelous thing was that Alistair Fontaine adopted the idea as his own. New York was a tattered dream, and Wichita was yet another cowtown quagmire, hardly better than Dodge City. But Denver, he declared after the Custers' stirring narrative, was the affirmation of an actor's prayer. He hadn't committed to a journey into the Rockies, but Lillian told herself it was only a matter of time. A gentle nudge here and there and he would talk himself into it.

Tonight's show was almost ended. Lillian was waiting in the wings for the finale, her last song of the evening. Her father was farther backstage, involved in a discussion with Frank Murphy. Chester approached her, glancing over his shoulder to make sure the conversation was still in progress. He gave her a dour look.

"Dad's back there grilling Murphy about Denver. You sure put a bee in his bonnet."

*"Me?"* Lillian said innocently. "The Custers got him started on it, not me."

"Yeah, sure," Chester scoffed, "and the moon's made of green cheese."

"Listen to me, Chester. However much Papa talks, we're never going back to New York. Denver is our only hope for a decent life."

"I know."

"You do?"

"Of course I do," Chester said. "The chances are nil of our ever getting a booking back East. Either we go to Wichita or we take a crack at Denver."

"Well . . ." Lillian was relieved. "I hope you favor Denver."

"Don't worry, we'll talk Dad into it."

"No, he thinks it's his own idea. Let him talk himself into it."

Chester smiled. "I can almost hear Mom saying the same thing. You remind me more and more of her lately."

"Oh, Chet . . ."

The piano player opened with her introduction. She gave Chester a quick kiss on the cheek and moved out of the wings. The fiddler joined the piano, and the crowd of drunken buffalo hunters greeted her with rowdy applause. She walked to the footlights, hoping they would appreciate her selection. She thought it a fitting end to the Christmas season. On the musicians' cue, her voice seemed to fill the night.

*Hark! the herald angels sing*
*Glory to the newborn King;*
*Peace on earth and mercy mild,*
*God and sinners reconciled!*
*Joyful all ye nations rise,*
*Join the triumph of the skies;*
*With th' angelic host proclaim*
*Christ is born in Bethlehem*

The saloon went silent. She saw Cimarron Jordan at the bar, and he nodded with an approving smile. The hide hunters, heathen or not, stared at her as though suddenly touched by memories past. To a man, their thoughts slipped from whiskey and whores to long-gone times of Christmas trees and family. Many snuffled, their noses runny, and one blubbered without shame, his features slack with emotion. A carol sung in a saloon took them back to better days, gentler times.

The hush held until her voice faded on the last note. Then they recovered themselves, and a roar went up, whistles and cheers and drumming applause. She curtsied, warmed by their reaction, and made her way offstage. They brought her back for another ovation, and then another, and she thought there was, after all, some glimmer of hope for buffalo hunters. Yet it was a passing thought, and one quickly gone. Her mind was fixed on Denver.

Later, after she'd changed, Jordan took her to a café for a late supper. The food was greasy, thick slabs of buffalo fried in a skillet, and she hardly ate a bite. But she chattered on with growing excitement as she related her conspiracy with Libbie Custer. Her eyes sparkled whenever she mentioned Denver, and she could scarcely contain herself. She bubbled with the thrill of it all.

"What about your pa?" Jordan asked, when she paused for breath. "Think he'll go for the idea?"

"Oh, I know he will. I just know it! He's talked of nothing else."

"Well, I'm pleased for you. Mighty pleased."

Lillian saw his downcast expression. She knew he was taken with her and chided herself for not being more sensitive. She touched his hand.

"You could always come visit me in Denver."

"Suppose I could," Jordan said, studying on it. "Course, they'll turn you into a big-city girl with fancy notions. Likely you wouldn't have time for a rough old cob like me."

"That simply isn't true," she said, squeezing his hand. "I'll always have time for you, Samuel. Always."

Cimarron Jordan wanted to believe it. But he was a pragmatist, and he told himself there was a greater truth in what he'd heard tonight. Come spring, there was no doubt in his mind.

Dodge City would see the last of Darlin' Lilly.

# Chapter 11

SPRING LAY across the land. The plains stretched onward to infinity, an emerald ocean of grass sprinkled with a riotous profusion of wildflowers. A late-afternoon sun heeled over toward the horizon.

Fontaine rode a bloodbay gelding. A Henry repeater was balanced behind the saddlehorn, and he wore a light doeskin jacket with fringe on the sleeves. Chester drove the buckboard, drawn by the mismatched sorrel and dun team, fat from a winter in the livery stable. Lillian was seated beside him, the brim of her bonnet lowered against the glare of the sun. They were three days west of Dodge City.

Lillian thought her father was in his glory. She glanced at him from beneath her bonnet, forced to smile at the striking figure he cut on the gelding. He rather fancied himself the intrepid plainsman and looked like he was playing a role that borrowed assorted traits from Daniel Boone and Kit Carson. She was amused that he played the part of stalwart scout with such élan.

Their immediate destination was Pueblo, Colorado. By her reckoning, she marked the date at April 18, and she hoped 1872 would prove more rewarding than the year just past. She had celebrated her twentieth birthday in February, and she felt immensely matured by her experiences in Abilene and Dodge City. So much so that she seldom fell into reverie about some grand and joyous return to New York. Her thoughts were on Denver.

By New Year's Day, Alistair Fontaine had sold himself on the idea. Over the next three months he'd devoted his time to planning their artistic assault on the Mile High City. The top nightspot in Denver was the Alcazar Variety Theater, and he had arranged for their New York booking agent to forward their notices and a glowing report on the show. The owner of the Alcazar had sent a lukewarm response, stating he was interested but offering no firm commitment. Fontaine, undeterred by details, went ahead with his plans. He was confident they would take Denver by storm.

George Armstrong Custer became their unofficial adviser. The Kansas Pacific railroad was laying track westward but had not completed the line into Colorado. The nearest railhead was Wichita, a week's journey to the east, and at least another week by train to Denver. The better route, Custer suggested, was to follow the Arkansas River overland, which would bring them to Pueblo within two weeks' time. From there, it was a short hop by train to Denver.

Cimarron Jordan considered the overland route to be foolhardy. He told Lillian, and then Fontaine, that Custer was playing daredevil with their lives. The country west of Dodge City, he explained, was a hunting ground for the Cheyenne, the Comanche, and other tribes. A strip of unsettled territory bordering their route, known as No Man's Land, was also haven to outlaws from throughout the West. He firmly believed they would be placing themselves in jeopardy.

Fontaine blithely ignored the warning. General Custer was a distinguished soldier and the greatest Indian fighter in the West. Jordan was a common buffalo hunter and, in the end, a man who lacked the wisdom of a military commander. To no small degree, Fontaine was influenced by Custer's derring-do and quixotic spirit. He saw the journey as another step in their westward adventure, and he cast himself in the role of trailblazer and scout. He declared they would take the overland route.

Their final week in Dodge City was spent in provisioning for the trip. Fontaine stocked all manner of victuals, including buffalo jerky, dried fruit, and four quarts of Irish whiskey. He purchased a ten-gauge shotgun, with powder and shot, announcing it was suitable for wild fowl or wild Indians. Then, in a picaresque moment, he bought a bloodbay gelding with fire in its eye and a quick, prancing gait. Custer, after seeing the horse, gave Fontaine a doeskin jacket taken in the spoils of war. He looked like a centaur with fringe on his sleeves.

Their departure brought out all of Dodge City in a rousing farewell. Custer was there, along with Libbie, who hugged Lillian with teary-eyed fondness and good wishes for the journey. Jordan and his crew of skinners accompanied them west for the first day and then turned south for the Cimarron River. Before they separated, Jordan again cautioned them to be wary at all times and to mount a guard over their livestock every night. Indians, he observed, might steal your horses and, rather than kill, leave you to a crueler fate. A man on foot would never survive the limitless plains.

Fontaine consulted his compass an hour or so before sundown. Encased in brass, indicating direction and azimuth without fail, the compass was largely a showpiece. The Arkansas River wound due west like a silver ribbon, and simply following its course would bring them to Pueblo. But Fontaine, immersed in his role as scout, wanted all the props to fit the part, and he'd bought a compass. After snapping the lid closed, he signaled Chester to a stand of cottonwoods along the riverbank. He announced they would stop for the night.

By now, they went about their assigned tasks with little conversation. Chester hobbled the horses and put them to graze on a grassy swale that bordered the river. Later, he would water them for the night and then place them on a picket line by the buckboard. Fontaine gathered deadwood from beneath the trees and kindled a fire with a mound of twigs. Lillian removed her cast-iron cookware and foodstuffs from the buckboard and began preparing supper. She planned to serve buffalo jerky, softened and fried, with beans and biscuits left over from breakfast.

Twilight settled over the land as she dished out the meal. The fire was like a beacon in the night, and they gathered around with tin plates and mugs of steaming coffee. She thought the scene was curiously atavistic, not unlike a primordial tribe, hunkered before a fire, sharing the end of another day. Three days on the trail had already toughened them, and though her father and Chester religiously shaved every morning, they appeared somehow leaner and harder. Every time she looked in her little vanity mirror, she got a fright. She was afraid the harsh plains sun would freckle her nose.

"Westerners do like their beans," Fontaine said, holding a bean to the firelight on the tines of his fork. "I've always found it amusing that they call them whistleberries."

"Oh, Papa," Lillian said, shocked. "That's disgusting."

"A natural function of the body, my dear. Beans produce wind."

"I really don't care to discuss it."

Lillian was still embarrassed by aspects of life on the trail. A call of nature required that she hunt down thick brush or hide behind a tree. Even then, she thought there was scarcely any privacy. She always felt exposed.

"Your modesty becomes you," Fontaine said understandingly. "In fact, it provides a lesson for us all. We mustn't allow ourselves to be coarsened by the demands of nomadic travel."

Chester laughed. "Buffalo jerky and beans are coarse all right. I'd give anything for a good steak."

"Capital idea!" Fontaine said. "The land fairly teams with wildlife. I'll set out on a hunt tomorrow."

Lillian was alarmed. Her father knew virtually nothing about hunting and even less about negotiating his way on the plains. She had visions of him becoming hopelessly lost on the sea of grass.

"Do you think that's wise, Papa?" she asked uneasily. "Shouldn't we stay together?"

"Have no fear," Fontaine said with a bold air. "I shan't stray too far from the river. Besides, I have my trusty compass."

Chester looked worried. "Lillian has a point. If we were separated somehow, we might never get back together. I can do without fresh meat."

"Nonsense," Fontaine said stubbornly. "You concern yourselves for no reason. The matter is settled."

Later, after the horses were picketed, they spread their bedrolls around the fire. Chester took the first shift of guarding the camp, stationed with his rifle near the buckboard. Fontaine would relieve him in two hours, and they would alternate shifts throughout the night. Neither of them would hear of Lillian standing guard. She was, after all, a girl.

Lillian was less offended than amused. They seemed to have forgotten that she'd killed a Kiowa warrior on the Santa Fe Trail last fall. But then, male vanity was as prevalent in the Fontaine family as any other. She was to be protected simply because she was a woman. Or in their minds, still a girl.

She snuggled into her bedroll. The sky was purest indigo, flecked with stars scattered about the heavens like shards of ice. She stared up at the Big Dipper, filled with wonder that they were here, roughing it on the plains, sleeping on the ground. Her father their scout and hunter.

She thought her mother would have been beyond laughter.

Fontaine rode out of camp at false dawn. He reined the bloodbay gelding north, toward a distant copse of trees bordering a tributary creek. He reasoned that deer would water there before sunrise.

Chester and Lillian, following his instructions, were to continue westward along the banks of the Arkansas. Fontaine was still touched by their concern for his welfare but nonetheless determined that plains travel was largely an exercise of the intellect. He planned to have his deer and rejoin them long before midday.

Hunting, he told himself, was a matter of intellect as well. He recalled reading somewhere—possibly Thoreau—that deer were by nature nocturnal creatures. So it made sense, after a night of foraging, they would water before bedding down for the day. He felt confident a fat buck awaited him even now at the creek.

The tree line was farther than he'd estimated. He reminded himself again that the vastness of the plains was deceptive; everything was more distant than it appeared to the eye. The sun burst free from the edge of the earth, a blinding globe of vermilion, just as he rode into the shade of the trees. He dismounted, tying the gelding to a stout limb. He moved into the shadows with the Henry repeater.

Fontaine was immensely pleased with himself. He'd taken equestrian lessons many years ago, and the rhythm of it had come back to him after a day or so in the saddle. He was armed with a rifle that shot true and perfectly capable of navigating across the vistas of open grassland. Everything considered, he felt the dime-novel exploits of Buffalo Bill and his ilk were greatly overrated, more myth than fact. Any man with a modicum of intelligence could become a plainsman, and the same was true of a hunter. All he needed was to spot—

A buck stepped out of the shadows across the creek, some fifty yards upstream. Streamers of sunlight filtered through the trees, glinting on antlers as the buck lowered his nose to the water. Fontaine thumbed the hammer on his rifle, slowly tucking the butt into his shoulder. His arms were shaking with excitement, and it took him a moment to steady the sights. He recalled a conversation with Cimarron Jordan, about the cleanest way to kill an animal. He aimed slightly behind the foreleg.

The gunshot reverberated like a kettledrum. The buck jerked back from the water, then whirled about and bounded off through the trees. Fontaine was too astounded to move, roundly cursing himself for having missed the shot. Before he could lever another cartridge into the chamber, the buck disappeared into a thicket far upstream. He lowered the rifle, still baffled by his poor marksmanship and struck by a vagrant, if somewhat unsavory, thought. There would be no fresh meat in the pot tonight.

The thud of hoofbeats sounded off to the east. Fontaine wondered if a herd of buffalo was headed his way, and in the next instant the notion was dispelled. Five Indians, drawn by the gunshot, topped the rise that sloped down to the creek and reined to a halt. Their eyes found him almost immediately, and for a moment he felt paralyzed, rooted to the ground. Then they gigged their ponies, whooping and screeching as they tore down the slope, and he scrambled to unhitch his horse. He flung himself into the saddle.

The Indians splashed across the creek. Fontaine had perhaps a hundred yards' head start, and he booted his horse hard in the ribs. The gelding responded, stretching out into a dead gallop, and he thanked the gods he'd bought a spirited mount. A quick glance over his shoulder brought reassurance that he was extending his lead, and he bent low in the saddle. Something fried the air past his ear, and a split second later he heard the report of a rifle from far behind. He thundered southwest toward the river.

Some twenty minutes into the chase Fontaine had widened the gap to a quarter-mile. He silently offered up a prayer that the gelding had stamina as well as speed, for if he faltered now all was lost. Then, as he rounded a bend in the river, he saw the buckboard not far ahead. Chester and Lillian turned in the seat as he pounded closer, and by the expression on their faces, he knew they'd seen the Indians. He frantically motioned them toward the riverbank.

*"Get down!"* he shouted. *"Take cover!"*

Chester sawed on the reins. He whipped the team off the grassy prairie and brought the buckboard to a skidding halt where a brush-choked overhang sheltered the streambed. He jumped to the ground, rifle in hand, as Lillian hopped out on the other side with the shotgun. Fontaine reined the gelding to a dust-smothered stop and vaulted from the saddle. His eyes were wild.

"Open fire!" he ordered. "Don't let them overrun us!"

The Indians galloped toward them at a full charge. The sight of a white woman and a buckboard full of supplies merely galvanized them to action. Fontaine and Chester commenced firing, working the levers on their rifles in a rolling staccato roar. The breakneck speed of the ponies made it difficult to center on a target, and none of their shots took effect. The warriors clearly intended to overrun their position.

Lillian finally joined the fight. After a struggle to cock both hammers on the shotgun, she found it required all her strength to raise the heavy weapon. She brought it to shoulder level, trying to steady the long barrels, and accidentally tripped both triggers. The shotgun boomed, the double hammers dropping almost simultaneously, and a hail of buckshot sizzled into the charging Indians. The brutal kick of the recoil knocked Lillian off her feet.

A warrior flung out his arms and toppled dead from his pony. The others swerved aside as buckshot simmered through their ranks like angry hornets. Their charge was broken not ten feet from the overhang, and Fontaine and Chester continued to blast away with their Henry repeaters. None of the slugs found a mark, but the Indians retreated to a stand of cottonwoods some thirty yards from the riverbank. They dismounted in the cover of the tree line.

"Help your sister," Fontaine said sharply. "I'll keep an eye on the red devils."

Lillian lay sprawled on the rocky shoreline. Her shoulder throbbed and her head ached, and there was a loud ringing in her ears. Chester lifted her off the ground and set her on her feet, supporting her until she recovered her balance. He grinned at her.

"You got one!"

"I did?"

"Look for yourself."

A gunshot from the trees sent a slug whizzing over their heads. They ducked beneath the overhang and quickly crouched beside their father. Fontaine gave them a doleful look.

"There are four left," he said. "They have only one rifle, but that is sufficient to keep us pinned down. I fear we're in for a siege."

"A siege?" Chester questioned. "You don't think they'll rush us again?"

"Not until nightfall," Fontaine remarked. "I daresay they are wary of Lillian's shotgun. You saved the day, my dear."

Lillian was still dazed. "Will they come after us tonight, Papa?"

"Yes, I believe they will. Chester, reload your sister's shotgun. We'll have need of our artillery."

Fontaine bent low behind the buckboard and tied his gelding to a wheel rim. He knew the Indians were as interested in their horses as in their scalps. A live horse was of equal value as a dead man.

He thought they were in for a long night.

# Chapter 12

A BALL of orange flame rose over the eastern horizon. The heat of the sun slowly burned off a pallid mist that hung across the river. Somewhere in the distance a bird twittered, then fell silent.

The clearing between the riverbank and the cottonwoods was ghostly still. Fontaine was crouched at the right of the overhang, with Lillian in the middle and Chester at the opposite end. Lillian's shoulder was sore and bruised, and Chester had relieved her of the shotgun. She was now armed with a Henry repeater.

They were exhausted. Three times in the course of the night the Indians had attempted to infiltrate their position. Twice, using stealth and the cover of darkness, the warriors had crept in from the flanks. The last time had been an abortive assault from the river, floating downstream and trying to take them from behind. They had fought off every attack.

A starlit sky proved to be their salvation. The light was murky but nonetheless adequate to discern movement and form. Fontaine's instructions were to fire at the first sign of danger, and Lillian and Chester, their nerves on edge, were alert to the slightest sound. Accuracy was difficult in the dim light, and yet it did nothing to hamper volley after volley of rapid fire. The Indians beat a hasty retreat in the face of flying lead.

The horses reared and pitched with every skirmish. But Chester, exhibiting foresight long before darkness fell, had secured the team to thick, ancient roots jutting out from the overhang. The bloodbay gelding, tied to the near wheel of the buckboard, kicked and squealed with a ferocity that threatened to snap the reins. Still, with the coming of daylight, the horses dozed off standing up, as if calmed by the relative quiet. The only sound was a bird that twittered now and again.

Fontaine removed his hat. He cautiously edged his head around the side of the overhang and peered across the clearing. He saw no movement in the stand of cottonwoods and wondered if the Indians had pulled out under cover of darkness. His eyes narrowed as he realized that, sometime during the night they had recovered the body of the warrior killed by Lillian. A spurt of smoke blossomed from the tree line and a slug kicked dirt in his face. He jerked his head back.

"How depressing," he said with a mild attempt at humor. "Our friends are a determined lot."

Chester grunted. "Hope we killed some of them last night."

"I rather doubt it, my boy. Unless they still had us outnumbered, I suspect they would have given up the fight."

"So what do we do now?"

"Well, it is somewhat like a game of cat and mouse, isn't it? We have no option but to wait them out."

"Some option," Chester said dourly. "We could be here forever."

"Isn't there another way, Papa?" Lillian asked. "I dread the thought of another night like last night."

Fontaine smiled. "My dear, you are the only soldier among us. Chet and I have yet to kill our first savage."

"I can't say I'm proud of it. Besides, it was an accident with that stupid old shotgun anyway. It's a wonder I didn't break my shoulder."

"Or your *derriere*," Chester added with a sly grin. "You hit the ground so hard the earth shook."

Lillian was too tired to bandy words. Her face was smudged with dirt and the smoke of gunpowder, and stray locks of hair spilled down over her forehead. She was scared to death and felt as though she hadn't slept in a week. She wondered if they would live to see Denver.

Fontaine stuck his rifle around the edge of the overhang and fired. He turned back to them with a crafty smile. "A reminder for our friends," he said. "We musn't let them think we're not alert."

"I don't feel very alert," Lillian said. "I honestly believe I could close my eyes and go to sleep right now."

"Excellent idea, my dear. We need to be fresh for tonight's war of wits. You and Chet try to catch a nap. I'll keep watch for a while."

"You must be exhausted, too, Papa."

"On the contrary, I've never felt more—"

A herd of horses thundered around the bend in the river. At first glance, Fontaine estimated there were fifty or more, their manes streaming in the wind. Then, looking closer, he was never more heartened in his life. There were six men driving the horses. Six *white* men.

The four remaining Indians exploded out of the cottonwoods. They whipped their ponies, galloping north from the river, clearly no less startled by the sudden appearance of the herd. Several of the drovers pulled their pistols, jolted by the sight of Indians, and prepared to open fire. A man on a magnificent roan stallion raised his hand.

"Hold off!" he bellowed. "You'll spook the gawd-damn herd!"

The men obediently holstered their pistols. They circled the herd and brought the horses to a milling standstill. One of them gestured off at the fleeing Indians.

"Them there's Comanche," he said in a puzzled voice. "Think they was fixin' to jump us, Rufe?"

"Tend to doubt it," the one named Rufe said. "Not the way they're hightailin' it outta here."

"Then what the blue-billy hell was they doin' here?"

Fontaine stepped around the overhang. Lillian and Chester followed him, all of them still armed. The six men stared at them as though a flock of doves had burst from a magician's hat. Fontaine nodded to the man named Rufe, the one who appeared to be the leader. He smiled amiably.

"Those heathens"—he motioned casually at the fast-departing Indians—"were here attempting to collect our scalps. You gentlemen arrived in the very nick of time."

"Who are you?"

"Alistair Fontaine. May I present my daughter, Lillian, and my son, Chester. And whom do I have the honor of addressing?"

"The name's Rufe Stroud."

"Well, sir," Fontaine said, the rifle nestled in the crook of his arm. "Never have I been more delighted to see anyone, Mr. Stroud. You are a welcome sight indeed."

Stroud squinted. "What brings you to this neck of the woods?"

"We are on our way to Denver."

"You picked a helluva way to get there. Them Comanche would've roasted you alive."

"All too true," Fontaine conceded. "You are, in every sense of the word, our deliverance."

"Mebbe so," Stroud said. "You folks on foot, are you?"

"Our buckboard is there on the riverbank."

One of the men rode to the overhang for a look. He turned in the saddle to Stroud. "Buckboard and three horses, Rufe. Got a bay gelding that's purty nice."

Stroud nodded. "I'm a mite curious," he said to Fontaine. "Why're you headed to Denver?"

"We are actors," Fontaine said in his best baritone. "We plan to play the Alcazar Theater."

"Your girl an actor, too?"

"Yes indeed, a fine actress. And a singer of exceptional merit, I might add."

"That a fact?"

Lillian felt uncomfortable under his stare. Fontaine smiled amicably. "From the size of your herd, I take it you are a horse rancher, Mr. Stroud."

"You take it wrong," Stroud said. "I'm a horse thief."

"I beg you pardon?"

"Drop them guns."

The men pulled their pistols as though on command. Fontaine looked at them, suddenly aware he was in the company of desperadoes. He dropped his rifle on the ground, nodding to Lillian and Chester, who quickly followed his lead. Then, ever so slowly, he fished the Colt .32 revolver from his jacket pocket and tossed it on the ground. He looked at Stroud.

"Those are all of our weapons. May I ask your intentions, Mr. Stroud?"

Stroud ignored him. "Shorty," he said to one of the men. "Get them into the buckboard and let's make tracks. Them Comanche might have friends hereabouts."

Shorty Martin was well named. He was hardly taller than a stump post, a thickset man with beady eyes. "Whyn't we kill'em now?" he said flatly. "They're just gonna slow us down."

Lillian's heart skipped a beat. She seemed unable to catch her breath as Stroud inspected them as if they were lame horses that might slow his progress. His eyes suddenly locked onto her and held her in a gaze that was at once assessment and raw lust. The look lasted a mere instant, though she felt stripped naked, and his eyes again went cold. He glanced at Martin.

"Do like you're told."

Martin knew an order when he heard one. Within minutes, the outfit proceeded west along the river. The Fontaines were in the buckboard, and the bloodbay gelding, now unsaddled, ran with the herd. Fontaine, nagged by a worrisome thought, wished he had kept the pistol.

He'd seen the way Stroud looked at Lillian.

The sun was high when they crossed the Arkansas. At a wide spot in the river, where the water ran shallow, they forded through a rocky streambed. Their direction was now almost due southwest.

Fontaine watched the operation with increasing vigilance. His mind was already exploring how they might escape, and he was committing the terrain and their direction to memory. Yet he discerned that the gang functioned like a military unit, relentlessly on guard and with an economy of commands. The men clearly knew what was expected of them.

The chain of command was clear as well. Stroud was the leader, and his orders were not open to question. The other men, though a rough lot, seemed wary of incurring his anger. Shorty Martin was apparently Stroud's lieutenant and nominally the second in command. But there was little doubt as to his place in the scheme of things. Every order originated with Stroud.

Lillian was frightened into stony silence. Her intuition told her that these men were far more dangerous than the Comanche warriors they'd fought off just last night. Their abductors were callous and openly cold-blooded, evidenced by the one who had so calmly suggested that killing them was the better alternative. Only by the whim of the gang leader were they still alive.

Their deliverance from the Indians seemed to her a harsher fate. She knew lust when she saw it, and she'd seen it all too plainly in Stroud's cool gaze. She thought they'd jumped from the frying pan into the fire, and all because of her. Some inner voice warned her that the lives of her father and Chester were hostage to how she behaved. She sensed it was only a matter of time until her virtue was tested.

Stroud called a halt at noon. A narrow creek lay across their path, and he ordered the horses watered. The men took turns watching the herd, some rolling themselves smokes while the horses crowded around the stream. Others dismounted, pulling their puds as if there weren't a woman within a hundred miles, and relieved themselves on the ground. Lillian kept her eyes averted.

Stroud rode over to the buckboard. Chester, whose face was white with fury, erupted in anger. "Don't your men have any decency? How can you let them. . . . do that! . . . in front of a woman?"

"Sonny, you'd best shut your mouth. I won't be barked at by pups."

"Listen here—"

"That's enough!" Fontaine broke in. "Do as he says, Chet. Say nothing more."

"Good advice," Stroud said. "Don't speak till you're spoke to. Savvy?"

"We understand," Fontaine assured him. "It won't happen again."

Stroud nodded. He hooked one leg around the saddlehorn and pulled the makings from his shirt pocket. After spilling tobacco from a sack into the paper, he licked the edges and rolled it tight. He popped a sulphurhead on his thumbnail and lit up in a haze of smoke. His gaze lingered on Lillian a moment as he exhaled. Then he looked back at Fontaine.

"I never met an actor," he said. "Go ahead, do something."

"Pardon me?"

"Let's see you act."

"Seated in a buckboard?"

"I ain't in the habit of repeatin' myself. Show me your stuff."

Fontaine realized it was a crude test of some sort. He knew he would have only one chance to make good and decided to give it his all. The other men, drawn by the spectacle, moved closer to the buckboard. His voice rose in a booming baritone.

*The quality of mercy is not strained,*
*It droppeth as the gentle rain from heaven*

*Upon the place beneath: it is twice bless'd;*
*It blesseth him that gives and him that takes:*
*'Tis mightest in the mightiest; it becomes*
*The throned monarch better than his crown;*
*His scepter shows the force of temporal power,*
*The attribute to awe and majesty,*
*Wherein doth sit the dread and fear of kings*

Stroud was silent a moment. He took a drag and exhaled a wad of smoke. Then he smiled. "I like that," he said. " 'The dread and fear of kings.' You just pick that out of thin air?"

Fontaine spread his hands. "I thought it appropriate to the occasion."

"The part about mercy wasn't bad, either. I can see you've got a sly way about you."

"A supplicant often petitions mercy. Under the circumstances, it seemed fitting."

Stroud turned to the men. "You boys ever hear Shakespeare before?"

The men traded sheepish glances, shook their heads. "Thought not," he said, flicking an ash off his cigarette. "Well, Mr. Fontaine, mebbe we won't have to kill you, after all. We're plumb shy on entertainment out our way."

Lillian thought he was evil incarnate. He was lithe and muscular, with square features and a bristly ginger mustache. His eyes were hooded and seemed to emanate menace. She found herself staring into them now.

"Your pa says you're—how'd he put it?—an exceptional singer."

"I try," she replied softly. "Some people think I have a nice voice."

"You be thinkin' up a good tune for when we camp tonight. I'll let you sing for the boys."

Stroud shifted his gaze to Chester. "What is it you do, sonny?"

Chester reddened. "I act in melodramas. And I do a soft-shoe routine."

"You'll be dancin' for your supper before we're done. Just don't gimme no more of your sass."

"We understand perfectly," Fontaine interjected. "You may depend on us for the spirit of cooperation."

Stroud snuffed his cigarette between thumb and forefinger. He gestured to his men. "Awright, we been jawbonin' long enough. Let's get them horses on the trail."

The men jumped to obey. Stroud swung his leg over the saddlehorn and jammed his boot in the stirrup. Fontaine cleared his throat.

"May I ask you something, Mr. Stroud?"

"Try me and see."

"Where, exactly, are you taking us?"

Stroud smiled. "Folks call it No Man's Land."

# CHAPTER 13

THREE DAYS later they crossed into No Man's Land. Their line of march was due southwest, through desolate country parched by wind and sun. On the fourth day, they sighted Wild Horse Lake.

Rufe Stroud seemed to unwind a little when they neared the outlaw camp. He rode beside the buckboard, suddenly talkative, almost genial, chatting with Fontaine. Lillian got the impression that it was all for her benefit, meant to impress her with the man and the place. He was in a bragging mood.

The remote strip of wilderness, Stroud told them, was all but uninhabited. Centuries ago Spanish explorers had called it *Cimarron*, which loosely translated meant "wild and unruly." Through a hodgepodge of confused and poorly written treaties, it now belonged to none of the Western states or territories. So it was aptly dubbed No Man's Land.

Despite the name, there was nothing confusing about its borders. Texas and Kansas were separated by its depth of some thirty-five miles, while its breadth extended nearly two hundred miles westward from Indian Territory to New Mexico Territory. Along its northwestern fringe, the isolated strip of grasslands formed a juncture with Colorado as well. To a large degree, the raw expanse of wilderness had been forgotten by God and government alike. There was no law, Stroud idly warned them, but his law.

Wild Horse Lake was his headquarters. Known to few white men, the spot was situated on the divide between the Beaver and Cimarron Rivers. A prominent landmark, it was the haunt of renegades and desperadoes from across the West. Those who came there were predators, wanted men on the dodge, and the law of the gun prevailed. A man survived on cunning and nerve and by minding his own business. Too much curiosity, Stroud explained, could get a man killed.

The lake itself was centered in a large basin. Somewhat like a deep bowl, it served as a reservoir for thunderstorms that whipped across the plains. Above the basin, sweeping away on all sides, was a limitless prairie where the grasses grew thick and tall. Wild things, the mustangs that gave the lake its name, no longer came there to feed and water. The basin was now the domain of men.

Outlaws found refuge there. A sanctuary where those who rode the owlhoot could retreat with no fear of pursuit. Not even U.S. marshals dared venture into the isolated stronghold, for lawmen were considered a form of prey anywhere in No Man's Land. Discretion being the better part of valor, peace officers stayed away, and a man on the run could find no safer place. There was absolute immunity from the law at Wild Horse Lake.

Several cabins dotted the perimeter of the lake. A trail from the east dropped off the plains and followed an incline into the basin. Lillian counted seven cabins and upward of ten men lounging about in the late-afternoon sunshine. Three men on hoseback were watering a herd of longhorns, and she noticed that the cattle wore fresh brands, the hair and hide still singed. She knew nothing of such matters, but it appeared to her that the old brands had somehow been altered. The men watched her with interest as the buckboard rolled past.

Stroud's headquarters was on the west side of the lake. There were three cabins, one larger than the others, and off on the south side a corral constructed of stout poles. The men hazed the horses into the corral, and a woman came running to slam and bolt the gate. Lillian saw two other women standing outside the larger cabin, and for a moment her spirits soared. But then, looking closer, she was reminded of the prostitutes she'd seen in Dodge City. She would find no friends at Wild Horse Lake.

One of the women walked forward. She was plump and curvaceous, with a mound of dark hair and bold amber eyes. Her gaze touched on Lillian with an instant's appraisal and then moved to Stroud. Her mouth ovaled in a saucy smile.

"Hello there, lover," she said. "Glad to see you back."

"Glad to be back."

Stroud stepped down from the saddle. The woman put her arms around his neck and kissed him full on the mouth. After a moment, she disengaged and nodded to the buckboard. "What've you got here?"

"They're actors," Stroud said, his arm around her waist. "The old man's pure hell on Shakespeare. The boy dances a little and the girl's a singer. Got a real nice voice."

"You plan to keep them here?"

"Don't see why not. We could stand some entertainment. Liven up the place."

She poked him in the ribs. "Thought I was lively enough for you."

"Course you are," Stroud said quickly. "Wait'll you hear the girl sing, though. She's damn good."

"Just make sure singing's all she does."

"C'mon now, Sally, don't get started on me. I'm in no mood for it."

She laughed a bawdy laugh. "I guess I know how to change your mood."

The order of things soon became apparent. Stroud and his woman, Sally Keogh, shared one of the smaller cabins. The other small cabin was occupied by Shorty Martin and a frowsy woman with broad hips and red hair. The largest of the cabins was a combination mess hall and bunkhouse for the remaining four men. The third woman appeared to be their communal harlot.

Martin quickly got a rude surprise. Stroud motioned him over to the buckboard. "The actors," he said, jerking a thumb at the Fontaines, "are takin' over your place. You and Mae move your stuff into the big cabin."

"For chrissake!" Martin howled. "You got no call to do that, Rufe."

"Don't gimme no argument. Get'em settled and quit your bellyachin'."

"There ain't no extra bunk in the big cabin!"

"Work out your own sleepin' arrangements. Just get it done."

"Yeah, awright," Martin grumped. "Still ain't fair."

Stroud turned to the buckboard. "Listen to me real good," he said, staring hard at Fontaine. "You mixin' with my men—'specially the girl—that's liable to cause trouble. So I'm givin' you a cabin to yourselves."

Fontaine nodded. "We appreciate the courtesy, Mr. Stroud."

"You're gonna see we don't have no padlock to put on your door. Before long, you might get it in your head to steal some horses and make a run for it."

"I assure you—"

"Lemme finish," Stroud said coldly. "You run, I'll let Shorty have his way with you. Get my drift?"

"Yes, I do."

"Then don't do nothin' stupid."

By sundown, the Fontaines were settled in the small cabin. Not long afterward, Fontaine and Chester were ordered to carry armloads of firewood into the big cabin. Lillian was assigned to the kitchen, which consisted of a woodburning cookstove and a crude table for preparing food. The other women, who were frying antelope steaks and a huge skillet of potatoes, gave her the silent treatment. But as the men trooped in, taking seats on long benches at a dining table, Sally Keogh sidled up to her. The woman's features were contorted.

"Stay away from Rufe," she hissed. "You mess with him and I'll slit your gullet."

"Why not tell him that?" Lillian said, suddenly angry. "All I want is to be left alone."

"Just remember you were warned."

Stroud broke out the whiskey. He waved Fontaine and Chester to the table and poured them drinks in enamel mugs. His amiable mood left them puzzled until they realized he wanted to celebrate a successful horse raid. He once again began bragging about his operation.

The whiskey and other essentials, he informed them, were imported to Wild Horse Lake from a distant trading post. There were three gangs who made the basin their headquarters, and his was the largest of the bunch. Some rustled cattle, others robbed banks and stagecoaches, but none dealt in stolen horses. Stroud reserved that right to himself, and the other gangs went along, aware that he would fight to protect his interests. No one cared to tangle with him or his outfit.

Fontaine mentioned he'd been told that the Comanche and Cheyenne tribes were active in this part of the country. He alluded specifically to Stroud and his men saving them from certain death at the hands of the Comanche raiding party. He asked how Stroud and the other gangs managed to operate so openly in a land where warlike tribes traveled at will. Stroud laughed loudly.

"We buy 'em off," he said. "Injuns would trade their souls for repeatin' rifles. Bastards think we hung the moon."

Lillian listened as she worked at the stove. She knew all his bragging was like the sounding of their death knell. He would never have brought them here or expounded at such length on his operation if there was any chance they would be released. Or any chance they might escape.

He was telling them that they would never leave Wild Horse Lake.

Stroud threw a party that night. He invited all the members of the other gangs headquartered at Wild Horse Lake. By eight o'clock, some twenty people were jammed into the big cabin.

The announced purpose of the shindig was celebration of still another profitable horse raid. Yet it was apparent to all who attended that Stroud was eager to show off his captives, the Fontaines. Or as he insisted on referring to them in a loud, boastful manner: The Actors.

Jugs of whiskey were liberally dispensed to the revelers. Stroud and the other gang leaders were seated at the head of the long dining table, the position of honor. Their followers were left to stand for the most part, though some took seats on the bunks. The party steadily became more boisterous as they swilled popskull liquor.

One of Stroud's men whanged away on a Jew's harp. With the metal instrument clamped between his teeth, he plucked musical tones that were surprisingly melodious. A member of another gang was no less proficient on a harmonica, and the sounds produced on the mouth organ complemented those from the Jew's harp. They soon had the cabin rollicking with sprightly tunes.

Fontaine felt like he was attending some mad festivity hosted by an ancient feudal lord. The only difference in his mind was that the men were armed with pistols rather than broadswords and crossbows. Somewhat sequestered, he stood watching with Lillian and Chester by the woodstove as liquor flowed and the party got rowdier. He sensed they were about to become the court jesters of Wild Horse Lake.

Not quite an hour into the revelry Stroud rose to his feet. His face was flushed with whiskey and his mouth stretched wide in a drunken grin. He pounded on the table with a thorny fist until the Jew's harp and the harmonica trailed off in a final note. The crowd fell silent.

"I got a treat for you boys," he said with a broad gesture directed at the Fontaines. "These here folks are professional actors, come all the way from Dodge City.

Song and dance and, believe it or not, Shakespeare!"

Monte Dunn, the leader of a band of robbers, guffawed loudly. He was lean, the welt of an old scar across his eyebrow, with muddy eyes and buttered hair. He gave Stroud a scornful look.

"Shakespeare?" he said caustically. "Who the hell wants to hear Shakespeare? Ain't no swells in this bunch."

Stroud glowered at him. "Don't gimme none of your bullshit, Monte. This here's my show and I'll run it any damn way I see fit. Got it?"

"Don't get your bowels in an uproar. I was just sayin' it ain't my cup of tea."

"Like it or lump it, you're gonna hear it."

Stroud nodded to Fontaine, motioning him forward. Fontaine walked to a cleared area at the end of the table and bowed with a grandiose air. "For your edification," he said, glancing about the room, "I shall present the most famous passage from *Julius Caesar*."

The outlaws stared back at him with blank expressions. The thought crossed his mind that he might as well be a minister preaching to a congregation of deaf imbeciles. Yet he knew that his audience was Stroud alone, a man with the power of life and death. His eloquent baritone lifted with emotion.

*Friends, Romans, countrymen, lend me your ears;*
*I come to bury Caesar, not to praise him.*
*The evil that men do lives after them,*
*The good is oft interred with their bones;*
*So let it be with Caesar . . .*

Fontaine labored on to the end of the soliloquy. When he finished, the crowd swapped baffled glances, as though he'd spoken in Mandarin Chinese. But Stroud laughed and pounded the table with hearty exuberance. "You hear that!" he whooped. "That there's art!"

No one appeared to share the sentiment. Chester was the next to perform, accompanied by the Jew's harp and the harmonica. He went into a soft-shoe routine, which was made all the more effective by the sandpaper scrape of his soles against dirt on the floor. He shuffled in place, executed a few lazy whirls, and ended with legs extended and arms spread wide. The outlaws whistled and hooted their approval.

Lillian was to close with a song. She asked the men on the Jew's harp and harmonica if they knew the ballad *Molly Bawn*. When they shook their heads, she suggested they follow her lead and try to catch the melody as she went along. She moved to the end of the table, hands folded at her waist, and avoided the leering stares of a crowd now gone quiet. Her husky alto flooded the room.

*Oh, Molly Bawn, why leave me pining,*
*All lonely, waiting here for you?*
*The stars above are brightly shining,*
*Because they've nothing else to do.*
*The flowers so gay were keeping,*
*To try a rival blush with you;*
*But Mother Nature set them sleeping,*
*Their rosy faces washed with dew.*
*Oh, Molly Bawn! Oh, Molly Bawn!*

The ballad ended on a heartrending note. There was a moment's silence; then the outlaws rocked the cabin with applause and cheers. Stroud looked proud enough to bust his buttons, grinning and nodding until the commotion died down. He climbed to his feet.

"Listen here, Lilly," he said expansively. "Let's give these boys a real show. What say?"

"I don't understand," Lillian said.

"That old rag you're wearin' don't do you justice. Go change into one of them pretty silk gowns. The ones I saw in your trunk."

"Now?"

"Yeah, right now," Stroud said. "Get dolled up and come give us another song."

Lillian looked at Fontaine, who shrugged helplessly. She turned away from the table, unwilling to anger Stroud, and moved toward the door, As she went out, the Jew's harp twanged and the harmonica chimed in on *The Tenderfoot*. The men poured a fresh round of drinks, clapping in time to the music.

"Good-lookin' gal," Monte Dunn said, glancing at Stroud. "How'd you like to sell that little buttercup, Rufe? I'd pay you a handsome price."

"What d'you think I am?" Stroud said indignantly. "I don't sell humans like some gawddamn slave trader."

"Well, I don't know why not. You stole her just like you stole them horses out in the corral. You're gonna sell them horses for a profit. Why not her?"

"She ain't for sale."

Dunn laughed. "Hell, anything's for sale. Name a price."

"Monte, you stink up a place worse'n a polecat. Think I'll get myself some fresh air."

Stroud walked to the door. Sally started after him and he waved her off. She'd overheard his conversation with Dunn, and she didn't believe a word of it. She thought he was after more than fresh air.

Outside, Stroud hurried off in the direction of the Fontaines' cabin. A coal-oil lamp lighted the window, and he paused, darting a look over his shoulder, before he opened the door. Lillian was clothed only in her chemise, about to slip into her blue silk gown. She backed away, holding the gown to cover her breasts. He closed the door behind him.

"Well, looky here," he said, advancing on her. "I knew you was hidin' something special under that dress."

"Get out!" Lillian backed up against the wall. "Get out or I'll scream."

"Naw, you ain't gonna scream. That'd bring your pa runnin' and I'd have to kill him."

"Please don't do this, I beg you. I'm not that kind of woman."

"You're my kind of woman," Stroud said, reaching for her. "You and me are gonna have some good times."

Lillian swatted his hand away. "Leave me alone! Don't touch me!"

"I'm gonna do more'n touch you."

The door burst open. Before Stroud could turn, Sally whapped him over the head with a gnarled stick of fire-wood. The blow drove him to his knees, and he saved himself from falling by planting a hand against the floor. She shook the log in his face.

"You son-of-a-bitch!" she screeched. "You try any strange pussy and I'll cut your balls off. You hear me?"

Stroud wobbled to his feet. "You ought'nt have hit me like that, Sal. I was just talkin' to her, that's all."

"You're a lying no-good two-timin' bastard!"

She shoved him out the door and slammed it behind her. Lillian sat down on the bunk, the gown still clutched to her breasts. Her heart was in her throat, and she had to gulp to get her breath. Yet a small vixenish smile dimpled the corner of her mouth.

She thought Sally really would cut off his balls.

# Chapter 14

Late the next morning, the first of the stolen horses was led to the branding fire. Outside the corral, thick stakes were driven into the ground several feet apart, and laid out near the fire were lengths of heavy-gauge wire and a lip twist. A wooden bucket, with a rag dauber fastened to a stick, was positioned off to the side.

The horse was thrown and the men swarmed over him. Within seconds, his legs, front and rear, were lashed to the stakes. One man held the gelding's head down, while two others kept his hindquarters from thrashing. The fourth man stepped into the fray with the twist. He attached the rope loop to the horse's lower lip, then began twisting it like a tourniquet. The pain, intensifying with every turn, quickly distracted the horse from all else.

Stroud stood watching with Fontaine and Chester. His eyes were bloodshot from last night's party, and his head pounded with a dull hangover. But he was proud of his operation, and he'd invited them to observe the crew in action. He wanted them to see how a stolen horse was transformed into a salable horse.

"Watch close now," he said. "Shorty's a regular brand doctor."

"Pardon me?" Fontaine said, curious despite himself. "A brand doctor?"

"Yeah, somebody that makes a new brand out of the old brand. He's a gawddamn wizard."

Shorty Martin walked to the fire. He studied the brand on the gelding's flank—Bar C—then selected a piece of wire. His hands worked the metal the way a sculptor fashions clay; with a twist here and a curl there, he shaped one end of the wire into a graceful but oddly patterned design. A quick measurement against the old brand apparently satisfied him.

"You gotta pay attention," Stroud urged. "Shorty works fast once't he gets started."

Martin pulled the length of wire, now cherry red, out of the fire. With a critical eye, he positioned the wire and laid it over the old brand. The smell of burnt hair and scorched flesh filled the air, and an instant later he stepped back, inspecting his handiwork. As if by magic, the original C̲ had been transformed into a Δ.

"Ever see the like!" Stroud crowed. "Touch here and a touch there, and we got a Triangle O."

"Amazing," Fontaine said, truly impressed. "Mr. Martin is something of an artist."

Chester's brow furrowed. "I don't mean to question his work, Mr. Stroud. But isn't the burning and the redness something of a tip-off?"

Stroud chuckled. "Keep your eyes peeled, sonny. You're fixin' to see why Shorty's a sure-enough doctor."

Martin hefted the bucket. He stirred the contents, which appeared thick as axle grease and had the faint odor of liniment. Then he turned to the horse, and with a quick stroke of the dauber he spread a dark, pasty layer across the new brand. The entire operation had taken less than five minutes.

"I'm still at a loss," Chester said. "What does that do?"

"Shorty's secret recipe," Stroud announced. "Heals the brand natural as all get-out in a couple of days. Jesus Christ himself couldn't tell it'd ever been worked over."

The gelding was released and choused back into the corral. One of the men roped another horse and led it toward the fire. Fontaine wagged his head.

"I must say, you have it down to a science. Very impressive indeed."

"Tricks of the trade," Stroud said. "Stealin' horses takes a sight of know-how."

"I'm curious," Fontaine said in a musing tone. "How do you sell the rebranded horses?"

"You'll recollect I told you curiosity could get you killed around here."

"I withdraw the question."

"No, come to think of it, what's the difference? You gents are gonna be with us till hell freezes over. It ain't like you'll ever be tellin' anybody."

"I take your point," Fontaine said. "We are, in a manner of speaking, residents of Wild Horse Lake."

"Like I said, you won't be tellin' tales out of school."

Stroud was in an expansive mood. He went on to liken his operation to a thimblerigger's shell game. Several livestock dealers, spread throughout surrounding states and territories, represented the pea under the pod. Every week or so the gang would conduct a raid into Kansas, Colorado, New Mexico, or Texas. The stolen horses were then trailed back to No Man's Land, where the brands were altered with Shorty's magic wire.

The stolen stock, Stroud elaborated, was never sold on home ground. Horses from Kansas were trailed to Colorado and those from Texas to New Mexico. To muddy the waters further, the order of the raids was rotated among the states and territories. Local ranchers were never able to establish any pattern to the random nature of the raids. Yet it was all very methodical, nearly impossible to defend against.

The shell game was played out on many fronts. After being trailed to different locations, never on home ground, the horses were sold by livestock dealers over a widespread area. Usually, there was a mix of altered brands, and to all appearances, the stock had been bought here and there by an itinerant horse trader. In the end, horses stolen in random order were the shells of the game, sold across the breadth of four states. The livestock dealers, the pea under the pod, were known only to Stroud and his gang. Not one had ever been caught selling stolen stock.

"Nothin's foolproof," Stroud concluded, "but this here's mighty damn close. Them horses are scattered to hell and gone, and nobody the wiser."

Fontaine could hardly argue the point. There was a logistical genius to the operation, which virtually eliminated any chance of being detected. Yet Stroud had revealed the inner workings of the scheme with what amounted to a veiled threat. The Fontaines would never leave Wild Horse Lake. Not alive.

Lillian was watching them from the kitchen window. She and the other women were preparing the noon meal, and she wondered why her father and Stroud were involved in such lengthy discussion. As she turned from the window, she saw that Sally had taken a break, seated at the table with a mug of coffee. She decided now was the time.

"May I speak with you?" she asked, moving to the table. "We haven't talked about last night and perhaps we should."

Sally looked at her. "What's on your mind?"

"Well . . ." Lillian seated herself. "I wanted to apologize for what happened. I was as surprised as you were."

"Wasn't any surprise to me. Rufe never could keep his pecker in his pants."

"Do you think he'll try again?"

"Damn sure better not," Sally said evenly. "If he does, I won't stop with his balls. I'll lop his tallywhacker off."

The term was new to Lillian. She considered a moment and suddenly blushed with understanding. Her mother had always referred to that part of a man's anatomy as his "dingus." She mentally committed *tallywhacker* to her vocabulary.

"You sound unsure," she said. "Does he really believe you would—you know . . . do that?"

"Oh, he believes it," Sally said with a wicked smile. "Trouble is, he'd risk it if he caught you off alone somewhere. He knows you'd never talk."

"Why on earth wouldn't I?"

"Did you tell your pa about last night?"

"No . . . I didn't."

"Because you knew he'd get riled and start trouble and Rufe would kill him. That about cover it?"

"Yes."

"Well, dearie, Rufe figures it the same way."

Lillian was silent a moment. She glanced quickly at the kitchen area, to make sure they wouldn't be overheard by the other women. Then, lowering her voice, she took a chance. "Will you help us escape?"

"You're off your rocker!" Sally said, flummoxed by the very thought. "Why would I do a fool thing like that?"

"You know why we were brought here. It has nothing to do with my father or my brother, or with the fact that we're entertainers. It has only to do with me."

"So?"

"So where will it end?" Lillian coaxed her. "Will you kill him when he finally manages to . . . to rape me? Will you kill me just to remove the temptation?"

"You're some piece of work. Either I help you escape, or somebody—you, Rufe, maybe even me—winds up dead. That the general idea?"

"Yes, exactly."

"Wish to hell you'd stayed in Dodge City."

"So you'll help us get away?"

Sally sighed wearily. "I'll think about it . . . no promises."

The cabin was cramped. There was a single bunk, wedged into a corner, and wall pegs for hanging clothes. Last night Fontaine had insisted that Lillian take the bunk while he and Chester made do with pallets on the floor. Yet it was their only haven from Stroud and the gang. The one place they could talk in privacy.

By early afternoon all the horses had been doctored with new brands. Stroud, finally tired by a morning of braggadocio on the stratagems of a horse thief, had dismissed Fontaine and Chester. Lillian helped the women clean up in the kitchen following the noon meal and afterward was left to her own devices as well. The family gathered in the relative security of the cabin.

Fontaine related the details of Stroud's windy discourse on the triumphs of the gang. His tone was one of grudging admiration, and he admitted that the outlaw chieftain had a natural gift for organization. He readily admitted as well that Stroud's garrulous revelations of how the operation worked had come at a high price. They were, for all practical purposes, consigned to spend the rest of their lives at Wild Horse Lake. Stroud would never release them.

"You should have heard him," Chester added, looking at Lillian. "He as much as said he was confiding in us because we would never be able to tell anyone. He would kill us before he'd let that happen."

"Not in those exact words," Fontaine amended. "He has a clever way of issuing a threat without stating it openly. But you are nonetheless correct, Chet. Our lives are at peril."

"I had the feeling that we were being sworn in as members of the gang."

"With the proviso, of course, that anyone who betrays the trust signs his own death warrant. I feel sure Mr. Martin would gladly carry out the sentence."

"Huh!" Chester grunted dismally. "Shorty Martin would kill us just to get this cabin back."

Fontaine nodded. "I daresay you're right."

Lillian listened with growing concern. She desperately wanted to tell them of her conversation with Sally Keogh. But she wondered how to do it without revealing last night's failed assault by Stroud. She decided to shade the truth.

"We may have an ally," she said. "I spoke with Sally this morning. She might help us."

"Oh?" Fontaine inquired. "Help us in what way?"

"To escape."

Fontaine stared at her, and Chester's mouth dropped open. A moment elapsed before Fontaine recovered his composure. "Why in God's name would you ever raise the subject with her? She is Stroud's woman."

"That was exactly the reason," Lillian said with more confidence than she felt. "Sally thinks Stroud is attracted to me and she's worried. She told me so herself."

"One moment." Fontaine stopped her with an upraised palm. "Are you saying she is concerned Stroud would turn her out for you? She would lose his . . . affections?"

"Yes, Papa, that's what I'm saying."

"And she broached the matter with you?"

"Not about the escape," Lillian said evasively. "She expressed her concern that she might lose Stroud. I suggested the way around that was to help us escape. She promised to think about it."

"Extraordinary," Fontaine muttered. "Wouldn't that rather place her in jeopardy with Stroud?"

"Not unless she's caught."

"What if *we're* caught?" Chester interjected. "We already know what Stroud would do to us. He'd kill us!"

Fontaine thought that was only partially true. He suspected Stroud would kill Chester and himself without a moment's hesitation. Lillian, on the other hand, would be spared only to become Stroud's concubine. But all of that might happen anyway, for he'd seen Stroud's covetous attitude toward his daughter. He told himself that escape was their only option.

"Let me understand," he said. "Do you have reason to believe Sally will help us? Did she say anything to that effect?"

"Nothing definite," Lillian admitted. "But I really do believe she will, Papa. She loves Stroud very much."

"Talk about a revolting thought," Chester said. "She certainly has poor taste in men."

Fontaine crossed to the door. He stood staring out at the bleak landscape, trying to puzzle through all of the ramifications. A movement caught his eye and he saw a rider approaching from the northwest. The man rode into the compound, dismounted, and left his horse hitched at the corral. He walked toward the big cabin.

Lost in his own thoughts, Fontaine dismissed the man from mind. Some while later, as the sun dropped steadily westward, he suggested they leave for the main cabin. The women would be preparing supper, he noted, and their appearance would be expected at the dinner table. He cautioned Lillian and Chester to act as normal as possible, particularly around Sally Keogh. The slightest misstep might alert Stroud.

On the way across the compound, they saw Sally stagger around the corner of the cabin. Her lip was split, blood leaking out of her mouth, and her left eye was almost swollen shut. She lurched, all but losing her balance, and managed to recover herself. Lillian rushed forward.

"Sally, my God, what happened?"

"Watch yourself, kiddo," Sally mumbled. "I tried, but it got nasty. Rufe's on a tear."

"He hit you?"

"Slugged me a couple of times. Knocked me flat on my ass."

"That's terrible!" Lillian said angrily. "Why would he hit you?"

"Ed Farley's here," Sally said. "He's always had a thing for me and I thought I could trust him. Turns out I was wrong."

"Wait, you aren't making sense. Who's Ed Farley?"

"Ed's a livestock dealer. He buys all the horses Rufe trails to Colorado."

"And you told him about us?"

Sally, dabbing at her split lip, briefly explained. She'd gotten Farley aside and told him what great entertainers the Fontaines were. She suggested that he buy them from Stroud and make them sign a contract appointing him their manager. She convinced him there was money to be made on the variety circuit.

"Wasn't a bad idea," she concluded. "I figured you could escape lots easier in Colorado than here. Trouble is, Rufe popped his cork and Ed lost his nerve. He told Rufe it was my idea."

Lillian gently touched her arm. "I'm so sorry I got you into this."

"Worry about yourself," Sally warned her. "Rufe's never gonna let you go. He's like a madman."

"Yes, but what about you? Will you be all right?"

"Honey, that's anybody's guess. Rufe knows I'll kill him if he touches you or any other woman. Maybe he'll be cooled down by the time he comes to bed."

Sally tottered off toward her cabin. Fontaine appeared unsettled by what he'd heard. He finally squared his shoulders. "We'll have to have our wits about us tonight. Under the circumstances, we cannot afforded to provoke Stroud."

There was a moment of turgid silence when they entered the cabin. The women busied themselves in the kitchen, their eyes fixed on their tasks. Stroud was seated at the table with Ed Farley and the other gang members. His features were set in a sphinxlike mask.

"Well, here's the actors," he said curtly. "Look'em over real good, Ed. Make me an offer."

Farley was a heavyset man with a full beard. He shook his head. "Rufe, I think I'll stick to horses."

Stroud studied Lillian as if trying to read her mind. His gaze abruptly shifted to Fontaine. "Don't matter which one of you put Sally up to that nonsense. It was a dumb move."

"Yes, it was," Fontaine agreed. "Very foolish indeed."

"I warned you twice about tryin' to escape. There's not gonna be a third time. You follow me?"

"Implicitly, Mr. Stroud."

"You and your fancy words," Stroud said with a tight smile. "Tell you what, actor; let's see you act. Show Ed some of your Shakespeare."

"I would be honored to do so."

Fontaine felt like an organ grinder's monkey. Yet he knew there was no choice but to perform on command. He struck a dramatic pose.

*"O, what a rogue and peasant slave am I . . ."*

# Chapter 15

THE LAKE was molten with sunlight. Stroud stood in the door of the main cabin with a mug of coffee. His gaze was fixed on the corral.

Four men, one of them Ed Farley, were saddling their horses. Farley finished tightening the cinch on his chestnut gelding and spoke to the men. One of them racked back the bolt on the gate while the others swung into the saddle. He led his horse toward the cabin.

"We're ready," he said. "Didn't forget to pay you, did I?"

"That'll be the day," Stroud said with a crooked grin. "You're off to an early start."

"Well, Rufe, I'm not a man of leisure. I've got a ways to go before those horses turn a profit."

"Don't give me no sob stories. You make out like a Mexican bandit."

Farley shrugged. "Guess I've got no complaints."

"Course you ain't." Stroud drained his coffee mug. "Make sure them boys head on back here when the job's done. I don't want'em lollygaggin' around whorehouses and such."

The men choused the stolen horses out of the corral. The herd now included Fontaine's bloodbay gelding and the team that had once pulled the buckboard. One of the men turned the lead horse, while the others circled from behind, and they drove the herd west from the cabins. Farley stepped into the saddle.

"Always good doing business with you, Rufe. See you in about a month."

"I'll be here."

Stroud moved back into the cabin. As the door closed, Farley and the three gang members pushed the herd up the western slope of the basin. Fontaine, watching from the door of his cabin, waited until the horses disappeared over the rim onto the plains. He shook his head with a frown.

"A pity," he said, almost to himself. "They've taken my horse and the buckboard team. We are, quite literally, afoot."

Chester laughed sourly. "Dad, that's how Stroud intended it all along. He knows we're not about to walk out of here."

"Quite so," Fontaine concurred. "Somehow, though, it makes me feel all the more a prisoner. I rather liked that horse."

Lillian was seated on the bunk. "We musn't despair, Papa. There has to be a way."

"Yes, of course, my dear. Spirits bright, for we are nothing without hope. I'm sure we will find a way."

Fontaine tried to sound optimistic. Still, given the circumstances, his spirits had never been lower. Last night, Stroud had made them perform until even the men grew bored. The lengthy show was punishment for their abortive escape attempt and a message as well. Their next attempt to flee would be their last.

For all that, Fontaine saw no alternative. Stroud, before too long, would try to force himself on Lillian. When that happened, Fontaine would resist, as would Chester, and they would both be killed. Even worse, Lillian would be doomed to a life of depravity and unremitting torment. Fontaine thought it preferable, if death was inevitable, to die trying to escape.

Lillian scooted off the bunk. "I think I'll go talk to Sally. Maybe she'll have another idea."

"Be very careful," Fontaine admonished. "We have no way of knowing what transpired overnight. She may report anything you say to Stroud."

"Oh, I doubt that very much, Papa. Not after the way he abused her."

"Exactly the point I'm trying to make. After last night, she may well fear for her own life."

"Don't worry, I'll be careful. I promise."

Lillian stepped out the door. Sally had failed to appear at breakfast that morning, and she was concerned about her. She was no less concerned about a means of escape, for she knew the stalemate with Stroud would not last much longer. Time was running out.

Sally was huddled in the bunk of her cabin. When Lillian entered, a bright shaft of sunlight filled the dim interior. Sally winced, her left eye swollen shut, bruised in a rosette of black and purple, and her lip caked with dried blood. She looked worse than last night.

"Close the door," she said. "I'm a sight not fit to see."

Lillian sat on the edge of the bunk. "I was worried when you didn't come to breakfast. Is there anything I can do to help?"

"No, thanks just the same. Time's the only thing that'll heal what I've got."

"Sometimes I wish I were a man. I'd give him a lesson he wouldn't forget."

"Honey, a half-dozen men sat there last night and watched him beat me. None of them said a damn word."

"Yes, but they're afraid of him."

"And you aren't?"

"Actually, I'm terrified," Lillian admitted. "I didn't sleep a wink worrying he might come for me."

Sally sniffed. "Rufe won't be comin' for you till he kills me. Not that he wouldn't, you understand."

"What happened?"

"I waited for him last night. Minute he got in bed, I put a knife to his throat. Told him if he ever hit me again I'd slit his gullet."

"You didn't!"

"Yeah, I did, too," Sally said hotly. "Told him it was him and me, or nothin'. I won't be thrown over for another woman . . . meanin' you, of course."

"Good heavens," Lillian breathed. "What did he say?"

"Oh, he tried to play lovey-dovey. Longer I held that knife to his throat, the more promises I got. But that don't mean a lot for either you or me."

"Why not?"

Sally went solemn. "Rufe's a born liar, that's why not. He might kill me to get at you." Her voice dropped. "Or he might turn you over to the men . . . just to spite me."

"The men?"

"Toss you to that pack of wolves in the big cabin. Way he thinks, that'd still give him the last laugh."

Lillian paled. She had been too worried about Stroud to conjure an even worse fate. The thought had never occurred to her that she might be forced to submit to the horror of several men, night after night. As she considered it now, she felt queasy and the bitter taste of bile flooded her throat. She silently swore she would kill herself first.

"Do you . . ." She faltered, groping for words. "There has to be some way we can escape from here. Do you know of anything that might have a chance?"

Sally looked defeated. "Wish I did. Trouble is, if I try anything else, Rufe *will* kill me. And it'd all be for nothing. He'd still get you."

"Oh, God, Sally, I feel so helpless."

"Honey, I've felt that way most of my life."

A distant gunshot brought their heads around. Then, in the space of a heartbeat, a rattling volley of gunfire echoed through the basin. Lillian rushed to the window, with Sally only a step behind. Across the way, they saw three columns of horsemen fanning out around Wild Horse Lake. One column was galloping directly toward Stroud's compound.

The attack caught everyone by surprise. Monte Dunn and his men, as well as the gang of cattle rustlers, were lounging in the sunshine outside their cabins. The men tried to put up a fight, but they were overwhelmed by sheer numbers. There appeared to be ten or more horsemen in each column, their pistols popping as they came on at a gallop. The outlaws were cut down in a withering maelstrom of lead.

Stroud ran out of the big cabin as the attack started from the southern rim of the basin. Shorty Martin and the other men followed him outside, guns drawn, their women watching from the door. They opened fire on the column headed toward the cabin, and then, too late, realized they were outnumbered. As they turned back to the cabin, Martin took a slug between the shoulders and pitched to the ground. The other men, riddled, dropped on the doorstep.

A swarm of bullets sizzled all around Stroud. His hat went flying and a slug clipped his bootheel, but somehow, miraculously, he was otherwise unscathed. Some visceral instinct told him he would be killed if he tried to make it into the cabin, and he abruptly gave up the fight. He flung his pistol into the dirt and stopped, still as a statue, his hands high overhead. He waited for a shot in the back, then the gunfire suddenly ceased. The riders reined to a halt before the cabin.

"My God," Lillian whispered. "Who are they?"

Sally swallowed hard. "I think you've just been saved."

"What do you mean?"

"I mean they're wearin' badges."

Capt. Ben Tuttle held court in front of the cabin. He was a large man, with the jaw of a bulldog and eyes the color of dead coals. The star of a Texas Ranger was pinned to his shirt.

Tuttle had been a Ranger for almost twenty years. He'd fought Comanche marauders who raided south of the Brazos and Mexican *banditos* who struck north of the Rio Grande. In his time, he had seen some strange things and yet nothing as strange as what he'd found at Wild Horse Lake. He thought it beggared belief.

The dining table had been brought outside and positioned before the cabin. Tuttle was seated behind the table, having adopted the role of judge and jury in today's hearings. The Rangers, throughout the organization's history, were notorious for dispensing summary justice in the field. Wild Horse Lake was no exception.

There were thirty Rangers in Tuttle's company. In the course of the raid, they had killed nine outlaws without suffering a casualty. They were now guarding the survivors, who were ranked before Tuttle's impromptu courtroom. Stroud waited with Sally and the other women off to one side. Monte Dunn, whose gang had been wiped out, was held with the two cattle rustlers. His left arm dripped blood from a bullet wound.

The Fontaines stood before the bench. Alistair Fontaine had just finished telling their saga of escaping wild Indians only to be taken captive by a band of outlaws. Lillian and Chester had said nothing, merely nodding affirmation as their father related one hair-raising exploit after another. Capt. Ben Tuttle, who knew a whopper when he heard one, considered them with a skeptical eye. He thought it was all a load of hogwash.

"Let me get this straight," he said. "You're being held here prisoner and forced to entertain this bunch, or they'd kill you. That about the gist of it?"

"Indeed so," Fontaine acknowledged. "You and your men were our very salvation. You have delivered us from certain death."

Tuttle scowled. "You never stole a horse, or rustled a cow, or robbed nobody. Have I got it right?"

"Never!" Fontaine intoned. "We are actors."

"And you're from New York City?"

"By way of Abilene and Dodge City."

"And George Armstrong Custer advised you to take the overland route to Denver."

"None other," Fontaine said. "General Custer and his wife Libbie are our very good friends."

Tuttle rolled his eyes. "That's the damnedest story I ever heard."

"Captain, I assure you every word of it is true."

"Your word don't count for much in this neck of the woods. I'll need some proof."

Fontaine assumed a classic profile. " 'O, I have passed a miserable night. So full of ugly sights, of ghastly dreams. That, as I am a Christian faithful man, I would not spend another such a night.' You may recognize a passage from *King Richard the Third.*"

"That ain't exactly proof," Tuttle said cynically. "Any dimdot might memorize himself some Shakespeare."

"Lillian, step forward," Fontaine prompted. "Sing something for the captain, my dear."

"Without music, Papa?"

"A cappella will do quite nicely."

Lillian composed herself. She knew all Texans were former Confederates, and she sang *The Bonnie Blue Flag*. Her clear alto voice finished on a stirring note.

> *Hurrah, hurrah, for Southern rights, hurrah!*
> *Hurrah for the Bonnie Blue Flag that bears the single star!*

"You sing right good," Tuttle complimented her. "Course, that don't mean you're a stage actress. I've heard near as good in a church choir."

"Like hell!" Sally interrupted loudly. "Not unless you're deaf as a post. She's the real article."

Tuttle squinted. "Who might you be?"

"Sally Keogh."

"You a singer, too, are you?"

"I'm his woman," she said, pointing at Stroud. "That's Rufe Stroud, all-round horse thief and woman beater. He abducted these folks, just like they told you."

Stroud blanched with rage. "You gawddamn lyin' bitch! Shut your mouth!"

Tuttle nodded to one of his Rangers. "Teach that rowdy some manners."

The Ranger whacked Stroud upside the jaw with a rifle butt. Stroud went down as though poleaxed, spitting blood and teeth. Tuttle looked pleased with the result.

"Mind your tongue," he said. "I won't have nobody takin' the Lord's name in vain in my courtroom."

"This ain't Texas!" Stroud said, levering himself to his knees. "This here's No Man's Land. You ain't got no . . . no . . ."

"Jurisdiction?"

"Yeah, you ain't got no jurisdiction here. You can't do nothin' to us."

"Don't bet on it," Tuttle said. "Time or two, I've taken jurisdiction across the border into Old Mexico. I reckon No Man's Land ain't no different."

"That's a crock!" Stroud sputtered, his front teeth missing. "You're breakin' the law yourself!"

"Have me arrested." Tuttle turned back to Fontaine. "Appears you folks was tellin' the truth, and this court won't hold you. You're free to go."

"Thank you, Captain."

Fontaine motioned Lillian and Chester away from the table. Tuttle riveted the outlaws with a look. "Rufe Stroud," he said, "we been huntin' you a long time now. Like your woman says, you're a top-notch horse thief."

"Go to hell," Stroud spat through bloody gums. "You ain't got nothin' on me."

"Monte Dunn." Tuttle fixed his gaze on Dunn. "Your name's pretty well known in Texas, too. Heard your description so often I would've knowed you in a crowd."

"You got the wrong man," Dunn blustered. "I never been in Texas in my life."

"There's many a stagecoach driver that would dispute that. You've robbed your last one."

"I'm tellin' you, I'm not your man!"

Tuttle straightened in his chair. "This here court sentences you gents to be hung by the neck till you're dead." He looked at the two cattle rustlers. "You boys are found guilty by the company you keep."

"You sorry sonovabitch!" Stroud roared. "You can't hang us without a trial!"

"Objection overruled." Tuttle got to his feet. "Let's get on with this business. Time's awastin'."

A lone oak tree stood between the cabin and the lake. Within minutes, the four men were bound, mounted on horses, and positioned beneath a stout limb. The Rangers tossed ropes over the limb and snugged them firmly to the trunk of the tree. The nooses were cinched around the necks of the doomed men.

Lillian turned away, unable to watch. Tuttle walked forward, staring up at the men. "You boys got any last words?"

"I do," Stroud said, glowering down at Sally. "Hope you're satisfied, you dumb slut. You got me hung."

"No, Rufe," she said in a teary voice. "You got yourself hung."

Tuttle motioned with his hand. The Rangers cracked the horses across the rumps, and the outlaws were jerked into the air. When the nooses snapped tight, their eyes seemed to burst from the sockets, growing huge and distended. They thrashed and kicked, their legs dancing, as though trying to gain a foothold. A full minute passed before their bodies went limp.

"We're done here," Tuttle called to his Rangers. "Get ready to move out!"

Fontaine was aghast. "Aren't you going to bury them?"

"We rode ten days to catch this bunch. I reckon we'll leave'em as warnin' to anybody that thinks they're safe in No Man's Land."

"I daresay that would be warning enough."

Tuttle studied him a moment. "You still set on headin' for Denver?"

"Yes, we are," Fontaine said. "Why do you ask?"

"Stroud's woman and them other two floozies. We don't take prisoners, specially women. You might want to cart 'em along to Denver."

"Good God!"

"Life's hell sometimes, ain't it?"

Lillian took Sally in her arms. She watched the Rangers mount, forming in a column, and ride out over the southern rim of the basin. In the silence, the creak of rope caught her attention, and she turned, staring at the bodies swaying beneath the tree. The brutal suddenness of it still left her in shock.

She prayed as she'd never prayed before for the bright lights of Denver.

# Chapter 16

The Arkansas River brought them at last to Pueblo. They had been on the trail twelve days, and the tale of the journey was told in their appearance. They looked worn and weary, somewhat bedraggled.

Fontaine was mounted astride Rufe Stroud's roan stallion. Beside him, Chester rode the frisky gelding formerly owned by Shorty Martin. They thought it only fitting that they had appropriated the horses of their now-deceased captors. The irony of it had a certain appeal.

The buckboard was drawn by two saddle horses, drafted into service as a team. Lillian drove the buckboard, with Sally seated beside her and the other two women in the rear. Fontaine promised himself that he would never again undertake overland travel with four women. He felt somewhat like the headmaster of a seminary on wheels.

Pueblo was situated in the southern foothills of the Rockies. The surrounding countryside was arid, despite the proximity of the Arkansas River to the town. Eastward lay a vista of broken plains, and to the west towering summits were still capped with snow. The mountains marched northward like an unbroken column of sentinels.

By 1872, Pueblo was the railway center of Southern Colorado. The road into town crossed the Denver & Rio Grande tracks, which extended some ninety miles northward to Denver. Directly past the tracks, Pueblo's main thoroughfare was clogged with wagons and buggies and the boardwalks were crowded with shoppers. The street was jammed with stores, and a block away the new courthouse was under construction. The arrival of the railroad had transformed a once-isolated outpost into a bustling mecca of commerce.

Lillian was all eyes. She hadn't seen anything so civilized since they departed New York almost nine months ago. Abilene, then Dodge City and No Man's Land seemed to her a journey through a wasteland most memorable for its bloodshed and violence. Several times she'd had nightmares about the brutal hangings, bodies dangling with crooked necks beneath a tree limb. She was determined never again to stray far from a city.

Sally asked her to stop as they neared the edge of the business district. She reined the team to a halt by the boardwalk, wondering why Sally wanted to stop short of the uptown area. Over the past twelve days they had become friends, confiding in each other and sharing secrets. She called out to her father and Chester, who rode back to the buckboard. Sally faced them with a sober expression.

"We'll leave you here," she said, nodding to the other women. "We're obliged for everything you've done."

"Why?" Lillian asked, openly surprised. "We've only just arrived."

"You don't want to be seen with the likes of us. Wouldn't do much for your reputation."

"Who cares about reputation? You're as new to Pueblo as we are. How will you manage?"

"Don't worry about us," Sally said with a rueful smile. "We'll do lots better here than we did at Wild Horse Lake."

"I won't hear of it!" Lillian said adamantly. "At least wait until we get settled."

"No, trust me, it's best this way. We'll likely see you before you leave for Denver."

Sally gave her an affectionate hug. Lillian's eyes puddled with tears as the women crawled out of the buckboard. They were poorly dressed, and their belongings, brought from Wild Horse Lake, were hardly any better. She knew they would become prostitutes or, if they were lucky, kept women. She knew as well that Sally was fibbing about getting together. She would never see them again.

The women walked away, Sally waving back over her shoulder. Fontaine waited a moment for Lillian to collect herself, then reined his horse around. Uptown, he quickly surveyed the street and led them toward the Manitou House Hotel. An imposing brick structure, three stories high, the hotel had two bellmen. They wrestled the steamer trunks off the buckboard and carried them inside. Fontaine turned to Chester.

"Lillian and I will register," he said. "Find the nearest livery stable and sell the lot. Horses, buckboard, everything."

"All right," Chester said. "What price should I ask?"

"Take whatever you're offered. I'm happy to say we have completed our last overland expedition. We will travel by train from now on."

"Dad, that sounds good to me. Hope I never see a horse again."

"I devoutly second the motion."

Fontaine engaged a suite on the third floor. After their travails, he informed Lillian, they were due some modicum of comfort. The suite contained a sitting room and two bedrooms, with windows overlooking the street. Lillian would take one bedroom, and Fontaine would share the other one with Chester. He ordered the bellmen to bring corrugated metal tubs for each bedroom and loads of hot water.

Lillian thought it grand enough for royalty. By the time she unpacked her trunk, the tub and hot water arrived. She spent the next hour luxuriating in steamy bliss, unable to remember when she'd been so content. Her very soul seemed encrusted with grime from No Man's Land and the overland trek, and she gave herself over to the cleansing of a good scrub and washing her hair. She stepped from the tub reborn.

Some while later she wandered into the sitting room. She was barefoot, wearing a fluffy robe, her hair wrapped in a towel. Fontaine, already bathed, shaved, and dressed, was attired in a suit he'd had pressed while he was in the tub. He was standing by the windows, staring out over the town, and turned when she entered the room. Before he could speak, Chester came through the door.

"I was becoming concerned," Fontaine said. "What took you so long, Chet?"

Chester grinned, pulling a leather pouch from his coat pocket. He dumped a mound of gold coins on a table by the sofa. "I finally talked them out of three hundred dollars."

"Three hundred!" Lillian yelped excitedly. "We're rich!"

"Bravo, my boy," Fontaine congratulated him. "You obviously have a gift for finance."

"I don't know about that." Chester shrugged modestly. "But I have to say, I enjoyed the dickering. It's fun to get the better of the deal."

"Yes, of course," Fontaine said. "Now, hurry along and have your bath. Lillian will be ready before you are."

"Where are we going?"

"Why, we're off to see the town. I'm looking forward to a decent meal."

Early that evening they emerged from an Italian restaurant recommended by the hotel. Fontaine was impressed by the service and, even more so, the food; they were stuffed on fresh garden salad, beef cannelloni, and a rich assortment of pastries. On the street, Fontaine suggested they have a look at some of Pueblo's variety theaters. He was interested to see what played well in the Rockies.

The sporting district was south of the business center. There, as in most western towns, the stage shows were mingled among saloons and gambling establishments. The largest, and by far the most crowded, was the Tivoli Variety Theater. A barnlike structure, the Tivoli boasted the longest bar in Pueblo, assorted games of chance, and a wide stage at the rear of the room. Fontaine arranged for a table near the orchestra.

A waiter seated them as a magician produced a rabbit from a top hat. Then, playing to the audience, he brought forth a pair of doves from a silk scarf. By the time Fontaine and Chester were served drinks, the headline act, billed as the Ethiopian Minstrels, pranced onstage. The troupe of twelve men, all in blackface, proceeded to rattle their tambourines while they sang and ribbed one another with colorful badinage. Fontaine was fascinated.

"I know this act," he said. "They played many of the theaters we did on the circuit back East."

"By golly, you're right," Chester remarked. "I remember we followed them into Syracuse one time. I forget the name of the theater."

"The Rialto."

Fontaine fell silent. He watched the minstrels clown and trade barbs, but his thoughts seemed elsewhere. His features were a study in concentration, and when the curtain came down, he scarcely bothered to applaud. He looked around at Lillian and Chester with a buoyant expression.

"I've just had a marvelous idea," he said. "Do you recall the roundabout message we got from the owner of the Alcazar Theater in Denver? That we would have to audition before he would consider booking us?"

"Yes, I do," Lillian replied. "You thought it was awfully stuffy of him."

"Well, a better plan occurs to me now. We will make our name here and then storm the gates of Denver."

"You mean . . . here . . . in Pueblo?"

"Exactly!"

"Oh, Papa, I so wanted to go on to Denver. Libbie Custer said it is absolutely cosmopolitan."

"Think a moment, my dear," Fontaine said earnestly. "We haven't yet made our name on the Western circuit. A short time here and we enter Denver with headliner billing."

"Listen to him," Chester encouraged her. "Pueblo may not be cosmopolitan, but it's the right place to start.

We need good notices going into Denver."

"No question of it!" Fontaine said vigorously. "We will make them *beg* for The Fontaines!"

Lillian knew she'd been outvoted. However disappointing, her father was wise in the ways of the theater. Pueblo really was the place to start.

Denver would have to wait.

Late the following morning they returned to the Tivoli. Bartenders were busy stocking the shelves, and one of them pointed toward the rear. The office was off to one side of the stage.

Nate Varnum, the owner, was a sparrow of a man. He was short and slight, with thinning hair and a reedy voice. At their knock, he invited them into the office and offered them seats. Fontaine went straight to the point.

"Mr. Varnum, I'm quite confident you are familiar with The Fontaines. We have been a headline act back East for many years."

"No, can't say as I am," Varnum commented. "How'd you wind up in Pueblo?"

"We decided to come West," Fontaine said evasively. "Naturally, we've heard a good deal about you and your theater. All of it quite complimentary, I might add."

"Hottest spot in town, that's for sure."

"And the very reason we are here. I see by the billboard that the Ethiopian Minstrels are closing tonight."

Varnum grimaced. "You know Foster and Davis, the comedy act?"

"Indeed we do," Fontaine said. "They were on the undercard when we played the Orpheum in New York."

"Well, they were supposed to open tomorrow night. But I got a wire from Burt Tully, he owns the Alcazar in Denver. Davis dropped dead last night in the middle of the act. Heart attack."

"I am most distressed to hear that, Mr. Varnum. Phil Davis was a consummate performer."

"Well, anyway, your timing's good," Varnum said. "I need an act and you pop up out of nowhere. What is it you folks do, exactly?"

Fontaine explained the nature of their show. Varnum listened, his birdlike features revealing very little. He gave them a pensive look when Fontaine finished.

"I'll have to see it," he said. "We're not open for business till noon. You got any objection to doing it now?"

"Not at all, my dear fellow. We would be delighted, absolutely delighted."

Varnum led them out to the theater. He was a middling piano player and offered to accompany Lillian. She sang *Wondrous Love* as her opening number, and then Fontaine delivered a soliloquy from *Hamlet*. Working as an ensemble, they next performed the melodrama *A Husband's Vengeance*. Lillian closed the show with an evocative rendition of *Molly Bawn*.

On the last note, Varnum smiled at her, nodding his approval. He swung around on the piano stool, facing Fontaine and Chester, who were seated at one of the tables. His expression was neutral.

"Lillian's a natural," he said. "Great voice, good looks, lots of emotion. Anybody ever think of calling her Lilly?"

"Yes, they have," Lillian said, descending a short flight of stairs beside the stage. "I was billed that way at our last two engagements."

"Good, that's what we'll use." Varnum rose from the piano stool. "Now, let's talk about your material. You can hold an audience only so long with love ballads. Don't you know any snappy tunes?"

"I usually sing selections similar to what you heard."

"Little lady, you have to be versatile to get to the top. So let me put it another way. Do you want to be a star?"

"Mr. Varnum, if you please," Fontaine interrupted. "My daughter will not lower herself to the vulgarian."

"Hush, Papa," Lillian said sharply. "Let him talk."

Fontaine was stunned into silence by her tone. Varnum glanced from one to the other, then turned to Lillian. He spread his hands in a conciliatory gesture.

"I don't mean dirty stuff," he said. "I'm talking about songs with some spirit, a little oomph. You want to leave the audience feeling good. End it on an upnote."

"Could you give me an illustration?"

"How about *Buffalo Gals*? Or maybe *Sweet Betsy from Pike*? Do you know songs like that?"

"Yes, I know them."

"Well?"

Lillian considered it, slowly nodded. "I could open the show with a ballad and close with something more lively. Would that work?"

"You bet it would!"

"Then it's settled."

"Not just exactly." Varnum's gaze swung around to Fontaine. "Lilly's fine and the melodrama ought to play well. But I can't use the Shakespeare."

Fontaine stiffened. "May I ask why not?"

"Shakespeare's too highbrow for our crowd. They want to be entertained."

"For your information, Shakespeare has been entertaining audiences for almost three hundred years. I rather think it will play well in your . . . establishment."

"Don't try to teach me my business, Fontaine. I said it's out and that's final. No Shakespeare."

"Then we've wasted your time," Lillian said forcefully. "Our act is as you've seen it, Mr. Varnum. All or nothing."

"There's no place for you in Pueblo but the Tivoli. I doubt the other joints would even take the melodrama."

"Yes, but that leaves you without a headliner tomorrow night . . . doesn't it?"

"You'd do that to save ten minutes of Shakespeare?"

"I believe I just have."

Varnum clenched his teeth. "You're tougher than you look, Lilly. I'll give you fifty a week for the whole act."

"A hundred," Lillian countered. "Not a penny less."

"You know, it's a good thing you sing as well as you do. Otherwise the whole bunch of you would be out on the street. All right, a hundred it is."

"Thank you very much, Mr. Varnum."

Arrangements were made for Lillian to rehearse with the orchestra the next morning. Then, after a cursory round of handshakes, Fontaine stalked out of the theater. Lillian and Chester followed along, and they turned back toward the hotel. Fontaine let go a bitter laugh.

"Shakespeare has no currency with our new employer. As he said, it is a good thing you sing so well, my dear."

"Oh, Papa," Lillian said, taking his arm. "You'll be just wonderful, wait and see. You always are."

"To quote the Bard," Fontaine replied. " 'When he had occasion to be seen, he was but as the cuckoo in

June. Heard, not regarded.' I am about to become the cuckoo of Pueblo."

Fontaine began drinking that afternoon. The more he drank, the more his perception of things became clear. He realized that, but for Lillian's voice, they would not open at the Tivoli tomorrow night. Even more, he toyed with the idea that the West was no place for a thespian and thought perhaps it was true. He felt as though he'd lost control of some essential part of his life and wondered where and how. By early evening, he was too drunk to stand.

Chester put him to bed shortly before seven o'clock. Lillian was waiting when he returned, seated on the sofa. Her features were taut with worry, and she looked on the verge of tears. She waited until he sat down.

"I feel like I'm responsible. Why didn't I let Father deal with Varnum? He must resent me terribly."

"No, you're wrong," Chester said. "It's something else entirely."

"What?"

"You're the only thing keeping this act together. Varnum was right when he said we'd be out on the street except for you. Dad finally saw it for himself today."

"Oh, that simply isn't true! I don't believe it for a minute."

"Yeah, it was true in Abilene and Dodge City, and it's true here. Like it or not, you'd better get used to the idea. You're the star of the show."

A tear rolled down Lillian's cheek. Her father was so proud and dignified, so defined by his years in the theater. A Shakespearean who had devoted his life to his art. She swore herself to an oath.

She wouldn't let him become the cuckoo of Pueblo.

# Chapter 17

A TEAM of acrobats gyrated around the stage. The Tivoli was packed for the opening night of the new headliners. Handbills had been plastered around town and an advertisement had appeared in the *Pueblo Sentinel*. The boldest line left no question as to the star of the show:

**LILLY FONTAINE & THE FONTAINES**

Lillian waited in the wings. She watched the acrobats as she prepared to go on with her opening number. Her hair was stylishly arranged in a chignon, and overnight she'd sponged and pressed her gowns. She looked radiant, her checks flushed with excitement.

Yet, appearances aside, she was worried. The Tivoli was the largest theater they'd played since leaving New York, and hopefully, their entrée to bigger things in Denver. Her father had read the ad in the newspaper and passed it along with no comment whatever about his second billing. She was deeply troubled by his silence.

The audience rewarded the acrobats with modest applause. The curtains swished closed as they bounded into the wings, and Lillian moved to center stage. As the curtains opened, she stood bathed in the glow of the footlights, and the orchestra segued into *We Parted By*

*The River Side*. Her voice sent a hush through the crowd.

The lyrics told the story of lovers biding fond adieu until they could be reunited. Lillian sang the ballad with ardent emotion, her eyes lingering here and there on members of the audience. Down front, seated at separate tables, she noticed two men dressed in frock coats and expensive silk cravats. Their attire set them apart from the other men in the crowd.

On the last note of the ballad, the audience exploded with applause. She bowed her way offstage, aware that the two well-dressed men were on their feet, trying to outclap one another. Her father was waiting in the wings, dressed in costume for *Macbeth*, and she gave him an encouraging kiss on the cheek. She smelled liquor on his breath.

Fontaine walked to center stage. He had been nipping at whiskey all day, and it had taken the edge off his hangover from last night. The liquor had dulled his dismal mood as well, for he was still unsettled by the ad in the morning newspaper. But he was determined that his sudden demotion to a supporting role would not affect his performance. His voice boomed out over the theater.

*Tomorrow, and tomorrow, and tomorrow,*
*Creeps in this petty pace from day to day,*
*To the last syllable of recorded time;*
*And all our yesterdays have lighted fools*
*The way to dusty death. Out, out, brief candle!*
*Life's but a walking shadow, a poor player*
*That struts and frets his hour upon the stage,*
*And then is heard no more; it is a tale*

*Told by an idiot, full of sound and fury,*
*Signifying nothing. . . .*

Lillian was overcome with emotion. Her eyes teared as she watched from the wings, never prouder of him than at this moment. She prayed there would be no catcalls or jeers from the crowd, and her eyes quickly scanned the theater. The two men she'd noted before, seated close to the stage, were following the performance with respectful interest. She got the impression that the audience, though restless, was looking to the men to set the example.

After a moment, she hurried backstage. She'd been given a tiny dressing room, and she began changing into her costume for the melodrama. She hung her teal gown on a hanger and slipped into the clinging cotton frock she would wear as a love-stricken young maiden. As she was brushed her hair to shoulder length, one of the chorus girls stopped in the doorway. Her name was Lulu Banes.

"Sweetie, I hafta tell you," she said with a bee-stung smile. "You got a real nice set of pipes."

"Why, thank you, Lulu."

Lillian had met her at rehearsal earlier in the day. Some of the chorus girls kept their distance, waiting to see if Lillian thought herself a prima donna. But Lulu was bubbly and outgoing, and they'd immediately hit it off. Lillian looked at her now in the mirror.

"Do you really think the audience enjoyed it?"

"Are you kiddin'?" Lulu said brightly. "You had those jokers eating out of your hand. They love you!"

"Oh, I hope so." Lillian paused with her hairbrush. "Did you see those nicely dressed gentlemen down near the front? The ones who look like bankers?"

"Spotted them, did you? That's Jake Tallant and Hank Warner, the biggest ranchers in these parts. And, sweetie, they're both rich as Midas!"

"I thought the crowd was watching them with unusual interest. Now I know why."

"No, that's not it," Lulu said archly. "Everybody was waiting to see which one pulled a gun. The crowd probably had bets down."

"Are you serious?" Lillian asked. "Do they dislike each other that much?"

"Hate would be more like it. Those two have been fighting a range war for almost a year. They're sworn enemies."

"Well, I must say I'm surprised. They look so refined."

"Not so refined they wouldn't shoot one another. They're on their good behavior tonight."

The stage manager called Lillian. She joined her father and Chester onstage for the melodrama *The Dying Kiss*. During the performance, she kept sneaking peeks at the two ranchers and found it difficult to concentrate on her lines. They were both handsome in their own way, one dark and the other fair, their mustaches neatly trimmed. She thought it a shame they were enemies.

The crowd applauded politely at the end of the melodrama. A juggler kept them entertained while Lillian rushed backstage and changed into her royal blue gown. She had rehearsed a new number most of the afternoon, and when the curtain opened her demeanor was totally changed. Hands on her hips, she gave the audience a saucy look as the orchestra launched into a sprightly melody. She belted out the tune.

*Oh, don't you remember sweet Besty from Pike*
*Crossed the great mountains with her lover Ike*
*With two yoke of oxen, a large yellow dog*
*A tall Shanghai rooster and one spotted hog!*

The lyrics about Betsy and Ike became suggestive, though never openly risqué. Lillian danced about the stage, with a wink here and a sassy grin there. She was enjoying herself immensely, and the audience, caught up in her performance, began clapping in time to the music. She ended with a pirouette, revealing a dainty ankle, her arms spread wide. The crowd went wild.

Lillian took four curtain calls. Finally, with the audience still cheering, she waved and skipped into the wings. Fontaine and Chester, along with Nate Varnum and the rest of the cast, were waiting backstage and broke out in applause. Her features were flushed with the thrill of it all—the freedom of letting go with a snappy, foot-stomping number—and she threw herself into her father's arms. His eyes were misty with pride.

"You were magnificent," he said softly. "How I wish your mother could have seen you tonight."

"Do you think she would have liked it, Papa?"

"My dear, she would have adored it."

A waiter appeared from the stairs by the stage. He nodded to Lillian. "Ma'am," he said formally. "Mr. Jacob Tallant sends his compliments. He requests you have champagne with him at his table."

A second waiter appeared. "Miss Lillian," he said, beaming. "Mr. Henry Warner extends his most sincere congratulations. He's asked you to join him and celebrate with champagne."

"Good God!" Varnum howled. "You can't pick one over the other, Lilly. We'll have a riot on our hands!"

Lillian shrugged. "Perhaps I should accept both invitations. The three of us could share a bottle of champagne."

"Never work," Varnum told her. "Jake Tallant and Hank Warner at the same table would be like lighting the fuse on a powder keg. They'd kill one another."

Fontaine stepped forward. "May I make a suggestion, my dear?"

"Yes, of course, Papa."

"There is no reason for you to become involved in other people's problems. Politely refuse both invitations."

"That'll work," Varnum quickly added. "Gets them off the premises without a fight. Smart thinking, Fontaine."

"You should read the Bard," Fontaine said with a mocking smile. "His plays are a treatise on the art of masterful scheming."

Lillian turned to the waiters. "Please inform Mr. Tallant and Mr. Warner that I decline their invitations—with sincere regrets."

Varnum heaved a sigh of relief. "Thank God."

"No, old chap," Fontaine reminded him. "Thank Shakespeare."

The *Pueblo Sentinel* gave the show rave notices. Fontaine and Chester were mentioned in passing, but Lillian was the centerpiece of the review. The editor rhapsodized at length on her voice, her stage presence, and her ethereal beauty. As though anointing a saint, he dubbed her the Colorado Nightingale.

Fontaine read the paper over breakfast. He'd arranged with the hotel to have room service in the suite every morning. The waiter brought the paper along with a serving cart loaded with eggs, ham, fluffy buttermilk biscuits, and coffee. The article was on the bottom fold of the front page.

Lillian wandered into the sitting room, still dressed in her robe and nightgown. Her face was freshly scrubbed, and her hair, cascading about her shoulders, was lustrous and tawny. Fontaine never ceased to marvel that she had the gift of awakening so exquisitely attractive that it took a man's breath. She was her mother's daughter.

Chester, who had finished reading the article, was slathering butter on a biscuit. He looked up as Lillian poured herself a cup of coffee. "Here she is," he said with a broad grin. "The Colorado Nightingale."

"Chet, really, it's too early for jokes."

"No joke," he said, spearing a hunk of ham with his fork. "Have a look at the paper."

Lillian sat down on the sofa. She placed her cup on the table and scanned the newspaper article. Then she read it again, more slowly. Her expression was pensive.

"Well, it's very nice," she said, folding the paper. "But I wasn't *that* good."

"Indeed you were," Fontaine corrected her. "I believe adding a number with quicker tempo inspirited your performance. You've found your true mêtier, my dear."

"Oh, Papa!" Her face was suddenly suffused with joy. "I'm so happy you think so. I felt so . . . so alive."

Fontaine nodded. "There is no question you held the audience enthralled. They would have listened to you sing all night."

"Why not!" Chester said, grinning around a mouthful of biscuit. "She's the Colorado Nightingale."

"I rather like it," Fontaine observed. "There's a certain ring to it, and it's catchy. Not to mention the metaphoric symmetry—the nightingale."

Lillian laughed. "I only wish it were true. I'd love to sound like a nightingale."

"Never underestimate yourself," Fontaine said, wagging his finger. "You have a lovely voice, and a range few singers ever attain. I see no limit to your career."

Lillian felt a stab of pain. She knew he was speaking as her father, and the pride was evident in his voice. Yet the newspaper article had scarcely mentioned his name or Chester's, and she sensed her father's hurt, the wound to his dignity. She sensed as well that she could offer no comfort, nothing to soothe his hurt. Anything she said would only make it worse.

"Aren't you going to eat?" Chester asked, buttering another biscuit. "A singer needs to keep up her strength. We're sure to pack the house tonight."

"Oh, nothing for me," Lillian said. "I'm having lunch with Lulu Banes. She's such a nice girl."

"Yes, I thought so, too," Fontaine remarked. "She struck me as a cut above the other girls. I'm delighted you've found a friend."

"She's really quite—"

A knock sounded at the door. Fontaine rose, crossed the room, and opened it to find a bellman in the hallway. The bellman gave him a sheepish smile.

"Sorry to bother you, Mr. Fontaine. We've got sort of a problem."

"Yes?"

"Well, sir, there's two cowhands downstairs. One sent here by Jake Tallant and the other from Hank Warner."

"How does that concern me?"

"Not you, your daughter," the bellman said nervously. "They've both got horses for Miss Fontaine."

Fontaine frowned. "Horses?"

"Yessir, outside on the street. Appears like Mr. Tallant and Mr. Warner both sent your daughter a present. Couple of real nice horses."

"One from each, is that it?"

"Yessir, and those cowhands are down there fit to fight. I mean to say, both of them showing up with horses at the same time. They're hot under the collar."

"Wait here a moment, young man."

Fontaine turned back into the suite. He looked at Lillian with a wry smile. "I believe you are being courted, my dear. Did you hear what was said?"

Lillian walked to the window. Fontaine and Chester followed, and they stared down at the street. Outside the hotel were two cowhands, studiously trying to ignore each other. One held the reins of a glossy sorrel gelding and the other those of a chocolate-spotted pinto mare.

"Horses!" Lillian said uncertainly. "What kind of gift is that?"

"Hardly the question," Fontaine advised. "More to the point, do you wish to accept gifts from men you've never met—albeit admirers?"

"No, I don't," Lillian said, after a moment's thought. "I think it would be inappropriate."

"Quite so."

Fontaine returned to the door. "If you will be so kind," he said to the bellman. "Inform the gentlemen downstairs that Miss Fontaine declines the gifts. They may so advise Mr. Tallant and Mr. Warner."

"Yessir, Mr. Fontaine," the bellman replied. "I'll tell'em just what you said."

"Thank you so much."

Lillian was flattered but nonetheless embarrassed. Chester attempted to josh with her about her new beaux, and she went to her bedroom. She stayed there the rest of the morning, emerging shortly before noon in a fitted cotton dress and carrying a parasol. She smiled at her father.

"I'm going to meet Lulu for lunch, Papa."

"Enjoy yourself, my dear."

"Take care, little sister," Chester called out. "Don't talk to men with strange horses."

"I wonder that I talk to you, Chester Fontaine!"

Lillian slammed the door. She was still steaming when she joined Lulu at a restaurant some ten minutes later. After a waiter took their orders, she told Lulu about the horses and how upset she was by the entire affair. Lulu was of a different opinion.

"Sugar, you ought to count your blessings. I wish I had those two scamps after me."

"Oh, honestly!" Lillian said. "Whoever heard of offering a lady *horses?* Everyone in town will be talking!"

"Who cares?" Lulu scoffed. "If they're wearing a skirt, they're just jealous. They'd give their eyeteeth to catch Jake Tallant or Hank Warner."

"Money isn't everything."

"A good-looking man with money is *definitely* everything. Take my word for it, sweetheart."

Lillian was silent a moment. "Tell me about them, will you? Why are they such enemies?"

Lulu quickly warmed to the subject. Jake Tallant was a widower, with two children, who owned an enormous ranch on the south side of the Arkansas River. Hank Warner, a bachelor, owned an equally large cattle spread on the north side of the river. For years, they had disputed water rights where the river curled through their separate spreads. Then, just within the last year, it had developed into a range war.

"I don't know all the details," Lulu concluded. "Something to do with one of those old Spanish land grants. You'd think either one had enough land for one man."

"How did the range war start?"

"Warner sued Tallant in court, and don't ask me what for. All that legal stuff makes me dizzy."

"How rich are they?"

"Sugar, they've both got more money than God!"

Lillian vaguely wondered why she'd even asked the question. She was still somewhat offended by the incident with the horses. Lulu finally uttered a sly laugh. "One thing's for sure."

"Oh?"

"Those two aren't through with you yet. The game has just started."

"What game?"

"Why, the game to see who wins your favor. You're the prize."

Lillian sniffed. "I have no intention of being anyone's prize."

"We'll see."

"What do you mean by that?"

Lulu smiled. "Get ready for the whirlwind, sugar. It's headed your way."

# CHAPTER 18

THE FONTAINES' second night at the Tivoli was standing-room-only. The crowd spilled out of the theater into the barroom and onto the street. Everyone wanted to see the Colorado Nightingale.

Jake Tallant and Hank Warner were again seated at tables in the front row. Neither of them appeared in the least daunted by the unceremonious refusal of their gifts. Their eyes were glued to Lillian every moment she was onstage.

Bouquets of wildflowers from both men were delivered backstage following the show. There were cards with the flowers, the script tactfully phrased, requesting the honor of calling on Lillian. She was flattered by their perseverance but again declined the invitations. Still, she considered flowers a more appropriate gift than horses. She put them in a vase in her dressing room.

The next morning she awoke expecting some new enticement to appear at the hotel. She was oddly disappointed when nothing was delivered to the suite and no messages were left at the desk. There was something titillating about being courted by suitors who were not only handsome but also enormously wealthy. She wondered if she had offended them by her seeming lack of interest. She wondered even more why she cared.

Early that afternoon there was a knock at the door. Chester admitted a man who wore the dog collar of a minister and, in fact, introduced himself as the Reverend Buford Blackburn. He was portly, with a thatch of hair the color of a pumpkin and the ever-ready smile of a preacher. His manner indicated that he was the very soul of discretion.

Fontaine was seated in an easy chair, reading the paper. Lillian came out of her bedroom, curious as to who might be calling. Chester ushered the minister into the sitting room and performed the introductions. There was an awkward moment while everyone got themselves arranged, Fontaine and Blackburn in overstuffed chairs and Lillian and Chester on the sofa. Fontaine opened the conversation.

"Well now, Reverend, a man of God is always welcome in our humble abode. To what do we owe the pleasure?"

"I am here on a mission," Blackburn ventured in an orotund voice. "One might say at the behest of Jacob Tallant and Henry Warner."

"Indeed?" Fontaine arched an eyebrow. "I take it this has to do with my daughter."

"Mr. Fontaine, I am the pastor of the First Methodist Church. Jake Tallant and Hank Warner are among my most loyal and devoted parishioners. They have asked me to act as their emissary."

"In what regard?"

"A truce keeper," Blackburn said with a small shrug. "Jake and Hank are fine, honorable men, true servants of Christ. Unfortunately, they are also the bitterest of enemies."

"So we are told," Fontaine allowed. "And what, precisely, is your mission with respect to Lillian?"

"These gentlemen hold your daughter in the highest esteem. They wish to call on her, and I am here to plead their case."

"A jolly plot indeed, Reverend. Shakespeare might have written it himself."

Blackburn smiled. "These are men of honorable intentions. In the most formal sense of the word, they wish to court your daughter."

"I see," Fontaine said. "Perhaps your remarks should be addressed to Lillian. She is, after all, the purpose of your mission."

"Yes, of course." Blackburn turned to her with a benign expression. "Miss Fontaine, let me assure you most earnestly that Mr. Tallant and Mr. Warner are sincere in their admiration of you. They wish only to be given the opportunity to call on you in person."

Lillian felt like hugging herself. She was all the more flattered that the men had sent a minister as their emissary. Their persistence as well spoke to the matter of sincerity and a guileless, rather unaffected admiration. Yet she was still wary.

"May I be frank, Reverend?" She waited until he nodded. "I understand Mr. Tallant and Mr. Warner are involved in what's known as a 'range war.' I have no interest in associating with violent men."

"Your fears are unjustified, Miss Fontaine. The range war you speak of is being fought in a court of law. Nothing of a violent nature has occurred."

"Everyone I've spoken with believes they might shoot one another on a moment's notice. You said yourself they are the bitterest enemies."

"And so they are," Blackburn conceded. "But these men are good Christians, and despite their differences, neither of them has resorted to violence. I have utmost confidence they will settle the matter in a peaceful fashion."

Lillian considered a moment. "Very well," she said at length. "You may tell them I will be most happy to have them call on me. You might also tell them of my aversion to violent men."

"I shall faithfully follow your wishes, Miss Fontaine."

"How will I decide which one to see first?"

"Oh, yes, that is a problem," Blackburn confessed. "Neither of them would want to feel slighted."

"That's simple enough," Chester broke in with an amused laugh. "Draw straws for the lucky man."

"Bully!" Blackburn exclaimed in quick agreement. "Certainly no one could object to a random draw."

Fontaine thought the Bard would have written it as a farce. Lillian went along, even though she felt somewhat the object of a lottery. Rev. Buford Blackburn, intent on his mission, would have agreed to anything short of blasphemy. A cleaning maid provided the broom straws.

Jake Tallant, his luck running strong, won the draw.

Lillian bought a new dress for the occasion. She was a perfect size 4, and the clerk at Mendel's Mercantile was delighted with her patronage. By now, she was something of a celebrity, and virtually every man in Pueblo knew her on sight. Her visit to the store caused a minor sensation.

The fabric of the dress was sateen, snugly fitted to complement her figure. Her black pearls against the dove gray material made the outfit all the more spectacular. Her hair was upswept and she wore a hat adorned with feathers the color of her dress. She looked stunning.

Tallant called for her at six o'clock. The plan was to have an early get-acquainted dinner and deliver her to the theater in time for the eight o'clock curtain. Fontaine and Chester greeted the rancher with cordiality and made small talk until Lillian swept into the sitting room. Her entrance, Fontaine wryly noted, was staged for maximum effect.

The restaurant Tallant chose was the finest in Pueblo. With impeccable service and an atmosphere of decorum, it was where men of influence and wealth took their wives for a night out. The tables were covered with linen, appointed with crystal and silver and the finest china. The owner greeted Tallant effusively, bowing to Lillian, and personally escorted them to their table. A waiter materialized with menus.

Lillian was charmed by all the attention. Tallant was a man of impressive bearing with a leonine head of dark hair, somewhere in his early thirties. His features were angular, set off by a sweeping mustache, and he wore a tailored charcoal suit with a patterned cravat. His manner was soft-spoken, though commanding, and he was gentlemanly in an old-world sort of way. She thought he was even more handsome up close.

Over dinner, he tried to draw her out about her life in the theater. She entertained him with a brief but amusing account of her adventures in the West. Ever so deftly, she then turned the conversation to his life and interests. He quietly explained that he was a widower and that his wife, a woman of Mexican heritage, had died of influenza just over a year ago. He had two children, a son and a daughter, ages nine and ten.

"How wonderful you had children," Lillian said, trying for a cheerful tone. "You have something of your wife in them. I'm sure they're adorable."

"Yeah, they're a pair," Tallant said proudly. "I'd like you to meet them sometime. Maybe you could come to Sunday dinner."

"I think that would be very nice."

"Don't let Hank Warner sour you on the idea. He won't have anything good to say about me."

"Oh?" Lillian was momentarily flustered by his directness. "You apparently know I'm having dinner with Mr. Warner tomorrow night."

"Reverend Blackburn told me," Tallant said with a faint smile. "He's keeping us both informed."

"Yes, I can understand that he would. He's very concerned about the difficulty between you and Mr. Warner."

"Well, that's a long story. Not a pretty one, either."

Lillian sensed he was dying to tell his version. She thought he'd raised Hank Warner's name for that very reason. Tonight was his night to impress on her the justness of his cause and the strength of his character. With only a little coaxing, she got him talking. She found it a fascinating story.

All land north of the Rio Grande had been ceded to the United States following the 1846 war with Mexico. By the Treaty of Guadalupe Hidalgo, the U.S. government agreed to respect the holdings of Mexican landowners. Yet the title to all property in the ceded zone had evolved from ancient land grants; the issue of who owned what was clouded by a convoluted maze of documents. To compound the problem, many of the grants overlapped one another.

Nowhere was the issue more confused than in Southern Colorado. Some Mexican landowners claimed that their holdings spilled over the New Mexico line into the southern reaches of the Rockies. At various times, land grants had been awarded by the king of Spain, the Republic of Mexico, and provincial governors who haphazardly drew a line on a map. Ownership was often nine points physical possession and one point law. For generations, the force to back the claim overrode legal technicalities.

"Maria, my wife, was the last of her line," Tallant explained. "The land had been in her family for over a hundred years, and when we were married, it became our land. No one disputed that until Warner filed his lawsuit."

"Good heavens," Lillian sympathized. "Are you saying his lawsuit is frivolous?"

"Well, he contends that the Treaty of Guadalupe Hidalgo didn't cover land grants in Colorado. Nobody ever questioned it before, so why now? He's just greedy, that's all."

"Does he have any chance of winning?"

"Not according to my lawyers," Tallant said. "They think he's plumb loco."

"And if they're wrong?" Lillian asked "What would you do then?"

"I won't be thrown off the land my wife's ancestors worked to build. Not by some scoundrel like Hank Warner."

"Yes, that would be terrible."

Lillian felt sorry for him. From what she'd just heard, there was every reason for bad blood between the two men. She halfway hoped Warner wouldn't appear at the theater for tonight's performance. But that was wishful thinking.

She knew he would be seated front and center.

Lillian was prepared to dislike Henry Warner. All she'd heard last night led her to believe he was an out-and-out rogue. But to her surprise, he was a very engaging rogue.

Warner was lithe and muscular, with sandy hair and a neatly groomed mustache. He was so personable that he charmed her father and Chester in a matter of moments. His magnetism all but took her breath.

They went to the restaurant where she'd dined last night. The owner was equally effusive in his greeting of Warner and made a production of escorting them to their table. The waiter was the same as last night, and he gave Lillian a conspiratorial smile. She hardly knew what to think.

Warner took charge. He ordered braised squab with wild rice for both of them. Then he selected a delicate white wine with a marvelous bouquet. When they clinked glasses, Lillian only sipped, but the taste was like some heady nectar. His vivid blue eyes pinned her like a butterfly to a board.

"Before anything else," he said in a deep voice, "I want to say you are the most beautiful woman I've ever seen. I intend to marry you."

Lillian was aghast. "Mr. Warner, you're frightening me."

"Call me Hank," he said jovially. "And no, Lillian—you prefer that to Lilly, don't you?—no, Lillian, I'm not frightening you. Am I?"

"How did you know I prefer Lillian?"

"Nate Varnum told me everything about you. I think he's in love with you himself."

"I somehow doubt that," Lillian said. "Do you always sweep the ladies off their feet?"

Warner chuckled, a low rumble. "As they say, the race goes to the swiftest. Jake Tallant probably convinced you I'm an immoral bounder." He paused, looking deep into her eyes. "Get to know me and you'll know better. I never toy with a lady's affections—especially yours."

Lillian tried to deflect his onslaught. "What Mr. Tallant and I discussed was your lawsuit. He is very disturbed you're attempting to take his ranch."

The remark seemed to amuse Warner. He wagged his head with a satiric smile. "Did Jake tell you about his wife?"

"Yes, as a matter of fact, he did. He said the land had been in her family for generations."

"Did he tell you that I was in love with her, too?"

"No." Lillian was visibly startled. "You were in love with another man's wife?"

"A long time ago." Warner hesitated, sipping his wine. "Jake and me were both courting Maria back in '61. Her folks were still alive then. Best people you'd ever hope to meet."

"And she married Mr. Tallant . . . Jake."

"Well, don't you see, I wasn't the lighthearted rascal that I am now. Jake beat me out."

Lillian suddenly realized it was all an act. Beneath the glib manner, there was nothing lighthearted about Henry Warner. She felt an outrush of sympathy.

"And having lost Maria, you never married?"

"Never saw her match," Warner said with a debonair grin. "Leastways, not till the night I saw you. I'm liable to propose any moment now."

The waiter appeared with a serving tray. He set their plates before them, succulent squab on beds of brown rice. Their conversation momentarily dwindled off as they took cutlery in hand and began dissecting the plump birds. Lillian savored her first bite.

"It's wonderful!" she marveled. "I've never had squab before."

"Stick with me and I'll show you a whole new world. How'd you like to go to Paris on our honeymoon?"

"I do believe you're an incorrigible flirt."

"A gentleman never lies," Warner said with a contagious smile. "You're the girl for me and no two ways about. I'm plumb smitten."

Lillian was silent for a moment. "May I ask you a personal question?"

"Darlin', for you, I'm an open book."

"Why did you wait until Maria died to sue Jake Tallant?"

Warner stopped eating. "You're a regular little firecracker. Don't miss much, do you?"

"I don't mean to pry," Lillian said with guileful innocence. "I was just curious."

"Well, what with you and me practically at the altar, I've got no secrets. I waited because I'd never have done anything to hurt Maria."

"What does that have to do with Jake's ranch?"

"Couple of things," Warner said, more serious now. "For openers, the river corkscrews all through our boundary lines. We've been fightin' over water rights for years."

Lillian looked at him. "But that isn't the main issue . . . is it?"

"No, it's not. There's an old Spanish land grant handed down through Maria. Did Jake tell you about it?"

"Yes, last night."

"Thing is, it'll never stand up in court. Jake knows it and I know it. He's just burned I opened his can of worms."

"Do you really want his ranch that badly?"

Warner grinned. "I don't want his ranch at all. I've got enough land of my own."

"I—" Lillian was shocked. "Why have you sued him, then?"

"Take a guess."

"Maria?"

"None other," Warner acknowledged. "Jake stole her away from me. Laughed about it for ten years to anybody that'd listen. I figure to have the last laugh."

Lillian thought she had never heard of anything so vindictive. But then, on second thought, she knew she'd heard a deeper truth. Henry Warner was a victim of the most powerful emotion imaginable. He had lived with a broken heart until the day Maria Tallant died. She felt his sorrow beneath the veneer of devil-may-care nonchalance.

"Do you still love her . . . even now?"

"No, ma'am," Warner said with a bold smile. "You are the light of my life. I hear the wedding bells ringing!"

Lillian wondered if he saw in her the ghost of a dead woman. She hoped not.

# Chapter 19

Lillian's dressing room was scarcely more than a cubicle. She was stripped to her chemise, seated before a tiny mirror lighted by small coal-oil lamps. She began applying kohl to her eyelids.

Following dinner, Hank Warner had dropped her off at the stage-door entrance. Her first number was usually around eight-thirty, after the juggler, the fire-eater, and a comic who told risqué jokes. That gave her an hour or so to finish her makeup.

Decent women never wore makeup in public. Lillian wished social conventions were different; she thought pinching one's cheeks to give them color was prudish and outmoded. She liked the way kohl enhanced her eyes and how nicely rouge accentuated her features. Still, she had to limit herself to nightly appearances on-stage. Only prostitutes wore makeup on the street.

There was a light rap at the door. She slipped into a smock she'd bought to cover herself backstage. She was proud of her figure but cautious around stagehands and male performers of any variety. Her mother had taught her that a girl's physical assets, if kept a mystery, were all the more a temptation. She tightened the belt on the smock. "Come in!" she called out. "I'm decent."

Lulu Banes stepped into the dressing room. She was in full war paint, wearing a skimpy peekaboo gown that left little to the imagination. The chorus line always opened the show, and the girls were usually costumed before anyone else. She paused inside the door.

"I couldn't wait till later," she said with a bee-stung smile. "How'd it go with Handsome Hank?"

"Oh, very nice," Lillian said, seating herself before the mirror. "He was a perfect gentleman."

"Honey, they all are till they get their way. C'mon, skip straight to the hot stuff."

By now, Lulu was her confidante. Last night, Lillian had related the details of her dinner with Jake Tallant. She'd never before had a close woman friend, and she was pleased to have someone to talk to. She knew Lulu thrived on gossip.

"You have to remember," she said, "everything is in confidence. You can't repeat a word to anyone."

"Cross my heart." Lulu drew a sign over her breast. "My lips are sealed."

"Well . . ." Lillian patted rouge on her cheekbones. "I know it will be hard to believe. . . ."

"Uh-oh, here it comes. What'd he say?"

"Hank was really quite open. He told me he doesn't want Jake's ranch. That isn't why he sued."

"Nooo," Lulu said slowly, with a look of undisguised amusement. "And you bought that?"

Lillian nodded. "I most certainly did."

"Sounds like malarkey to me."

"Not when you know the reason. Hank was in love with Maria Tallant, Jake's wife. He waited until she died to bring legal action."

*"Omigod!"* Lulu's eyes went round. "He was having an affair with Tallant's wife?"

"No, no," Lillian said dismissively. "They were rivals for her affections long before she married Jake. Hank has loved her all this time."

"You lost me there, kiddo. What's that got to do with the lawsuit?"

"Hank wants Jake to suffer the way he's suffered. How tragic that they both loved the same woman . . . and lost her."

"Uh-huh." Lulu raised a skeptical eyebrow. "Sounds to me like Hank is after revenge. Don't you think?"

"Yes, perhaps a little," Lillian admitted. "But only because he'd loved her all these years. I mean, think about it, he never married!"

"Sweetie, I hate to say it, but you're a soft touch. That's the most cockamamy story I ever heard."

"I think it's rather romantic."

Lulu *humphed.* "Are you going to see him again?"

"Saturday," Lillian said. "He invited me to see his ranch. I accepted."

"And you're having Sunday dinner at Jake Tallant's ranch? You're an awfully busy little bee."

"Yes, but they're both such nice men. How could I refuse?"

"Far be it from me to give you advice. . . ."

"Oh, don't be silly, go ahead."

"Whatever sad tale they tell you . . . ?"

"Yes?"

"Forget a grain of salt, honey. Take it with a spoon."

Later that evening, Lillian went on for her opening number. Tallant and Warner, as usual, were seated at tables down front. They applauded mightily even as she stood bathed in the footlights, each trying to outdo the other. She blushed, avoiding their eyes, as the maestro lifted his baton and led the orchestra into *Aura Lee*. Her voice floated dreamily across the theater.

*Aura Lee, Aura Lee*
*Maid of golden hair*
*Sunshine came along with thee*
*And took my heart for fair*

Lillian thought the song was suitable to the moment. Never before had she had two such handsome and pleasantly wealthy men vying for her attention. She told herself that Lulu was simply too protective, perhaps too cynical. There was no need for a grain of salt.

No need for salt at all.

Hank Warner called for her the next morning. He was attired in range clothes, whipcord trousers stuffed in his boots and a dark placket shirt. His hat was tall-crowned, roweled spurs on his boots and a Colt pistol strapped on his hip. He looked every inch the cattleman.

Lillian wore a muslin day dress, a gay little bonnet atop her mound of curls. She carried her parasol and snapped it open as he assisted her into a buckboard drawn by a matched team of sorrel mares. The sun was in their faces as they drove east from town.

"I'm so excited," she said happily. "I've never seen an honest-to-goodness ranch."

Warner smiled secretly. "Well, you're in for a treat today. I arranged a surprise."

"Oh, I love surprises! What is it?"

"Wouldn't be a surprise if I told you, would it? You'll just have to wait and see."

"Will it be worth the wait?"

"I've got a notion you'll approve."

Near the edge of town, they had to wait until a train pulled out of the railroad station. As they crossed the tracks, she gave him a quick sideways inspection. He caught the look.

"What?" he said. "Something wrong?"

"Nothing really." Lillian titled her parasol against the glare of the sun. "It's just that I've never seen you wear a gun before."

"You've never seen it because I was wearing a suit. I carry it tucked in my waistband. You shy of guns?"

"No, not in the right hands."

"Well, I have to say, I'm right handy."

"I think you are making fun of me."

"You're too pretty to make fun of. I'm plumb struck blind."

"In that event"—Lillian playfully batted her eyelashes—"I insist you tell me your surprise."

Warner laughed, "Now that would spoil the fun. Wait till we get there."

The ranch was located some five miles east of Pueblo. Warner explained that he owned nearly a hundred thousand acres of grazeland, all of it north of the Arkansas River. The range was well watered, sheltered from plains blizzards by the walls of a canyon, and covered with lush grama grass that fattened steers. He ran about ten thousand head of cattle.

Lillian was stunned into silence. She couldn't imagine anyone owning so much land, and as the road wound along the canyon, she was mesmerized by vast herds of cattle grazing beneath a forenoon sun. The headquarters compound, situated leeward of the canyon walls, consisted of a main house, a large bunkhouse, and a corral. The buildings were stout log structures.

"Not the grandest in the world," Warner said, halting the buckboard in front of the main house. "But it's warm in the winter and cool in the summer. Built to last, too."

"Yes, I can see." Lillian thought it looked like a fort with windows. "It's really very nice."

She realized he was trying to impress her. The land, the cattle, the house, an empire built on an ocean of grass. There were at least thirty men gathered outside the bunkhouse, and Warner explained that they were some of the cowhands on his payroll. A whole steer, cleaved down the middle, was being roasted over a bed of coals. The day, he told her, had been planned to honor her visit to the ranch. Later they would celebrate with a traditional Western feast.

The festivities started with an exhibition by Warner's top broncbuster. A buckskin renegade was blindfolded with a gunnysack while Alvin Johnson, the broncbuster, got himself mounted. When the sack was removed, the horse exploded at both ends, like a stick of dynamite bursting within itself. All four feet left the ground as the buckskin swapped ends in midair and sunfished across the corral in a series of bounding catlike leaps. The battle went on for what seemed an eternity, with the men whooping and shouting as the horse whirled and kicked with squeals of outrage. Johnson rode the bronc to a standstill.

"Bravo! Bravo!" Lillian cried, clapping loudly when it was over. "I've never seen anything so exciting in my life. It was just wonderful!"

Warner seemed pleased. "No doubt about it, Alvin's the best. Glad you liked it."

"Your surprise really was worth waiting for."

"There's more to come, lots more. All for you."

The men took turns aboard pitching broncs. None of them were as good as Alvin Johnson, and most got thrown off. But there was a spirit of camaraderie about it, and everyone hooted and cheered when a rider got dumped. After the broncbusting, there was a demonstration of fancy work with a lariat. Longhorns were hazed onto open ground near the corral, and horsemen would cast loops at a dead run, snaring the steers' horns and hind legs, and neatly drop them in midstride. Lillian applauded the men's feats like a young girl at her first circus.

Late that afternoon the feast was served. Cooks sliced choice cuts off the roasted steer and loaded plates with beef, beans, and sourdough biscuits fresh from a Dutch oven. The men scattered about the compound, wolfing down their food, while Lillian and Warner were served at a table in the shade of a leafy oak tree. Afterward, Warner gave her a tour of the house, which, much as she expected, was a masculine domain. The parlor was dominated by a huge stone fireplace with a bearskin rug and lots of leather furniture.

Warner drove her back into town as sunset fired the sky beyond distant mountains. Lillian was exhilarated, still bubbling with excitement, and yet oddly reflective. She had the feeling she'd spent the day auditioning for a role. Mistress of the manor or perhaps queen of the cowboys.

She wasn't sure it was the part for her.

The Fontaines were invited to Jacob Tallant's for dinner the following day. The noon meal on Sunday, commonly called dinner by country folk, was considered the occasion of the week. Fontaine rented a buggy and team at the livery stable.

The ranch headquarters was located some three miles east of Pueblo. On the drive out, Lillian thought Jake Tallant was playing the diplomat by inviting her father and Chester. His intent, clearly, was to win over the entire Fontaine family. His designs on her would only be furthered by her father's blessing.

The *casa grande* reflected its Mexican heritage. The main house was one-story, constructed of native adobe, with broad wings extending off the central living quarters. Beneath a tile roof, hewn beams protruded from walls four feet thick. The window casements gleamed of tallowed oak, and the double doors were wider than a man's outspanned arms. The effect was one of old-world gentility.

The house, which overlooked the river to the north, commanded the ranch compound. The buildings formed a quadrangle, grouped with a symmetry that was at once functional and pleasing to the eye. Corrals and stables, flanked by storage sheds, angled off to the south. A commissary and an open-sided blacksmith forge were situated on a plot central to a compound that covered several acres. It looked like a small but prosperous village.

Fontaine brought the team to a halt in front of the house. Tallant hurried outside and assisted Lillian from the buggy. "Welcome to my home," he said cordially. "I trust you had a good drive from town."

"Yes, we did," Lillian replied. "The views are simply marvelous along the river."

"Quite an operation," Fontaine said, gesturing about the compound. "How large is your ranch?"

"Just over a hundred thousand acres. We run in the neighborhood of ten thousand head."

"How do you keep up with that many cows?"

"Mr. Fontaine, I often wonder myself. Please, won't you come inside?"

The interior of the house was even more impressive than the outside. The floors were tiled, and off the foyer was an immense parlor with furniture crafted of rich hardwood. Waiting in the parlor were Tallant's children, dressed in their Sunday best. The girl was nine, with the olive complexion of her mother and hair the color of a raven's wing. The boy, who was ten, favored his father, with dark, curly hair. Their eyes fixed immediately on Lillian.

"This is Jennifer," Tallant introduced them, "and this is Robert. And I warn you, they're dying of curiosity."

Lillian smiled warmly. "I'm so happy to meet you, Jennifer and Robert. Thank you for having us to your home."

"Father says you're a singer," Jennifer said, overcome with curiosity. "Will you sing something for us?"

"Why, yes, of course I will. Do you have a favorite song?"

"Father likes *Aura Lee*," Robert said with boyish enthusiasm. "He told us how you sang it the other night. He likes it a lot."

"Mind your manners," Tallant broke in. "Perhaps Miss Fontaine will favor us with a song after dinner. Although I'm afraid we don't have a piano."

"Miguel plays the guitar," Robert reminded him. "Want me to run down to the bunkhouse?"

"Not just yet, Son. I think it'll wait till we've eaten."

Dinner was served in a spacious dining room. There were two servants, a man and a woman, and they brought from the kitchen platters of spicy Mexican dishes. Fontaine, as well as Lillian and Chester, found the food delicious, if somewhat zesty to the palate. Jennifer and Robert peppered them with questions throughout the meal, eager to learn everything about their life in the theater. Fontaine, playing to a wide-eyed audience, gave them a running discourse on the wonders of Shakespeare.

After dinner, Miguel was summoned from the bunkhouse. Lillian hummed the melody for him, and he quickly found the chords on his guitar. Everyone got themselves seated in the parlor, and with Miguel strumming softly, she sang *Aura Lee*. The children were fascinated, watching her intently, and applauded wildly on the last note. When they clamored for more, Fontaine stepped into the breech, delivering a stirring passage from *Hamlet.* As her father's baritone filled the room, Lillian joined Tallant, who was standing behind the sofa. He gave her an apologetic shrug.

"I hope you don't mind," he said. "They get carried away sometimes."

"I think they're wonderful," Lillian said graciously. "You should encourage them in the arts. They enjoy it so much."

"Well, I don't have to encourage them about you. I've never seen them take to anyone so fast."

"Jennifer is so beautiful, and Robert is the very image of you. You must be very proud."

"Never more so than today, Lillian."

The afternoon sped past. Tallant gave them a tour of the compound, explaining the many facets of how a ranch operates. The children clung to Lillian, and she sensed they were starved for a woman's affection. Before anyone quite knew it, the sun heeled over to the west, and it was time to leave. Fontaine told them that actors, unlike the Lord, were allowed no rest on the Sabbath. The show, he noted jovially, must go on.

Tallant and the children saw them off. Jennifer and Robert hugged Lillian, begging her to return, and ran alongside until the buggy picked up speed. On the way into town, Lillian was silent, playing the afternoon back in her mind. Fontaine finally broke into her reverie, looking at her with an amused expression. He shook his head.

"I believe the Bard said it all," he observed wryly. " 'She's beautiful and therefore to be wooed. She is a woman, therefore to be won.' You have captured their hearts, my dear."

Lillian ignored the jest. She stared off into the fading sun and suddenly felt the race was too swift for her liking. All the more so after a visit to the Tallant ranch.

She thought she was too young to be a mother. Perhaps too young to be a wife.

# Chapter 20

Lillian wrestled with her uncertainty all through Sunday night. Neither Tallant nor Warner attended the evening performance, and she was relieved by their absence. She needed time to sort out her feelings.

Her ambivalence was unsettling. She genuinely liked both men, though they were as different as night and day. One lived like an old-world Spanish *grandee* and the other like a devil-may-care plains buccaneer. She'd never known two men so dissimilar.

All of which was part of a larger problem. She had never been courted, and she'd never known any man intimately. Her experiences with men were of a flirtatious nature, a stolen kiss that never led to anything more. Her mother had imparted wisdom about men, but Lillian had no actual experience. She felt oddly like a vestal virgin in ancient Rome. Chaste, even wise, but nonetheless ignorant.

She wasn't sure she wanted to lose that ignorance to either of them. Jake Tallant was a gentleman of the old school, kind and considerate, almost chivalrous in manner. Yet his children, however delightful, posed the worrisome question of overnight motherhood. Hank Warner was perhaps more debonair, a puckish bon vivant with a devilish sense of humor. Still, for all his protests, he lived with the memory of a dead woman. A wife would never displace the ghost of Maria Tallant.

Lillian's ambivalence was underscored by an even more personal dilemma. Over the course of her Western odyssey, she had found some essential part of herself in the theater. She loved the audiences and the thrill of it all, the wave of adulation that came to her over the footlights. She thought she loved it more than she might ever love a man, and she wasn't willing to trade one for the other. Her stage career was, at least for now, her life.

By Monday morning, she had arrived at a partial solution. She wrote discreet notes to both Tallant and Warner, explaining that she felt overwhelmed by their attentions. The notes were identical except for the salutations, tactfully phrased word-for-word appeals for patience. She emphasized that she needed time, needed to be alone with her thoughts, for it had all happened too fast, too quickly. She asked that they not contact her until she was able to reconcile her own feelings.

The notes were secretly delivered to each of the men by Chester. He caught them separately, as they were entering the Tivoli Monday evening, and slipped them the notes in the course of a handshake. That night, and for the three days following, the men honored her wishes. They attended her performances every evening, seated at their usual tables, following her about the stage with the eyes of infatuated schoolboys. True to her request, neither of them attempted to contact her.

Friday morning she awoke with a vague sense of disquiet. Her father and Chester went out to attend to personal errands, and she was left alone with her thoughts. She couldn't identify the source of her unease, apart from the fact that she somehow felt lonely. She inwardly admitted that she missed the company of the men, Tallant for his courtly manner and Warner for his waggish humor. She wondered if a woman, after all, needed a man in her life.

Fontaine returned shortly before noon. He found her moping about, still dressed in her housecoat, staring listlessly out the window. She didn't move as he crossed the sitting room and stopped at her side. Her expression was pensive, vaguely sad. He tried for a light note.

"What's this?" he said. "I planned to take you out for lunch. Why aren't you dressed?"

"I just haven't gotten around to it."

"Come now, my dear, that is hardly an answer. What's wrong?"

"Oh, Papa." Her voice wavered. "I'm so confused."

Fontaine studied her with concern. "Need I ask the source of your confusion? Something to do with men, is it?"

"I was standing here thinking I miss them. And then I thought how perfectly ingenuous. How naive."

"No one would ever accuse you of naïveté. You are much more the sophisticate than you realize."

"Am I?" Lillian said with a tinge of melancholy. "One minute I want them out of my life, and the next I wish they were knocking on the door. How sophisticated is that, Papa?"

"You punish yourself unnecessarily," Fontaine said. "Quite often logic dictates one thing while the heart dictates another. Are you in love with either of these men?"

"No, of course not."

"And the stage is still your beacon?"

"Yes, more than anything."

"Then logic prevails, my dear. There are simpler ways to resolve matters of the heart."

Lillian turned from the window. "I'm not sure I understand, Papa. What is it you're suggesting?"

"Nothing unseemly," Fontaine assured her. "You are lonely for male companionship and nothing could be more natural. Amuse yourself without becoming involved."

"Wouldn't that be unfair to them?"

"I'm sure your mother educated you about the whys and wherefores of men. A woman need not worry about trifling with their affections."

"Yes, but how would—"

Chester burst through the door. His face was flushed and he looked as though he'd just run a marathon. He hurried across the room, gesturing wildly.

"Your gentleman friends just shot it out! Not five minutes ago in front of the bank."

Lillian appeared to stagger. "Hank and Jake?"

"None other," Chester said. "I saw it myself."

"Are they . . . dead?"

"Warner got it in the arm and Tallant lost a piece of his ear. They're both lousy shots."

Fontaine put an arm around Lillian's shoulders. He looked at Chester. "How did it happen?"

"Warner started it," Chester said. "Tallant was coming out of the bank and Warner stopped him on the street. They exchanged insults, and next thing you know, they pulled their guns. Wounded one another with the first shot."

"Unfortunate," Fontaine remarked. "I assume it had to do with Warner's lawsuit?"

"No, Dad, it was literally an *affaire de coeur.* They were fighting over Lillian."

"Me!" Lillian was nonplussed. "Why would they fight over me?"

Chester suppressed a grin. "Warner used some dirty language. Accused Tallant of stealing your affections."

"That's ridiculous!"

"You haven't heard the rest of it. Tallant cursed Warner out and accused him of the same thing. That's when they went for their guns."

"How dare they!" Lillian fumed. "I never gave either of them reason to believe I favored one over the other. I asked both of them to leave me alone!"

"Not to hear them tell it," Chester informed her. "They each think the other one stole your heart away. Talk about jealousy."

"I feel like a common streetwalker. Men fighting over me, for mercy's sake! It's disgusting."

A knock sounded at the door. Chester opened it and admitted Lulu Banes. She rushed across the room to Lillian.

"Have you heard?"

"Chester just finished telling me. I can't believe it."

"Believe it," Lulu said archly. "Lucky the fools didn't kill one another."

"I wrote each of them notes," Lillian said with a dazed expression. "And they weren't love notes, either. I told them to stay away."

"Honey, you think they compare dance cards?"

"What do you mean?"

"I mean your notes had the opposite effect. They both thought you ditched one for the other."

"Well, that's absurd," Lillian protested. "Neither of them has any claim on me. I made that very clear."

Lulu chuckled. "Not clear enough, sugar. They just got through fighting a duel for you. How's it feel to be fought over?"

"Absolutely revolting! I wish I'd never met either of them."

"And I'd give anything in the world to be in your place. How I wish, I wish, I wish."

Lillian sniffed. "You're welcome to them."

"Not in this lifetime," Lulu said woefully. "They've only got eyes for you, kiddo."

"Then I'll have to persuade them otherwise, won't I?"

"What are you talking about?"

"Lulu, I mean to put an end to it—permanently!"

* * *

*For God's sake, let us sit upon the ground*
*And tell sad stories of the death of kings:*
*How some have been depos'd, some slain in war,*
*Some haunted by the ghosts they have deposed,*
*Some poison'd by their wives, some sleeping kill'd;*
*All murder'd: for within the hollow crown*
*That rounds the mortal temples of a king*
*Keeps Death his court . . .*

Fontaine plowed on with the soliloquy from *King Richard II.* The patrons of the Tivoli were by now resigned to his nightly orations from Shakespeare. For the most part, they ignored him, milling about and carrying on conversations interspersed with laughter. He might have been playing to an empty house.

Two members of the audience were nonetheless attentive. Jake Tallant was seated at his usual table, his right ear heavily bandaged with gauze. Across the aisle, Hank Warner sat with his left arm cradled in a dark sling that matched the color of his suit. Fontaine was surprised to find them in the crowd, for their wounds were still fresh from the morning gunfight. He suspected their attendance had little to do with Shakepeare.

The magician kept the audience entertained between acts. The curtain then opened on the melodrama of the evening, *The Dying Kiss*. Lillian was all too aware of Tallant and Warner, for their tables were just beyond the orchestra, near the stage. She noted that they studiously ignored each other, but she thought their presence was scandalous. The eyes of every man in the room were on her, and she knew what they were thinking. She was the temptress who provoked men to gunfights.

After the melodrama, she hurried backstage to change for her final number. She was still seething as she slipped into her teal gown and tried to repair her makeup. When she went on, her face was scarlet and she had little doubt that everyone in the theater looked upon her as a scarlet woman. She was, in all likelihood, branded the lover of the two men seated down front. The orchestra led her into a lively tune.

*I came from Alabama*
*With a banjo on my knee*
*I'm going to Louisiana*
*My true love for to see*

*It rained all night the day I left*
*The weather it was dry*
*The sun so hot I froze to death*
*Susanna, don't you cry*
*Oh! Susanna, oh don't you cry for me*
*I've come from Alabama with a banjo on my knee*

The crowd gave her a rousing ovation. Tallant, undeterred by his mangled ear, applauded mightily. Warner, limited to one good arm, pounded the table with the flat of his hand. She took three curtain calls, then bowed offstage into the wings. Nate Varnum was standing nearby, and she asked him to invite Tallant and Warner backstage. Her look was such that he restrained himself from questioning her judgment. He hurried off.

Fontaine and Chester were finished removing their greasepaint. They exchanged glances, having overheard her conversation with Varnum, and joined her near her dressing room. Fontaine appeared troubled.

"Do you think this is wise?" he asked. "Bringing them together so soon after their altercation?"

"Their welfare doesn't concern me," Lillian said. "I intend to put an end to it here—tonight."

"I hope you know what you're doing, my dear."

"Yes, I know very well, Papa."

Varnum came through the door at the side of the stage. Warner was directly behind him, followed by Tallant. Everything came to a standstill as the cast—chorus girls, acrobats, jugglers, and the magician—paused to watch. Varnum led the ranchers backstage and stopped outside Lillian's dressing room. The men seemed disconcerted by her summons, nodding to her with weak smiles. Her eyes flashed with anger.

"Look at you!" she said in a stinging voice. "You should be ashamed of yourselves."

Tallant and Warner ducked their heads like naughty urchins. Lillian felt a momentary pang of sympathy, for they were proud men being humbled in public. But she was determined to see it end. She lashed out at them.

"Do you have any idea how you've humiliated me? Fighting like common thugs in the street. And all in my name!"

"Lillian, listen," Warner said, thoroughly abashed. "I wouldn't offend you for anything in the world. I just wasn't thinking straight."

Tallant nodded his head rapidly. "That goes double for me. I'm as much to blame as Hank."

"Yes, you are," Lillian said shortly. "Now, I want you both to shake hands. Let it end here."

Warner and Tallant swapped a quick glance. After a moment, Tallant stuck out his hand and Warner clasped it in a firm grip. Lillian allowed herself a tight smile.

"I hope you can behave like gentlemen from now on. You might even become friends."

"I tend to doubt it," Warner said.

Tallant grunted. "Yeah, not too likely."

"Well, you won't have me as an excuse." Lillian looked from one to the other. "I am leaving Pueblo and I never want to see you again. Either of you."

"Hold on!" Warner barked, and Tallant added a hasty, "Let's talk about this!"

Fontaine stepped forward. "Gentlemen, I believe my daughter—"

"Please, Papa," Lillian cut him off. "I have to do this myself."

"Of course, my dear."

"Goodbye, Hank. Goodbye, Jake." Lillian permitted herself a softer smile. "Please don't say anything to make it more difficult. Just leave now. Please."

Tallant and Warner seemed on the verge of arguing it further. But then, under her cool stare, they mumbled their goodbyes and turned away. No one said anything as they crossed backstage and went out the door. Fontaine looked at Lillian.

"Leaving Pueblo?" he said. "Wasn't that what you told them? I recall no discussion to that effect."

"Yes, Papa, we are leaving."

"You might have consulted me first."

"I'm sorry," Lillian said evenly. "I've had my fill of ruffians, Papa. It's time to go on to Denver."

Fontaine nodded judiciously. "Certainly our notices merit moving onward and upward. You may have a point."

"Just a damn minute!" Varnum jumped in. "You can't run off and leave me high and dry."

"Indeed?" Fontaine said, suddenly testy. "For a man who dislikes Shakespeare, you take umbrage rather too quickly. Do we have a contract with you, Mr. Varnum?"

"I gave you your start!" Varnum objected loudly. "And besides, it's not professional."

"Hmmn." Fontaine feigned deep consideration. "Never let it be said that the Fontaines are less than professional. What say, my dear, shall we give him another week?"

Lillian sighed. "One week, Papa, but no more. I'm anxious to see Denver."

"I concur," Fontaine said, gesturing idly in Varnum's direction. "There you have it, my good man. One week and we bid you *adieu*."

"Godalmighty," Varnum groaned. "I'll never find a headliner act in a week."

"Nor will you find one to replace The Fontaines, my dear fellow. We are, in a word, singular."

Lillian turned toward her dressing room. Lulu was waiting by the door and gave her Kewpie-doll smile. "Sugar, you sure know how to end a romance. I never saw two chumps dusted off so fast."

"I hope I wasn't too harsh on them. Although I must say they deserved it."

"Well, who knows, maybe I'll snag one of them while he's sobbin' in his beer. But whether I do or don't, I'm gonna miss you, kiddo."

"Oh, Lulu, I'll miss you, too."

"Yeah, but I can always say I knew you when. You're on your way to the big time now."

"Do you think so, honestly?"

"Sugar, I'd lay odds on it."

Theatrical people were superstitious and rarely counted their good fortune until it came true. Yet Lillian, who was caught up in the moment, cast her superstitions aside. She already knew it was true.

She saw her name in lights.

# Chapter 21

The engineer set the brakes with a racketing squeal. A moment later the train rocked to a halt before the Denver stationhouse. Towering skyward, the Rockies rose majestically under a noonday sun, the snowcapped spires touching the clouds. Lillian thought it was a scene of unimaginable grandeur.

Passengers began deboarding the train. Fontaine signaled one of the porters who waited outside the stationhouse. When the baggage car was unloaded, the porter muscled their steamer trunks onto a cart and led them across the platform. In front of the depot, Fontaine engaged a carriage and told the cabbie to take them to the Brown Palace Hotel. From all he'd heard, the hotel was an institution, the finest in Denver. He planned to establish residence in proper style.

On the way uptown Lillian noted that the streets were cobbled and many of the buildings were constructed of brick masonry. She recalled Libbie Custer telling her that a town founded on a gold strike had become a center of finance and commerce. Over the years, the mining camp reproduced itself a hundredfold, until finally a modern metropolis rose along the banks of Cherry Creek and the South Platte River. Denver was transformed into a cosmopolitan beehive, with opera and a stock exchange and a population approaching 20,000. The city was unrivaled on the Western plains.

The Brown Palace was all they'd been led to expect. Thick carpets covered the marble floor of the lobby, and a central seating area was furnished with leather chairs and sofas. The whole of the lobby ceiling glittered with an ornate mural, and a wide, sweeping staircase ascended to the upper floors. The place had the look and smell of wealth, home away from home for the upper class. At the reception desk, Fontaine noted a calendar with the date May 25, and he marked it as an auspicious day. Their journey had at last brought them to Denver.

"Good afternoon," he said, nodding to the clerk. "You have a suite reserved for Alistair Fontaine."

"Yes, sir," the clerk replied. "How long will you be staying with us, Mr. Fontaine?"

"Indefinitely."

"Welcome to the Brown Palace."

"Thank you so much."

Fontaine signed the register with a flourish. Upstairs, led by a bellman, they were shown into a lavish suite. A lush Persian carpet covered the sitting room floor, and grouped before a marble fireplace were several chairs and a chesterfield divan. There were connecting doors to the bedrooms, both of which were appointed in Victorian style and equipped with a private lavatory. A series of handsomely draped windows overlooked the city.

Lillian whirled around the sitting room. "I can hardly believe we're here. It's like a dream come true."

"Indeed, my dear," Fontaine said. "Far more civilized than anything we've seen in our travels, hmmm?"

"And running water," Chester added, returning from the bedroom. "I think I'm going to like Denver."

"I'm going to *love* it!" Lillian said gaily. "Papa, when will we see the theater? Could we go this afternoon?"

"Tonight, I believe," Fontaine said. "We'll take in the show and get a feel for the crowd. No need to rush."

"I'm just so anxious, that's all. I wish we were opening tonight."

"What is one night more or less? We will have a long run in Denver, my dear. You may depend on it."

Fontaine exuded confidence. By telegraph, he'd spent the last week negotiating with Burt Tully, owner of the Alcazar Variety Theater. Their notices from Pueblo, just as he'd predicted, had made Tully eager to offer them headliner billing. Though Tully's principal interest was in Lillian, Fontaine had nonetheless struck a lucrative deal for the entire act. Their salary was $300 a week, with a four-week guarantee.

Early that evening, they took a stroll through the sporting district. For reasons lost to time, the district was known locally as the Tenderloin. There, within a few square blocks of Blake Street, gaming dives and variety theaters provided a circus of nightlife. Saloons and gambling, mixed with top-drawer entertainment, presented an enticing lure. Sporting men were attracted from all across the West.

One block over was Denver's infamous red-light district. Known simply as the Row, Holladay Street was a lusty fleshpot, with a veritable crush of dollar cribs. Yet while hook shops dominated the row, there was no scarcity of high-class bordellos. The parlor houses offered exotic tarts, usually younger and prettier, all at steeper prices. Something over a thousand soiled doves plied their trade on Holladay Street.

Hop Alley satisfied the more bizarre tastes. A narrow passageway off Holladay, it was Denver's version of Lotus Land. Chinese fan-tan parlors vied with the faint sweet odor of opium dens, and those addicted to the Orient's heady delights beat a steady path to this back-street world of pipe dreams. To a select clientele, dainty China dolls were available day or night. Vice in every form was available at a price.

Fontaine cut short their tour of Holladay Street. He realized within a block that they had strayed from the more respectable section of the sporting district. Lillian kept her gaze averted, though she felt shamelessly intrigued by the sight of so much sin for sale. Chester, on the other hand, oogled the girls and mentally marked a few bordellos that looked worthy of a visit. They quickly found themselves back on Blake Street.

The Alcazar Variety Theater was the liveliest spot in town. A two-story structure with leaded-glass windows, if offered diverse forms of entertainment for the sporting crowd. On the first floor was the bar and, through an arched doorway at the rear, the theater. The stage was centered on the room, with seating for 400, and a gallery of private booths circled the mezzanine. The upper floor of the club was devoted exclusively to gambling.

Their entrance was not altogether unnoticed. Lillian, though she was dressed in a simple gown, drew admiring stares from men at the bar. Fontaine purchased tickets to the theater and slipped the doorman a gold eagle, which resulted in a table near the orchestra. The audience was composed primarily of men, and waiters scurried back and forth serving drinks. As they were seated,

Fontaine saw a man emerge from a door leading backstage. He nodded at Lillian.

"Unless I'm mistaken," he said, "there goes our employer, Mr. Tully."

Lillian followed his look. The man was stoutly built, with salt-and-pepper hair and a handlebar mustache, attired in a dark suit and a colorful brocade vest. He stopped here and there, greeting customers seated at tables, and slowly made his way to the rear of the theater. She glanced back at her father.

"Shouldn't we introduce ourselves, Papa?"

"No need, my dear," Fontaine said idly. "We aren't expected until tomorrow. Time enough, then."

"Yes, I suppose," Lillian said. "He certainly has a nice theater."

"Let us hope he's a good showman as well."

The orchestra thumped into a spirited dance number. As the curtain opened, a line of chorus girls went high-stepping across the stage. The lead dancer raised her skirts, revealing a shapely leg, and joined them in a prancing cakewalk. The dance routine was followed by a comic, a sword swallower and his pretty assistant, a contortionist who tied himself in knots, and a team of nimble acrobats dressed in tights. The audience applauded appreciatively after every act.

The headliner was billed as The Flying Nymph. A trapeze bar flew out of the stage loft with a woman hanging by her knees. She was identified on the program as Darlene LaRue, and she wore abbreviated tights covered by flowing veils. She performed daring flips and at one point hung by her heels, all the while divesting herself of a veil at a time. The orchestra built to a cresendo as she swung by one hand, tossing the last veil into the audience, her buxom figure revealed in the footlights. The curtain swished closed to applause and cheers.

"Good Lord!" Fontaine muttered. "I thought I'd seen everything. That is positively bizarre."

Chester laughed. "Dad, it's the show business. You have to admit she's different."

"So are dancing elephants," Fontaine said. "That doesn't mean it is art." He turned to Lillian. "Don't you agree, my dear?"

Lillian thought Denver was no different than Pueblo. Or for that matter, Abilene and Dodge City. Men were men, and they wanted to be entertained rather than enlightened. Opera would never play on a variety stage.

"Yes, Papa, I agree," she said. "No dancing elephants."

Fontaine gave her a strange look. "Pardon me?"

"I won't sing from a trapeze, either."

"I should think not!"

She decided to humor him. His art was his life and not a subject for jest. Alistair Fontaine was who he was.

She hoped Shakespeare would play in Denver.

Springtime was the best of times in the Rockies. The air was invigorating, and on the mountains green-leafed aspens fluttered on gentle breezes. The slopes sparkled below the timberline with a kaleidoscope of wildflowers.

A horse-drawn streetcar trundled past as the Fontaines emerged from the hotel. The sun was directly overhead, fixed like a copper ball in a cloudless sky. Fontaine, who was in a chipper mood, filled his lungs with air. He exhaled with gusto.

"I do believe I'm going to like it here. There's something bracing about the mountain air."

"Not to mention the streetcars," Chester said. "Give me a city anytime, all the time."

"I endorse the sentiment, my boy."

Lillian shared their spirited manner. The sidewalks were crowded with smartly dressed men and women attired in the latest fashions. Everywhere she looked there were shops and stores, and the city seemed to pulse with an energy that was all but palpable. She thought she'd already fallen in love with Denver.

Fontaine set off briskly down the street. They were on their way to meet with Burt Tully, the owner of the Alcazar. Fontaine and Chester looked dapper in their three-piece suits, freshly pressed for the occasion. Lillian wore her dove gray taffeta gown, her hair upswept, a parasol over her shoulder. She had never felt so alive, or more eager to get on with anything. She was excited by their prospects.

"I'm looking forward to this," Fontaine said, waiting for a streetcar to pass. "From what we saw last night, Tully's establishment needs a touch of class. That is to say, The Fontaines."

Lillian took his arm. "Papa, will you do something for me?"

"Why, of course, my dear. What is it?"

"Try not to lecture Mr. Tully."

"Lecture?" Fontaine said in a bemused tone. "Why on earth would I lecture him?"

"You know," Lillian gently reminded. "What we were talking about last night? Dancing elephants and trapeze ladies."

"I see no reason to raise topics of an unpleasant nature. After all, we have Mr. Tully exactly where we want him."

"We do?"

"Yes indeed," Fontaine said confidently. "Three hundred a week speaks to the fact that we have the upper hand. His first offer, as you will recall, was rather niggardly."

"Papa, we mustn't let him think we're overbearing. Won't you be tactful . . . for me?"

"I shall be the very soul of discretion. You may depend on it."

Lillian exchanged a look with Chester. He tipped his head in an imperceptible nod. "Listen to her, Dad," he urged. "Denver's our big break and we don't want to spoil it. We might end up in Pueblo again."

Fontaine laughed it off. "Never fear, my boy, we have seen the last of Pueblo. Leave everything to me."

Some ten minutes later they entered the Alcazar. A bartender told them that Tully's office was on the second floor, at the rear of the gaming room. Upstairs, they found a plushly appointed room with faro layouts, twenty-one, chuck-a-luck, roulette, and several poker tables. Though it was scarcely past the noon hour, there were men gathered around the various gaming devices. The girls serving drinks wore peekaboo gowns that displayed their cleavage to maximum effect.

The office looked more suited to a railroad mogul. A lush carpet covered the floor, the furniture was oxblood leather, and the walls were paneled in dark hardwood. Burt Tully was seated at a massive walnut desk; a large painting of sunset over the Rockies hung behind his chair. He rose after they knocked and came through the door. His mouth lifted in a pleasant smile.

"Let me guess," he said, extending his hand. "You're the Fontaines."

Fontaine accepted his handshake. "A distinct pleasure to meet you at last, Mr. Tully. May I introduce my daughter, Lillian, and my son, Chester."

"An honor, Miss Fontaine," Tully said, gently taking her hand. "I've heard a good deal about the Colorado Nightingale. Welcome to the Alcazar."

Lillian smiled winningly. "Thank you so much, Mr. Tully. We're delighted to be here."

"Please, won't you folks have a seat?"

There were two wingback chairs before the desk. Fontaine took one and Chester stepped back, motioning Lillian to the other. He seated himself on a leather sofa against the wall, casually crossing his legs. Tully dropped into his chair behind the desk.

"Allow me to congratulate you," Fontaine said. "You have a very impressive operation here."

"I don't mean to brag—" Tully spread his hands with a modest grin. "The Alcazar is the top spot in the Tenderloin. We pack them in seven nights a week."

"And well you should, my dear fellow. You offer the finest in entertainment."

"All the more reason you're here. Darlene LaRue closes tonight and you open tomorrow night."

"Indeed!" Fontaine said jovially. "I'm sure we will fill the house."

"No doubt you will." Tully paused, his gaze shifting to Lillian. "I have ads starting in all the papers tomorrow. Everyone in town will want to see the Colorado Nightingale."

Lillian detected an unspoken message. There was no mention of The Fontaines but instead a rather subtle reference to the Colorado Nightingale. She returned his look.

"Are you familiar with the way we present our act?"

"Yes, of course he is," Fontaine interrupted. "I covered all that in our telegrams. Didn't I, dear fellow?"

"Let's talk about that," Tully said seriously. "You realize your daughter is the attraction? The real headliner?"

"I—" Fontaine seemed taken aback. "I would be the first to admit that Lillian draws the crowds. Was there some other point?"

Tully steepled his hands. "I have no objection to the melodrama. We haven't held one in a while and it ought to play pretty well." He hesitated, his features solemn. "I'd like you to consider dropping the Shakespeare."

"Nate Varnum said the same thing in Pueblo. Shakespeare played well enough there."

"No, Mr. Fontaine, it didn't. I exchanged telegrams with Nate, and he told me—you'll pardon my saying so—the crowd sat on their hands. The same thing will happen here."

Fontaine reddened. "You signed The Fontaines to an engagement, and The Fontaines are here. I expect you to honor the terms of our agreement."

"Think about it," Tully suggested. "Your daughter has a great career ahead of her. She's doing two songs a show, and she should be doing three or four. Without the Shakespeare, she could."

"Mr. Tully."

Their heads snapped around at the tone in Lillian's voice. She shifted forward in her chair. "Father speaks for The Fontaines. You have to accept us as we are . . . or not at all."

There was a moment of intense silence. Tully finally shook his head. "You're doing yourself a disservice, Miss Fontaine. Your father knows it and I know it. And you know it, too, don't you?"

"As I said, we are The Fontaines. Shakespeare is part of our act."

"Just as you wish," Tully said in a resigned voice. "I'll go along only because I want the Colorado Nightingale at the Alcazar. For you, personally, I think it's a big mistake."

Lillian smiled. "You won't think so tomorrow night. We'll fill the house."

"Yes, I'm sure *you* will, Miss Fontaine."

Tully arranged a rehersal schedule for her the next morning. After a perfunctory round of handshakes, they left his office. Outside, walking along Blake Street, it was apparent that Fontaine's chipper mood had vanished. He appeared somehow diminished, head bowed and shoulders hunched. Lillian knew he was crushed.

"Papa—"

"Later, my dear."

"Are you all right?"

"I think I need a drink."

# CHAPTER 22

LILLIAN STROLLED along Larimer Street. The central thoroughfare of Denver, it was lined with shops and stores, banks and newspaper offices, and all manner of business establishments. She turned into Mlle. Tourneau's Dress Shop.

The shop was airy and pleasantly appointed, with a large plate glass window fronting Larimer Street. Dresses were displayed on mannequins, and from the rear, behind a partition, she heard the whir of sewing machines. A small woman with pince-nez glasses walked forward as the bell over the door jingled. She nodded amiably.

"Good afternoon," she said with a trace of an accent. "May I help you?"

"Are you Mademoiselle Tourneau?" Lillian asked.

"*Oui.*"

Lillian thought the accent was slightly off and wondered if the woman was really French. She smiled politely. "The manager at the Brown Palace told me you are the finest dressmaker in Denver."

"M'sieur Clark is very kind," Mlle. Tourneau said. "And whom do I have the privilege of addressing?"

"My name is Lillian Fontaine."

"*Enchanté*, Mademoiselle Fontaine. How may I serve you?"

"I'm in desperate need of some gowns. I hoped you might design them for me."

"But of course, with pleasure. What type of gowns do you require?"

"Stage gowns," Lillian replied. "I'm an actress and a singer. I open tomorrow night at the Alcazar Variety Theater."

Mlle. Tourneau laughed coyly. "There is much talk about you, I believe. You are the one called the Colorado Nightingale. *Non?*"

"Well, yes, that is how they have me billed."

"How very exciting! I will be honored to design your gowns."

Mlle. Tourneau began spreading bolts of cloth on a large table. As she prattled on about the quality of the fabrics, Lillian ran her fingers over the material, pausing to study various colors and textures. Finally, hardly able to choose from the delicate fabrics, she made three selections. The bolts were set aside.

Scarcely drawing a breath, Mlle. Tourneau pulled out a large pad of paper and a stick of charcoal shaved to a point. She began sketching gowns, rapidly filling in details as the charcoal flew across the paper. One was to be done in embroidered yellow tulle, another in Lyon silk with white lace trim, and the third in pleated ivory satin with guipure lace. She completed the last sketch with a flourish.

*"Voilà!"* she announced dramatically. *"C'est magnifique!"*

Lillian studied the sketches. She had given considerable thought to remarks made by both theater owners and stage performers over the last several months. The more discreet had alluded to the aura of innocence she projected onstage and how irresistible that was to men. The more plainspoken advised naughty but nice, a peek here and a peek there to heighten the sense of mystery. She decided now that some of both would enhance the overall effect.

"Here," she said, a fingernail on the sketch. "Perhaps we could lower it slightly . . . to here."

"Ahhh!" Mlle. Tourneau peered over her pince-nez. "You wish to accentuate the décolletage. *Tres bien*!"

"And here." Lillian pointed to the bottom of the gown. "Perhaps we could raise this just a . . . touch."

"*Mais oui!* You wish a tiny display of the ankle. How very daring."

"Nothing vulgar, you understand."

"*Non, non!* Never!"

Mlle. Tourneau led her to the fitting room. Lillian disrobed to her chemise and the dressmaker began taking measurements. She ran the tape around hips, waist, and bust, and her eyes went round. She clucked appreciatively.

"*Extraordinaire!*" she said merrily. "You will look absolutely lovely in these gowns. I predict you will break hearts. Many hearts."

"Well . . ." Lillian studied herself in the full-length mirror and giggled. "I'll certainly try."

"*Fait accompli, mon cher*. Men will fall at your feet."

"I have to ask you a favor, mademoiselle."

"Anything in my power."

"The ivory gown . . ." Lillian waited until she nodded. "I'll need it by tomorrow evening. I just have to have it for my opening show."

"*Sacre bleu!*" Mlle. Tourneau exclaimed. "Tomorrow?"

"Won't you please?"

Lillian looked at her with a beseeching gaze. Mlle. Tourneau's stern expression slowly gave way to a resigned smile. Her eyes blinked behind her pince-nez.

"How could I refuse you? I will work my girls throughout the night. You must be here first thing in the morning for a fitting. But you will have your gown. *Certainment!*"

"Oh, thank you! Thank you!"

The measurements completed, Mlle. Tourneau suggested an accessory to complement the outfit. She carried a line of low-cut slippers with a medium heel, which she could cover in the same fabric as the gown. She laughed a wicked little laugh.

"Show the shoe, show the ankle. Eh?"

"I think it's perfect!"

A short while later Lillian left the shop. She returned to the hotel, tingling with excitement at the thought of her new gown. When she entered the suite, her father was slumped in an easy chair, a bottle of whiskey at hand on a side table. His jaw was slack and his eyes appeared glazed. He lifted his glass in a mock toast.

"Welcome back to our cheery abode, my dear. How went the shopping?"

Chester was seated on the divan. As she crossed the room, he looked at her with an expression of rueful concern, wagging his head from side to side. She stopped by the fireplace. "I ordered a lovely gown," she said, forcing herself to smile. "I'll have it for the opening tomorrow night."

"Marvelous!" Fontaine pronounced in a slurred voice. "Never disappoint your public."

Lillian saw that he was already drunk. He laughed as though amused by some private joke and poured himself another drink. The bottle wobbled when he set it back on the table, and he watched it with an indifferent stare. He took a slug of whiskey.

"Papa," Lillian said tentatively. "Don't you think you've had enough to drink?"

Fontaine waved her off with an idle gesture. "Have no fear," he said. "John Barleycorn and I are old friends. He treats me gently."

"I worry anyway. Too much liquor isn't good for you."

"I am indestructible, my dear. A rock upon which a sea of troubles doth scatter to the winds."

Lillian knew he was trying to escape into a bottle. His optimism about their prospects in Denver and his pride in negotiating such a lucrative engagement at the Alcazar—all that had been dashed by their meeting with Burt Tully. Her father had heard all over again that no one was interested in Shakespeare. Or Alistair Fontaine.

She felt guilty about her own good fortune. The accolades accorded the Colorado Nightingale, first in Pueblo and now in Denver, had pushed her father out of the limelight and ever deeper into the shadows. She suddenly felt guilty about her new gowns, for while she was happy, her father was drunk and disconsolate. She simply didn't know how to erase his pain.

"Papa, listen to me," she temporized. "You're only hurting yourself, and I hate to see you like this. Won't you please stop . . . for me?"

Fontaine grunted. " 'Men's evil manners live in brass; their virtues we write in water.' I believe the Bard penned the line for me. Yes, indeed, quite apropos."

Lillian was reduced to silence. She looked at Chester, and he again shook his head in dull defeat. Fontaine downed the glass of whiskey, muttering something unintelligible, and slumped deeper in the chair. His eyes went blank, then slowly closed, and his chin sank lower on his chest. The glass dropped from his hand onto the carpet.

Lillian took a seat on the divan. She stared at her father a moment, listening to his light snore. "I feel so terrible," she said, tears welling up in her eyes. "Surely there's something we can do."

"Like what?" Chester said. "You know yourself, he lives and breathes Shakespeare. Tully might as well have hit him over the head with a hammer."

"Yes, you're right, he was just devastated. He thought Denver would be so much more cultured. His hopes were so high."

"Maybe he'll sleep it off and come to his senses. He's always bounced back before."

"I'm not sure sleep will solve anything."

"You tell me then, what will?"

"Perhaps Tully was wrong about the audiences. Perhaps they will appreciate Shakespeare."

"Anything's possible," Chester said with no great confidence. "I guess we'll find out tomorrow night."

"Oh, Chet, I feel so helpless."

"Let's cross our fingers and hope for the best."

Lillian thought they would need more than luck.

Denver turned out for opening night. The theater was full by seven o'clock, and men were wedged tight in the barroom. The crowd spilled out onto the sidewalk, and a police squad was brought in to maintain order. The backlit marquee blazed outside the Alcazar.

## LILLY FONTAINE THE COLORADO NIGHTINGALE

Lillian complained to Burt Tully. The marquee made no reference to her father or Chester, and she was upset by the oversight. Her father had sloughed it off, but she knew he was offended and hurt. Tully told her it was no oversight and then repeated what he'd said the day before. The crowd was there to see her, not The Fontaines. She was the headliner.

Before her opening number, she stopped by the dressing room her father shared with Chester. Fontaine was attired in the costume of a Danish nobleman, and his breath reeked of alcohol. His eyes were bloodshot, and though he tried to hide a tremor in his hand, he seemed in rare form. He nodded affably and inspected her outfit, the teal gown with the black pearls. He arched an eyebrow.

"What's this?" he said. "Not wearing your new gown?"

Lillian smiled. "I'm saving it for the closing number."

"Excellent thinking, my dear. Contrary to common wisdom, the last impression is the one most remembered."

"Are you all right, Papa?"

"I am in fine fettle," Fontaine said grandly. "I shall acquit myself admirably indeed."

Lillian kissed him on the cheek. "You will always be my Hamlet."

"And you the sweet voice in the darkness of my night."

"I have to go."

"Leave them enraptured, my dear. Hearts in their throats!"

A juggler came offstage as she moved into the wings. She walked to center stage, composing herself, hands clasped at her waist. The orchestra glided smoothly into *Nobody's Darling* as the curtain opened to reveal her awash in a rose-hued spotlight. Her voice brought an expectant hush over the audience.

*They say I am nobody's darling*
*Nobody cares for me*
*While others are radiant and joyful*
*I'm lonely as lonely can be*
*I'm lonely indeed without you*
*But I know what I know in my heart*
*Dreaming at morning and evening*
*Of meeting, oh never to part*

On the last note there was a moment of almost reverent silence. Then the crowd stood, everyone in the theater on their feet, their applause vibrating off the walls. She curtsied, her eyes radiant, and slowly bowed her way offstage. The uproar went on unabated, and the audience brought her back for four curtain calls. Her face was flushed with joy when at last the commotion subsided.

Fontaine was waiting in the wings. His eyes were misty and he hugged her in a fierce outpouring of pride. She again smelled liquor on his breath, and then he marched, shoulders squared, to the center of the stage. The curtain swished open, and he raised one hand in a dramatic gesture, caught in the glow of a cider spotlight.

He hesitated an instant, staring out over the audience, and launched into a soliloquy from *Hamlet.* His rich baritone resonated across the theater.

> *Neither a borrower, nor a lender be;*
> *For loan oft loses both itself and friend,*
> *And borrowing dulls the edge of husbandry,*
> *This above all: to thine own self be true,*
> *And it must follow, as the night the day,*
> *Thou canst not then be false to any man . . .*

The crowd watched him with a look of dumb bemusement. There was a sense of some misguided gathering come upon a man speaking in a tongue foreign to the ear. When he delivered the last line, they stared at him as though waiting for a summation that would make it all comprehensible. Then, just as Burt Tully had predicted, they sat on their hands. Their applause was scattered, quickly gone.

Fontaine took no curtain calls. The acrobats bounded onstage as he walked, head bowed, to his dressing room to change costumes. A few minutes later he joined Lillian and Chester in the presentation of the melodrama *A Husband's Vengeance.* All through the performance Lillian's concentration was on her father rather than on the play. She knew, even if the audience never would, why he had selected that particular passage from *Hamlet.* He wanted to deliver the one line that personified Alistair Fontaine.

> *To thine own self be true.*

The crowd responded favorably to the melodrama. Following the performance, Fontaine's spirits seemed somewhat restored. He changed into his street clothes, leaving Chester backstage, and moved quickly to the door leading to the theater. Lillian came out of her dressing room just as he went through the door. She was wearing her new gown, resplendent in ivory, her hair loose to her shoulders. She saw Chester standing outside his dressing room, his face screwed up in a puzzled frown. She hurried forward.

"Chet?" she said anxiously. "Where did Papa go?"

"To the bar." Chester appeared troubled. "He said he'd watch your performance from there. He just rushed off."

"I'm worried about his drinking. Will you find him and stay with him?"

"The way he acted, I'm not sure he wants company. He didn't invite me along."

"Yes, but he shouldn't be left alone. Not tonight."

"You're right. I'll go find him."

Chester walked away. The stage manager motioned frantically to Lillian as the chorus line pranced offstage. She moved through the wings, taking her position at center stage, and struck a coquettish pose. The curtain opened as the orchestra swung into *Buffalo Gals* and the spotlight made her a vision in ivory. Her cleavage and the sight of a dainty ankle brought shouts from the audience. She performed a cheeky dance routine as she zestfully banged out the lyrics.

*Buffalo gals, won't you come out tonight*
*Come out tonight, come out tonight*

*Buffalo gals, won't you come out tonight*
*And we'll dance by the light of the moon*

Lillian twirled around the stage, her ivory slippers lightly skipping in time to the music. Her voice was animated and strong, every mirthful stanza of the song followed by the rollicking chorus. She spun about in a playful pirouette on the last line and ended with her arms flung wide and her hip cocked at a saucy angle. The uproar from the crowd rocked the theater with applause and cheers and shrill whistles of exuberance. A standing ovation drummed on through five curtain calls.

The cast surrounded her backstage. She was jubilant with the wild reception from the audience, and congratulations from the other performers made it all the more heady. Burt Tully pulled her into a smothering bear hug and told her she would play the Alcazar forever. As he let her go, she saw her father and Chester, followed by another man, come through the door from the theater. She threw herself into her father's arms.

"Oh, Papa!" she cried. "Wasn't it just wonderful!"

Fontaine was glassy-eyed with liquor. He kissed her with drunken affection. "You bedazzled them, my dear. You were magical."

"I could have sung forever and ever! And Papa, five curtain calls!"

"Yes, indeed, you brought the house down."

"Oooo, I'm so excited!"

"I'd like you to meet someone." Fontaine motioned the other man forward. "Permit me to introduce Otis Gaylord. I've invited him to join us for supper."

Gaylord was a man of imposing stature. He was tall, lithely built, with sandy hair and pale blue eyes. He took her hand in his and lifted it to his lips. He caressed it with a kiss.

"I am your most ardent admirer, Miss Fontaine. Your performance left me thoroughly bewitched."

Lillian smiled graciously. He wasn't the handsomest man she'd ever seen. But he was devilishly good-looking, strongly virile, with a cleft chin and rugged features. She thought she might drown in his pale blue eyes.

"Otis favors Irish whiskey," Fontaine said with a tipsy chortle. "I can think of no finer attribute in a friend. And lest I betray a secret, my dear—he is smitten with you."

Gaylord laughed. "I would be a liar if I said otherwise."

Lillian sensed they would celebrate more than her triumph tonight.

# Chapter 23

Lillian was the toast of Denver. Her first week at the Alcazar Variety Theater was a sellout every night. The Colorado Nightingale was front-page news.

Articles appeared in the *Denver Tribune* and the *Rocky Mountain News*. The stories gushed with accolades and adjectives, unanimous agreement that she was a sensation, a singer with the voice of an angel. She was the talk of the town.

The response was overwhelming. Loads of flowers were delivered to her dressing room every night, with notes expressing adulation and all but begging her attention. Every man in Denver was seemingly a rabid admirer and intent on becoming a suitor. She was an object of adoration, the stuff of men's dreams.

Otis Gaylord was the envy of her many admirers. He managed to monopolize her time and squired her around town at every opportunity. Today, she joined him for lunch in the restaurant at the Brown Palace, and the maître d' greeted them with the fanfare reserved for the hotel's resident celebrity. Heads turned as they were led to their table.

Lillian was taken with Gaylord's urbane manner. He was courteous, thoughtful, and attentive to her every wish. His wit amused her, and if he was not the handsomest man she'd ever known, he was nonetheless the most attractive. So much so that she declined dozens of invitations every night, for she was drawn to him by an emotional affinity she'd never before felt. And apart from all that, he was enormously wealthy.

Gaylord was a mining investor. As he explained it, he owned blocks of stock in several gold mines in Central City, which was located some thirty miles west of Denver. The mining camp was called the richest square mile on earth, and upward of a hundred thousand dollars a week was gouged from the mountainous terrain. A shrewd financier might easily quadruple his investment in a year or less.

For Lillian, Otis Gaylord seemed the answer to a girl's prayers. Nor was she alone in that sense, for fortune had smiled on Chester as well. Earlier in the week he'd met Ethel Weaver, who kept the books at her father's store, Weaver's Mercantile. The girl was cute as a button, and to hear Chester tell it, she was one in a million. He spent every spare moment in her company, and he acted like a man who had fallen hard. He talked of nothing else.

Lillian's one concern was her father. His spirit seemed broken by the theater crowd's yawning indifference to Shakespeare and to him as an actor. His drinking had grown worse over the past week, starting in the morning and ending only when he fell into bed at night. His mind was fogged with alcohol, and on two occasions he'd forgotten his lines in the course of the melodrama. His escape into a bottle, just as Lillian had feared, was sapping him mentally and physically. He seemed a shell of his former self.

Gaylord tried to write it off as a momentary lapse. He enjoyed Fontaine's sardonic wit, and even more, he respected his integrity as an actor. Gaylord counseled Lillian to patience, and today, when she seemed particularly distressed, he assured her that her father, given time, would come to grips with the problem. No more had he offered his assurances than James Clark, the manager of the Brown Palace, interrupted their luncheon. He rushed into the dining room.

"Pardon the intrusion," he said earnestly. "Miss Fontaine, your father has been injured. Your brother asked that you come immediately to the suite."

Lillian pushed back her chair. "What kind of injury?"

"I'm afraid I haven't any details. I saw your brother and several men carry your father in from the street. He asked me to find you."

Lillian hurried from the restaurant. Gaylord escorted her upstairs, and three men came out of the suite as they arrived. They found Chester nervously pacing around the sitting room. He turned as they entered.

"Thank God you're here," he said. "Dad got run over by a lumber wagon. I was on the way to lunch with Ethel and I saw it. He just stepped off the curb into the path of the horses."

"How bad is he?" Lillian demanded. "Have you sent for a doctor?"

"There was a doctor there. On the street, on his way to lunch, I mean. He and some other men helped me carry Dad back here."

"The doctor's here, now?"

"Dr. Macquire." Chester motioned to the closed bedroom door. "Dad was unconscious when we brought him in. He didn't look good."

Lillian sagged and Gaylord put his arm around her shoulders. "Steady now," he said. "No need to think the worst."

"Oh, Otis, I feel so terrible. Drinking the way he does, he shouldn't have been on the street. I should have known better."

Chester grimaced. "We would have to keep him under lock and key. Or hide the whiskey."

The bedroom door opened. Dr. Thomas Macquire moved into the sitting room, his features solemn. He nodded to Lillian and Chester. "Your father has the constitution of an ox. Of course, in a way, being drunk was a lucky thing. Drunks can absorb more damage than a sober man."

Lillian stepped forward. "Are you saying he'll be all right?"

"There are no broken bones, and so far as I can tell, there's no internal injuries. I'll have to keep an eye on him for a few days."

"Has he regained consciousness?"

"Miss Fontaine, not only is he awake, he asked for a drink."

Lillian walked to the bedroom. Her father's features were ashen, a discolored bruise on his jaw and a large knot on his forehead. His eyes were rheumy and his breathing raspy. He looked at her with a forlorn expression.

" 'If I must die,' " he said in a slurred voice, " 'I will encounter darkness as a bride, and hug it in mine arms.' Send for a priest, my dear."

"You aren't going to die, Papa. Not as long as you can quote Shakespeare."

" 'The stroke of death is as a lover's pinch'! I could quote the Bard from my grave."

"Dr. Macquire says you'll live."

"What do doctors know?" Fontaine said dismissively. "I need a drink and a priest. Would you oblige me, my dear?"

"Try to get some rest," Lillian said, turning away. "We'll talk later, Papa."

She closed the door on her way out.

Lillian carried on the show by herself. She was forced to cancel the melodrama, as well as the Shakespearean act, for the immediate future. Neither could be performed without her father.

Burt Tully was almost deliriously happy. The crowds jamming the Alcazar shared the sentiment to a man. Lillian was now singing five songs a night, and the theater was sold out a week in advance. A cottage industry sprang up with street hustlers hawking tickets for triple the box office price.

Chester, much to Lillian's surprise, took it all in stride. He told her he was available to resume stage work whenever their father recovered. But he promptly obtained a job as a clerk in Weaver's Mercantile and seemed content to spend his days in close proximity to Ethel Weaver. His nights were spent in her company as well.

Dr. Macquire, at Fontaine's insistence, got the clergy involved. The Reverend Titus Hunnicut, pastor of the First Baptist Church, became a regular at Fontaine's bedside. The actor and the minister sequestered themselves, talking for hours at a time. A male nurse was hired to tend to Fontaine's physical needs, and Reverend Hunnicut tended to his spiritual needs. Fontaine, to Lillian's utter shock, stopped drinking.

Three days after the accident, Fontaine was on the mend. Dr. Macquire pronounced his recovery remarkable, for he'd been trampled by the horses and the lumber wagon had passed over his right leg. He was alert and sober, his cheeks glowing with health, and positively reveling in all the attention. Even more remarkable, he'd taken a vow of abstinence, swearing off demon rum forever. He basked in the glory of the Lord.

Lillian returned from rehearsing a new number late that afternoon. Reverend Hunnicut was on his way out and stopped to chat with her for a moment. A slight man, with oily hair and an unctuous manner, he seemed forever on the pulpit. He nodded as though angels were whispering in his ear.

"Praise the Lord," he said in a sepulchral voice. "Your father has been delivered from the damnation of hell's fires. He is truly blessed."

"How wonderful," Lillian demurred. "Thank you for all your concern, Reverend."

"I am but a humble servant of Christ, Miss Fontaine. God's will be done!"

"Yes, of course."

Lillian showed him to the door. The male nurse, who was seated on the divan reading a newspaper, started to his feet. She waved him down with a smile and proceeded on into the bedroom. Her father was propped up against a bank of pillows.

"Hello, Papa," she said, bussing him on the cheek. "How are you feeling?"

"Quite well." Fontaine studied her with an eager look. "I have something to tell you, my dear. Reverend Hunnicut convinced me it was time."

"Oh?"

"The day the wagon ran over me—actually it was that evening—God spoke to me in the moment of my death."

"You weren't dying, Papa. And since when have you become so devout?"

" 'Ye of little faith,' " Fontaine chided her. " 'They that wait upon the Lord shall renew their strength; they shall mount up with wings as eagles.' " He paused, holding her gaze. "I have been spared death for a greater mission in life."

"A greater mission?"

"Yes indeed, my dear. I shall carry the word of our Lord to the infidels in the mining camps. Their immortal souls are but a step away from perdition."

Lillian was never more stunned in her life. "Are you serious, Papa?"

"I most certainly am."

"What about the stage?"

"All the world's a stage." Fontaine's eyes burned with a fervent light. "I shall be an actor for our Lord Jesus Christ."

"Really?" Lillian said dubiously. "You intend to give up Shakespeare to become a preacher?"

" 'To every thing there is a season, and a time to every purpose under the heaven.' That comes from Ecclesiastes, not Shakespeare."

"Yes, but how can you forsake the stage?"

"On the contrary, the stage has forsaken me. I go now to spread the word of Him who so oft inspired the Bard."

"Are you certain about this, Papa?"

"I have been called," Fontaine said with conviction. "The Gospel will light my way."

Lillian returned to the sitting room in a daze. The male nurse rose from the divan and went past her into the bedroom. As she sat down, the door opened and Chester entered the suite. She gave him a look of baffled consternation.

"Papa has decided to become a preacher."

"I know," Chester said, crossing to the divan. "He's been working himself up to telling you. I found out last night."

"And you didn't say anything?" Lillian was astounded. "Do you think he's lost his mind? I have to talk to the doctor."

"Think about it a minute and you'll understand. What he lost was his faith in himself as a Shakespearean. He's adopted a new role in life—a man of God."

"Oh, Chet, how can you say that? He's an actor, not a preacher."

"As the Bard said," Chester quoted, " 'one man in his time plays many parts.' I'm taking on a new part myself."

"You?" Lillian said. "What are you talking about?"

"I've decided to quit the stage."

"I don't believe it!"

Chester sat down beside her. "You know yourself I was never much of an actor. I stayed with it because it was sort of the family tradition. I think it's time to move on."

Lillian's head was reeling. "Move on to what?"

"I really believe I was cut out to be a merchant. I can't tell you how much I enjoy working in the store. Ethel's father says I have a head for business."

"For business or for Ethel?"

"Well, her, too," Chester said with a goofy smile. "But the point is, what with the act breaking up, I have no future on the stage. Time to make a new career for myself."

"I'm speechless." Lillian felt dizzy and somehow saddened. "Papa a preacher and you a merchant. Where will it end?"

"As for Dad and myself, who's to say? You're the only sure bet in the family."

"I'd so much rather have you and Papa onstage with me."

"You don't need us where you're going, little sister. You never did."

Lillian snuggled close in his arms, her head on his shoulder. A tear ran down her cheek and she wondered how they'd come so far to have it end this way. So abruptly, so unforeseen. So final.

The end of The Fontaines.

* * *

*My wild Irish Rose*
*The sweetest flower that grows*
*You may search everywhere*
*But none can compare*
*With my wild Irish Rose*

Lillian's voice was particularly poignant that night. She was thinking not of the lyrics but of her father and Chester. Her eyes shone with tears, and the emotion she felt inside gave the song a haunting quality. She got hold of herself for the last refrain.

*My wild Irish Rose*
*The dearest flower that grows*

*And someday for my sake*
*She may let me take*
*The bloom from my wild Irish Rose*

A momentary lull held the audience in thrall as the last note faded away. Then the house rocked with applause, men swiping at their noses, their eyes moist with memories evoked by her performance. The noise quickened, went on unabated, the crowd on their feet, bellowing their approval. She left them wanting more with a fifth curtain call.

Some while later Otis Gaylord met her at the stage-door entrance. She was dressed in a gossamer satin gown, a fashionable Eton jacket thrown over her shoulders, her hair pulled back in a lustrous chignon. A carriage took them to Delmonico's, one of the finer restaurants in Denver. The owner personally escorted them to their table.

"That was some performance," Gaylord said when they were seated. "You had the boys crying in their beer."

"I feel like crying myself."

"What's wrong?"

Lillian told him about her afternoon. Gaylord was no less amazed to hear that her father was to become a preacher. The news of her brother was no great surprise, for he'd always felt Chester was the least talented of the family. She ended on a rueful note.

"Nothing will ever be the same again. We've been an act since I was a little girl."

"Yeah, it's a shame," Gaylord agreed. "Of course, maybe it's the best thing for Alistair, and Chester, too. You have to look on the bright side."

"What bright side?" Lillian said. "We'll be separated now."

"Only on the stage. Sounds to me like Alistair and Chester will be doing something that makes them lots happier. Think of it that way."

The waiter appeared with menus. Lillian thought about Gaylord's advice, and after they ordered, she looked at him. Her eyes crinkled with a smile.

"I was being selfish," she said. "If they're happy, why should I be sad? Isn't that what you meant?"

Gaylord chuckled. "I think I put it a little more tactfully. But yeah, that's the general idea."

"Well, you were right, and I feel like a ninny I didn't see it for myself. No more tears."

"Maybe this will cheer you up even more."

Gaylord took a small box from his pocket. He set it before her on the table, his expression unreadable, and eased back in his chair. She opened it and saw a gold heart-shaped locket bordered with tiny diamonds, strung on a delicate chain. Her mouth ovaled with surprise.

"Oh, it's beautiful!" she said merrily. "No one ever gave me anything so nice!"

"We'll have to correct that," Gaylord said. "Lots of pretty presents for a pretty lady. I like it when you laugh."

Lillian batted her eyelashes. "Are you trying to ply me with favors, Mr. Gaylord?"

"I'll ply you any way I can, Miss Fontaine. I intend to be the object of your affections."

"Do you?"

"No question about it."

"Well . . ." She gave him a sultry look. "We'll see."

Gaylord ordered champagne. Lillian strung the locket around her neck, aware that he was watching her. She wondered if tonight was the beginning of what would lead to a proposal. She certainly wasn't going to surrender herself without a wedding band on her finger. But then, on second thought, she wasn't at all sure that love and marriage were the same thing. She felt awfully old to still be a virgin. Too old.

The waiter poured champagne, then moved away. Gaylord lifted his glass, staring at her over the rim. "To us," he said in a seductive voice. "And the future."

Lillian laughed vivaciously. "Yes, to the future."

# Chapter 24

Some days mark a passage in time. Lillian was never to forget June 12, 1872, the day her world turned topsy-turvy. She felt alone for the first time in her life.

Alistair Fontaine stood at the curb in front of the Brown Palace Hotel. He was dressed in a black frock coat, with dark trousers and a white shirt, the crown of his hat rounded in a dome. His horse, a swaybacked gelding donated by the church, was black as well. Fontaine looked every inch the part of an itinerant preacher.

Lillian and Chester waited while he checked his saddlebags. Over the past week he had recovered fully from his encounter with the lumber wagon. By now, after daily sessions with Reverend Hunnicut, he virtually had the Bible memorized, and the paperwork, properly endorsed, had been submitted to have him ordained. He was a man of God.

Watching him, Lillian thought he'd never looked so fit. He held himself tall and straight, and there was fire in his eyes, the zealotry of a man reborn in faith. The saddlebags held all his worldly possessions, and he pulled the strap tight with a firm hand. He turned to face them with an expression that was beatific, at peace with himself.

"Come now," he said, looking from one to the other. "Will you send me off with dreary faces?"

"Oh, Papa!" Lillian sniffled, on the verge of tears. "We'll miss you so."

"The Spirit of the Lord God is upon me. I go forth to give light to them that sit in darkness. I am blessed among men, my dear."

"Dad, I'd like to hear your first sermon," Chester said, grinning. "You'll probably convert those miners in droves."

Fontaine chortled. "I will try to save my first wedding ceremony for you and Ethel."

Chester was himself like a man with a new lease on life. After a whirlwind courtship, he'd announced that morning his betrothal to Ethel Weaver. Her father, who knew a natural-born tradesman when he saw one, welcomed Chester into the family. They were to be married in October.

"God bless you both and keep you safe until I return."

Fontaine hugged Lillian and shook hands with Chester. He stepped into the saddle, tipping his hat with a jaunty air, and rode off along Larimer Street. They stood watching until he rounded the corner and turned west toward the distant mountains. Lillian dabbed at her eyes with a hankie.

"How things change," she said. "I expected him to leave us with a quote from Shakespeare. Something properly dashing, or adventurous."

"Actually . . ." Chester paused, nodding to himself. "I was thinking of Cervantes. A line he wrote in *Don Quixote* strikes me as perfect: 'Many are the ways by which God leads His children home.' "

"For a storekeeper, you're still very much the actor. Are you sure you've given up on the stage?"

"Never more sure of anything. And speaking of the store, I have to get back. I'll see you later."

Chester hurried off down the street. Lillian turned into the hotel, feeling lonely and blue. Upstairs, she wandered through the empty suite, reminded of her father everywhere she looked. She wished she had a rehearsal, or a dress fitting, anything to take her mind off the overwhelming loneliness. She thought she might go to the theater early tonight.

A short while later there was a knock at the door. Lillian was staring out the window, brooding, and she welcomed the distraction. She moved across the sitting room, opening the door, and found two men standing in the hall. One was short and stocky, the other one tall and lean, both attired in conservative suits. She nodded pleasantly.

"May I help you?"

"Miss Fontaine?"

"Yes."

"I'm David Cook," the short one said, "and this is my associate, Jeff Carr. I wonder if we might speak with you a moment."

"May I ask what it regards?"

"A personal matter involving Otis Gaylord."

Lillian invited them inside. Once they were seated, Cook explained that he was head of the Rocky Mountain Detective Association, located in Denver, and currently retained by Wells Fargo. Jeff Carr, he went on, was the county sheriff from Cheyenne, Wyoming. They wanted to ask her a few questions about Otis Gaylord.

"I don't understand," she said. "Why are you interested in Mr. Gaylord?"

Lillian would later discover that David Cook and Jeff Carr were renowned manhunters. Cook, the chief operative of the Rocky Mountain Detective Association, had tracked fugitives all across the West. Carr, who had killed several men in gunfights, was reputed to be the only lawman who had ridden into Hole-in-the-Wall, the outlaw sanctuary, and ridden out alive. Cook looked at her now.

"We have reason to believe that Gaylord's real name is Earl Miller. He's wanted for robbery and murder."

"You're mistaken," Lillian said tersely. "Mr. Gaylord is a mining investor. He's quite wealthy."

"Guess he oughta be," Jeff Carr said. "He robbed a Wells Fargo stagecoach outside of Cheyenne. Got forty-three thousand in gold bullion and killed the express guard."

"And those investments?" Cook added. "We checked out the story he uses, about owning mines in Central City. Nobody there ever heard of him."

Lillian sniffed. "That isn't proof. There could be any number of explanations."

"How's this for proof?" Cook said. "Gaylord sold almost forty thousand in gold bullion to Ed Chase for seventy cents on the dollar. Our informant saw the transaction."

Everyone in Denver knew the name Ed Chase. He was the underworld czar who controlled the rackets and ruled the Tenderloin with a gang of thugs. One of his sidelines was operating as a fence for stolen goods.

"I don't believe you," Lillian said tartly. "If you have evidence, why haven't you arrested Mr. Gaylord? Why come to me?"

Cook informed her that the gold bars, once in the hands of Ed Chase, were untraceable. As for Earl Miller, the robber and murderer, he always wore a bandanna mask and had yet to be positively identified. The break in the case came when they were informed of the underworld sale of the gold.

"We know of your relationship with Gaylord," Cook went on discreetly. "We hoped to solicit your assistance in identifying him."

"Really?" Lillian countered. "Why would I help you?"

"The man's a killer," Carr said bluntly. "Because of him that express guard left a widow and three kids. How's that for a reason?"

"And you might be doing Gaylord a service," Cook argued. "If he's not Earl Miller, you could clear his name. Prove we've got the wrong suspect."

Lillian was less certain of herself than a moment ago. Yet she couldn't believe that Otis Gaylord was a robber, not to mention a murderer. Still, the lawmen were determined, and unless he was cleared, they might very well destroy his reputation. She decided to cooperate.

"What do you want me to do?"

Cook told her what they had in mind.

Gaylord maintained rooms at the Windsor Hotel. Lillian sent a note by messenger, asking that their usual late supper be changed to an early dinner. She suggested their favorite restaurant, Delmonico's.

All afternoon she fretted over what seemed to her a conspiracy. For more than two weeks now, Gaylord had been her lone suitor and her constant companion. She wasn't in love with him, but she thought that might come with time. He was immensely attractive, and she'd even had wicked dreams about him. Wild, delicious dreams.

By five o'clock, she had all but convinced herself that she was betraying him. However much she rationalized it, the plot hatched with Cook and Carr left a bitter taste in her mouth. She went over it again as she was dressing for dinner and forced herself to justify it as a means to an end. Tonight, she would clear Gaylord's name!

Gaylord called for her at six. As they walked to the restaurant, she excused the early dinner by saying she was lonely. She told him about her father's departure that morning and Chester's announcement of his impending marriage. She was happy for them, for one had found salvation in God and the other with the girl of his dreams. But she'd never felt so alone, and a little lost. She missed her father terribly.

Over dinner, Gaylord sympathized with her sense of loss. She felt all the more guilty because he was so considerate and understanding, hardly the traits of a robber and murderer. Finally, when she declined dessert and Gaylord ordered chokecherry pie she knew she was unable to avoid it any longer. She waited until he was served, then leaned forward on her elbows. She lowered her voice.

"Today, two men called on me at the hotel . . . a detective and a sheriff."

"Oh?" Gaylord said curiously. "What was the purpose of their call?"

Lillian composed herself. "The detective works for Wells Fargo and the sheriff is from Wyoming. They're searching for a robber."

"That's the strangest thing I ever heard of. Why would they ask you about a robber?"

"I'm afraid they were asking about you. They said your name is really Earl Miller."

Gaylord's fork paused in midair. She saw something flicker in his eyes, and then he recovered himself. He forked the bite of pie into his mouth and looked at her with an open expression. He chewed away, seemingly puzzled.

"Well, I've been called many things, but never a robber. It must be a case of mistaken identity."

Lillian held his gaze. "They have a witness."

"A witness to what?"

"Someone who saw you sell the gold from the robbery to Ed Chase. And they know you haven't any mining properties in Central City."

"Lillian—"

"You are Earl Miller, aren't you?"

Gaylord placed his fork on his plate. "I'm sorry, more sorry than you'll ever know. I'd hoped to start fresh here in Denver."

"Omigod," Lillian whispered. "I wasn't sure until just now. I prayed it wasn't so."

"And I forgot what a good actress you are. They sent you here to get a confession, didn't they?"

"I thought I could clear your name. How silly of me."

"Where are they now?"

"Sitting right over there."

David Cook and Jeff Carr were seated at a table across the room. Gaylord looked at them and they returned his look with flat stares. He glanced back at Lillian.

"Time to go," he said with an ironic smile. "Wish I could stick around and see how we made out. I think it would've worked."

"Wait, please!" Lillian pleaded. "You musn't try to run."

"Didn't they tell you I killed a man?"

"Yes—"

"I won't be hung."

"Otis, please—"

"So long, Lillian."

Gaylord swung out of his chair. He walked quickly toward the front of the restaurant, snaring his hat off a wall rack. As he neared the door, Cook and Carr got to their feet. Carr pushed a waiter aside.

"Earl Miller!" he commanded. "Halt right there!"

Miller, alias Otis Gaylord, stopped at the door. His hand snaked inside his jacket and came out with a Colt Navy revolver. He whirled, bringing the Colt to bear, and found himself a beat behind. Jeff Carr, pistol extended at shoulder level, fired.

The slug struck Miller dead-center in the chest. His shirt colored as though a small rosebud had been painted on the cloth by an invisible brush. A look of mild surprise came over his face, and he staggered back, dropping the Colt, slamming into the door. His knees buckled and he slumped to the floor.

Lillian stared at him as though she'd been shot herself. Her mouth opened in a soundless scream and for a moment she couldn't get her breath. She buried her head in her hands.

Her low, choking sob was the only sound in Delmonico's.

The theater was mobbed. Within the hour, the news of the shooting had spread throughout the Tenderloin, and the star of the Alcazar became even more sensational.

Everyone wanted a glimpse of the woman assumed to be the dead man's paramour. The Colorado Nightingale.

Lillian somehow got through her first four numbers. She felt wretched about Gaylord's death and oddly guilty for having exposed him as an outlaw. But she kept reminding herself of what her father—and her mother—had always taught as the cardinal tenet of the theater. No matter what, the show must go on.

The oldest bromide in the business was her lodestone. A trouper, barring earthquake or flood, went out on the stage and performed. She sang the ballads with heartfelt emotion for Gaylord (she still couldn't think of him as Earl Miller, robber and murderer). And she belted out the snappy tunes with an insouciance that belied her sorrow.

A comic came offstage as she waited in the wings. Her final number for the evening was *Lily of the West*, which played well off her own billing. She walked to center stage, steeling herself to hold it all together and close out the night on a high note. She put on a happy face as the curtain opened and the orchestra swung into the tune. Her voice was bubbly and spirited.

*When first I came to Denver*
*Some pleasure here to find*
*A damsel fresh from Durango*
*Was laughter to my mind*
*Her rosy cheeks, her ruby lips*
*Set things aflutter in my chest*
*Her name so sweet and dear was Dora*
*The Lily of the West . . .*

The audience began clapping in time to the music. Her ivory gown shone in the spotlight as she whirled and skipped about the stage, revealing her ankles in a sprightly dance routine. She finished the song with a winsome smile and playfully threw kisses to the crowd, bowing low when she curtsied for a mischievous display of cleavage. The applause swelled into a standing ovation that brought her on for five—then six—curtain calls.

Backstage, she nodded politely to congratulations from the other performers. Burt Tully had earlier offered his condolences about Gaylord, and she hoped she'd seen the last of him for the night. She wanted nothing more than to hurry back to the hotel and climb into bed and hide. She thought she might burst into tears at any moment.

Before she could undo her gown, there was a light rap on the door. She sighed, thinking it was Tully, or Chester come to express his sympathy, and sulked across the room. When she opened the door, a man in his early thirties, dressed in an impeccably tailored suit, stood outside. His mouth flashed in an engaging smile.

"Miss Fontaine," he said in a modulated voice. "I'm Victor Stanton, from San Francisco. May I speak with you a moment?"

Lillian held her ground. "What is it you want, Mr. Stanton? How did you get backstage?"

"I talked my way past Burt Tully. As to my purpose, I own the Bella Union Theater. Perhaps you've heard of it."

Everyone in show business had heard of the Bella Union. Even in New York, which was considered the center of the universe for theater, the Bella Union was fabled for its opulent productions. Victor Stanton, the impresario, was considered a showman second to none. Lillian suddenly placed the man with the name.

"Yes, of course," she said pleasantly. "Won't you please come in?"

There was a small, sagging sofa against the wall. Lillian got him seated and took her chair by the dressing table. "How nice of you to drop by," she said, trying to gather her wits. "What brings you to Denver?"

"I come here once or twice a year," Stanton said amiably. "I'm always scouting for new acts, and I must say, tonight was my lucky night. You were absolutely brilliant, Miss Fontaine."

"Why, thank you!" Lillian gushed. "I'm very flattered you would say so."

"Let me ask, are you familiar with San Francisco?"

"Well, no, not really."

"We like to think of it as the Paris of North America. Even more cosmopolitan than New York."

Stanton went on like a civic booster, extolling the virtues of the City by the Bay. As he talked, Lillian noticed his dapper attire, his polished manner and his chiseled features, and the fact that he wore no wedding ring. A fleeting thought crossed her mind about the rotten luck she'd had with men on her odyssey through the West. She wondered if her fortunes might change.

"There you have it," Stanton said. "A city worthy of your remarkable talent."

Lillian realized she was focused on the man rather than his words. "Pardon me?"

"Miss Fontaine, I'm offering you star billing at the Bella Union. How much is Tully paying you?"

"Why . . . three hundred a week."

"I'll make it five hundred," Stanton said without hesitation. "With a one-year contract and my personal guarantee of fame beyond your wildest expectations. What do you say?"

"I . . ." Lillian thought she might faint. "I have almost two weeks left on my engagement here."

"Then you'll open at the Bella Union on Independence Day. We'll introduce you to San Francisco with fireworks on July Fourth! I couldn't think of anything more fitting."

Lillian felt a sudden rush of memory. Abilene and the Comique and Wild Bill Hickok. Dodge City and George Armstrong Custer and Cimarron Jordan. Pueblo and Denver and her long run as the Colorado Nightingale. And now, her name in lights in the City by the Bay.

"You'll love it there," Stanton said, staring directly into her eyes. "I can't wait to show you all the sights, Telegraph Hill and the Golden Gate. I predict you'll never leave."

"I've always heard it's very nice."

"Do you prefer to be called Lilly or Lillian?"

"All my friends call me Lillian."

"And mine call me Victor. I think this is the start of something big, Lillian. Do you feel it, too?"

Lillian all but melted under the warmth of his gaze. The Bella Union, her name in lights, and maybe, with just a little luck, Victor Stanton. Yes, she told herself with the wonder of it all . . .

San Francisco, here I come.

# Epilogue

Victor Stanton made good on his promise. Lillian was billed simply as *The Nightingale*, and she quickly became the star of the Bella Union. By early summer of 1873, she was the sweetheart of stage and song.

Lillian loved San Francisco. The city was wondrously nestled in a natural amphitheater, with steep hills surrounding the center of the community. The bay was the finest landlocked harbor on the continent, and westward along the peninsula, through the Golden Gate, sailed tall-masted clippers and oceangoing steamers from around the world. The trade had transformed the City by the Bay into one of the richest ports on earth.

A profusion of cultures, it was also the premier city of the West. Along the waterfront was the infamous Barbary Coast, a wild carnival of dance halls and brothels where sailors were shanghaied onto ships bound for the Orient. Chinatown, an exotic city within a city, was like being transported backward in time to Old Cathay, where ancient customs still prevailed. The Uptown Tenderloin, a district reserved for society swells, was filled with theaters and cabarets and plush casinos. To Lillian, it was all a storybook come to life.

The Bella Union, located in the heart of the Uptown Tenderloin, was on O'Farrel Street. There was a casino for affluent high rollers upstairs and on the ground floor an ornate barroom fronting the building. Beyond the bar was a spacious theater, with a sunken orchestra pit and the largest proscenium stage west of Chicago. The floor was jammed with linen-covered tables for 500, and a horseshoe balcony was partitioned into private boxes for wealthy patrons. Crowds flocked there every night of the week to see The Nightingale.

Lillian's dressing room was decorated in pale blue. The furnishings were expensive and tasteful, a Louis XIV sofa and chairs and a lush Persian carpet. Victor Stanton, as was his custom, lounged on the sofa while she changed behind a silk screen that was all but translucent. For her last number of the night, she slipped into a bead-embroidered gown of lavender crepe de chine. When she stepped from behind the screen, Stanton stared at her as though spellbound. The gown clung like silken skin to her sumptuous figure.

"Do you like it?" she said, posing for him. "I ordered it especially for you."

Stanton seemed short of breath. "You have never looked lovelier," he said, his eyes glued to her. "I deeply regret I must share you with the audience."

"How gallant!" She laughed a minxish little laugh. "Perhaps I'll wear it only for you."

"No, no," Stanton said, ever the showman. "You owe it to your public, my dear. You are, after all, The Nightingale."

"Then you won't mind sharing me with the audience?"

"I smother my desires to the good of the show."

"Sweet Victor, you really are a naughty man. I somehow doubt your resolve will hold after the show."

Lillian was a very chic and sophisticated twenty-one. She was not a maiden any longer, but neither was she a fallen woman. Any number of times, Victor had asked her to become his bride and share his mansion in the posh Nob Hill district. She was content instead to be his lover, what the society grand dames, given to tittering euphemism, called his inamorata. She enjoyed her freedom.

On Telegraph Hill, her little house was done in the French style, with a magnificent view of the bay. No less than her own home, she loved the independence of $9,000 in the bank and a growing portfolio of railroad stocks. She had renegotiated her contract with Victor three times and now received 5 percent of the box office receipts at the Bella Union. She often thought there was a bit of the extortionist in every successful chanteuse.

Letters from Colorado merely added to her sense of well-being. Chester was happily married, his wife in a family way, and almost certainly destined to become the merchant prince of Denver. Alistair Fontaine, now an ordained minister, reveled in his role as an itinerant preacher in the mining camps. To hear him tell it in his letters, he had Satan on the run and waged war on sinners with the battle cry of "Onward Christian Soldiers." She suspected God had never had a warrior quite like her father. A Shakespearean was, in the end, more than a match for Satan.

"I've arranged supper at the Palace," Stanton said as she checked herself in the mirror. "I thought it only appropriate for our celebration."

"Oh?" Lillian adjusted the bodice of her gown. "What are we celebrating?"

"Why, it's June 28, the anniversary of your arrival from Denver. Surely you haven't forgotten?"

"How could I forget a year together? And because

of you, dear, sweet Victor . . . the happiest year of my life."

"Well, selfish fellow that I am, I planned it that way. I told you the night we met you would never leave San Francisco."

"Yes, it's true." Lillian turned, kissed him soundly on the mouth. "I will never leave."

"Does that mean you'll accept my proposal?"

"One day, someday, maybe a Sunday. We'll see."

"You're a little vixen to keep me waiting."

"I know!"

Stanton, as he did every night, walked her to the wings for her last performance. Onstage, a squealing troupe of dancers was romping through the 'Frisco version of the French *cancan.* Their frilly drawers and black mesh stockings were laughingly exposed as they went into the finale and flung themselves rump first to the floor in *la split.* Then, screaming and tossing their skirts, they leaped to their feet and raced offstage as the curtain closed. The crowd rewarded them with thunderous applause.

Lillian moved to center stage. The orchestra segued into *A Cozy Corner*, and when the curtain opened, she stood framed in a creamy spotlight. Her clear alto voice filled the theater, and she glided around the stage, pausing here and there with a dazzling smile and a saucy wink. She played to every man in the room.

*A cup of coffee, a sandwich and you*
*A cozy comer, a table for two*
*A chance to whisper and cuddle and coo*
*With lots of loving and hugging from you*
*I don't need music, laughter or wine*

*Whenever your eyes look into mine*
*A cup of coffee, a sandwich and you*
*A cozy corner, a table for two*

San Franciscans were fond of saying there was only one nightingale in all the world. Her name was Lilly Fontaine.